ELEVEN PLAYS

OF

William Butler Yeats

ELEVEN PLAYS

OF

William Butler Yeats

*Edited
with an Introduction
and Notes
by*
A. Norman Jeffares

COLLIER BOOKS
New York, New York

SECOND PRINTING 1971

The Macmillan Company
866 Third Avenue, New York, N.Y. 10022
Printed in the United States of America

Contents

Introduction

WE think of Yeats primarily as a poet, yet throughout his life he devoted much of his energy to writing plays and for many years his time was taken up as Manager of the Abbey Theatre with "theatre business, management of men." The second (posthumous) edition of his *Collected Plays* (1952), though it does not include all his published dramatic work,[1] contains over seven hundred pages of text, and this gives some indication of the scope of his dramatic work.

Yeats began to write play after play in imitation of Spenser and Shelley in his teens. His father, who exercised a strong influence over him at this period of his life, used to read aloud the most dramatic passages of whatever play or poem was at the time engaging his capacity for acute, original, speculative appreciation. His son read his own lines aloud as he wrote them; as he did not understand prosody, he discovered that, in order to create some common music for his lines, he needed a listener, an audience. He developed a habit of acting what he wrote and spoke. Indeed, when he left the High School and joined the School of Art in Dublin he sometimes adopted an artificial stride, seeing himself as a kind of Hamlet seeking for heroic self-possession as he was torn by inner struggles.

His concern in drama was largely with the heroic. His early plays were romantic and mournful, preoccupied with loneliness and beauty. *The Island of Statues* of 1885,[2] for instance, though cast in dramatic form, was a romantic poem with little dramatic content. About 1886, under the influence of John O'Leary and his own developing nationalism, he had decided

[1] For details of some unpublished MSS. see G. B. Saul, *Prolegomena to the Study of Yeats's Plays* (1958), pp. 99–100.

[2] Included in *The Dublin University Review*, April, May, June, and July 1885.

to write out of his emotions; he had come to believe a new kind of Irish literature was needed. As he began to explore through translations a new world of Gaelic literature, and also to build up a deep knowledge of nineteenth-century Irish writing in English, he left behind conventional themes and derivative romance.

The Countess Kathleen (1892)[3] bears witness to this change in his style and aims. His falling in love with Maud Gonne in 1889 and his realisation that he would need "a very public talent" to commend himself to this beautiful, violent, and ruthless revolutionary were reasons for his writing this verse play for her. But he was also deeply impressed by Florence Farr's verse speaking in John Todhunter's *A Sicilian Idyll* (1890), performed at Bedford Park in 1890. He based *The Countess Cathleen* on a story he had found and thought suitable for a poetic drama when he was preparing his *Fairy and Folk Tales of the Irish Peasantry* (1888). He drafted it in prose, beginning work in February or March 1889, and finishing the first version in verse in October 1891.

The play has a simple episodic plot. The Countess leaves her dreams for the reality of life; she opposes the efforts of two demon-merchants to buy the souls of her starving peasants. Finally she sells her own soul to prevent this. Yeats wrote *The Countess Cathleen* out of a general ambition to create a "great distinctive poetic literature" out of Ireland's pagan and Christian traditions: in contrast to his long poem *The Wanderings of Oisin* (1889), which was concerned with pagan legends, this play was to mingle his personal thought and feeling with the beliefs and customs of Christian Ireland. He regarded the pagan and Christian elements in Irish tradition as a kind of double fountain head of inspiration. His personal feelings are contained in the play, when the poet Kevin vainly attempts to sell his own soul to prevent the Countess from selling hers. He believes that she should leave the ultimate salvation of the peasants to the builder of the heavens, that

[3] The original spelling, Kathleen, was altered to Cathleen in 1895; the latter spelling is subsequently used in this edition.

her concern should be with marriage and children. This was an indirect message for Maud Gonne, which becomes stronger in later versions of the play, when Kevin, altered to Aleel, puts the claims of subjective life (the beautiful life of artists which Yeats dreamed of for Maud Gonne) as opposed to the grey realities of "the evil of the times."

Yeats revised the text extensively, in 1895, 1901, 1912, and 1919, making minor alterations at other times. The first of these major revisions[4] was stimulated by the performance in 1894 of *The Land of Heart's Desire* (1894) at the Avenue Theatre. Yeats wrote this slight play at Florence Farr's suggestion, so that her niece Dorothy Paget could play the rôle of a fairy child who tempts a young woman away from a respectable cottage marriage to the timelessness of life with the faery host.

The Shadowy Waters (1900),[5] also a much revised play, on which Yeats worked from 1885 to 1905 or later,[6] explores a different kind of situation: it is a study of the heroic gesture, the union of hearts. More a ritual than a play, according to Yeats, it is a symbolic drama of escape, in which the hero and heroine, lily and rose, seek death and life respectively. The symbols are meant—like those in his poems of the 'nineties— to carry a weight of cryptic meaning. Through their shadows they suggest the lovers' contrasting dreams of love and also they symbolise a love beyond this, of superhuman kind.

Yeats's twilight *fin de siècle* weariness changed into a new harsh realism after the turn of the century, and he devoted most of his energy and a great deal of courage to launching, administering, and championing the Irish dramatic movement. He had met Lady Gregory in 1896 and spent subsequent summers in Coole, gathering folk lore with her in the West of Ireland, and finding in her the ally he sought in creating an Irish theatre. Together they established the Irish

---

[4] They are described in Peter Ure, *Yeats the Playwright* (1963), pp. 13–15.

[5] First published in the *North American Review*, May 1900.

[6] It was first produced at the Molesworth Hall, Dublin, on 14 January 1904. The acting version was first published in 1907.

Literary Theatre, with Edward Martyn and George Moore as co-directors, and in 1899 Martyn's *The Heather Field* and Yeats's *The Countess Cathleen* were performed in Dublin. There was a baptism of fire for *The Countess Cathleen*, which incurred moral, political, and religious opposition on the grounds that the people of Ireland would never sell their souls, and the play was performed with police protection.

The Irish Literary Theatre continued to function until the end of 1902: by then Martyn and Moore dropped out of the movement, but not before Yeats and Moore had quarrelled violently over their joint play *Diarmuid and Grania*[7] and then over a story intended to provide the basis for further collaboration. Yeats hastily wrote *Where There is Nothing* (1902)[8] to stop Moore using the subject. This was an account of an anarchistic country gentleman who, after joining a group of tinkers, marries one of them, disassociates himself from his respectable neighbours, enters a monastery where he becomes heretical, is banished and finally killed by a mob. Nietzsche, whom Yeats began reading in 1902, may well have influenced the superman element in this hero.

The Irish National Dramatic Society, with Yeats as its president, replaced the Irish Literary Theatre; this new group contained the Fay brothers, and it provided Yeats with the Irish actors and actresses he had wanted. He gave it his *Cathleen ni Hoolihan* (1902), and Maud Gonne acted in the title-rôle. The play was almost terrifyingly successful in its revolutionary message, in its portrayal of Ireland as the traditional wronged old woman, calling on her children for help. On the news of the landing of a French force at Killala,[9] she is suddenly seen as a young girl with "the walk of a queen." The play is simple and dramatically very effective indeed. In old age Yeats,

[7] The text has been published by W. Becker, *The Dublin Magazine*, April–June 1951.

[8] First published as supplement to the *United Irishman*, 1 November 1902.

[9] The play is based on the *Shan Van Vocht*, a well-known street ballad which celebrated French aid for Irish rebellions. General Humbert landed his men at Killala in 1798.

remembering its startling effect on the audience, wondered

> Did that play of mine send out
> Certain men the English shot?[10]

The Pot of Broth (1904)[11] was an adaptation of a folk tale for which Lady Gregory wrote some dialogue. *The Hour-Glass* (1903), originally a prose morality play, in which a Wise Man humbles himself to a Fool and receives salvation,[12] was re-written in verse. These plays are due to the aim Yeats and Lady Gregory had formed of bringing the poetical tradition contained in the speech of the countryside to the city. They, along with Synge, thought

> All that we did, all that we said or sang
> Must come from contact with the soil, from that
> Contact everything Antaeus-like grew strong.[13]

Synge's first plays to be performed in Dublin were *In the Shadow of the Glen* (1903) and *Riders to the Sea* (1904). The melancholia and vitality of Synge's genius (which Yeats felt he had discovered and guided into its right channels) made for a different use of peasant speech and idiom, and Yeats fully realised and wrote enthusiastically of its merits.[14] He and Lady Gregory fought unselfishly for Synge's work, especially *The Playboy of the Western World* (1907), the exuberant yet profound sense of comedy of which aroused

[10] W. B. Yeats, "The Man and the Echo," *Collected Poems* (1956), p. 393.

[11] First published in *The Gael*, September 1903; then in *The Hour-Glass and Other Plays* (1904).

[12] It was founded on a story, "The Priest's Soul," recorded in Lady Wilde, *Ancient Legends of Ireland* (1887), I, ll. 60–67.

[13] W. B. Yeats, "The Municipal Gallery Revisited," *Collected Poems*, p. 368.

[14] Cf. W. B. Yeats, *Plays in Prose and Verse* (1922), p. 421: "The first use of Irish dialect, rich, abundant and correct, for the purposes of creative art, was in J. M. Synge's *Riders to the Sea* and Lady Gregory's *Spreading the News*."

vociferous hostility from a section of Irish and later Irish-American public opinion. The poetical quality of Synge's prose drama was, however, *sui generis*, and when, after the success of Yeats's *The Countess Cathleen*, *The Pot of Broth*, and *The Hour-Glass*, and Lady Gregory's *Twenty Five* in London in 1903, the Abbey Theatre was opened in Dublin in 1904 Yeats was writing a very different kind of play.

The King's Threshold (1904) was first performed in 1903. This play was founded upon a middle-Irish story of the demands of the poets at the court of King Guaire at Gort, Co. Galway; it also owed something to Edwin Ellis's play *Sancan the Bard* (1905). It marks, according to S. B. Bushrui,[15] the point at which Yeats abandoned passivity—the idealism of Kevin in *The Countess Cathleen*, the isolation of Forgael in *The Shadowy Waters*—and descended into the world of reality. In this play Seanchan the bard is prepared to become part of the real world and struggle with its trivialities in order to assert his view of the place of poetry in the life of the nation. This is an aristocratic view of poetry. It has moved away from any desire to become an instrument of nationalistic politics. As J. I. M. Stewart remarked, "Yeats was at least as shrewd as he was mystical," and must have realised that the forces Maud Gonne wished to unleash would be as hostile in the end to Coole Park as to Dublin Castle.[16]

Yeats's romantic dreams were over once Maud Gonne had married John MacBride in 1903. His new love poetry, now devoid of decorative trappings, recorded movingly the losses caused by his barren passion. Maud Gonne had not understood his aims for Ireland and Ireland itself seemed not to want the new culture he and his friends were creating. Like Seanchan, Yeats was ready to enter the real world; he became Manager of the Abbey and soon his heartfelt curse lay on plays

15 " 'The King's Threshold': A Defence of Poetry," *A Review of English Literature*, IV, 3, July 1963, p. 83.
16 *Eight Modern Writers*, Oxford History of English Literature (1963), p. 326.

> That have to be set up in fifty ways
> On the day's war with knave and dolt, . . .[17]

But despite Yeats's preoccupation with the fascination of what was difficult his own verse plays were not popular with the Abbey audience:

> When we are high and airy hundreds say
> That if we hold that flight they'll leave the place.[18]

The audience preferred realism, and Yeats was unselfish enough to work for the kind of play the younger dramatists were writing. But his own preoccupation was still with the heroic.

In 1892 he had written "The Death of Cuchulain," a poem based largely on folk-tale sources and on the work of Sir Samuel Ferguson and Standish O'Grady. Cuchulain continued to occupy his mind as a subject throughout his life, especially at critical periods in it.[19] In 1901 he was working on the play *On Baile's Strand* (1903),[20] which also deals with Cuchulain's unwitting killing of his own son. Birgit Bjersby has shown how Cuchulain grows older in Yeats's work along with Yeats himself; in the revised version of *On Baile's Strand* of 1905 (when Yeats was forty) we are told he is about forty, though, traditionally, he was twenty-seven when he died.[21] This, then, is a play with reflections of Yeats's frustrated love and frustrated desire for a son: in it he is beginning to stylise the form of the play, and to make the characters reflect the abstract

[17] W. B. Yeats, "The Fascination of What's Difficult," *Collected Poems*, p. 104.

[18] W. B. Yeats, "At the Abbey Theatre," *Collected Poems*, p. 107.

[19] There were seven main treatments: "The Death of Cuchulain" (poem, 1892); *On Baile's Strand* (1903); *The Golden Helmet* (1908) and *The Green Helmet* (1910); *At the Hawk's Well* (1917), *The Only Jealousy of Emer* (1919), and *Fighting the Waves* (1934); *The Death of Cuchulain* (1939) and "Cuchulain Comforted" (poem, 1939).

[20] First published in *The Seven Woods* (1903).

[21] *The Interpretation of the Cuchulain Legend in the Works of W. B. Yeats* (1950), p. 79.

ideas that were persecuting him,[22] for the Fool and the Blind
Man are shadows of Cuchulain and Conchubar, and are later
to become important symbols in A Vision (1926; 1937). They
affect the play's events and yet are detached from it: they
reveal Yeats's increasing interest in extremes and oppositions.
The play has a sense of impending doom; its irony and in-
exorability inevitably remind us of Greek tragedy.

In Deirdre (1907) Yeats attempted a more difficult subject,
concentrating into one act the treachery and terror which kill
Naoise, the pity provoked by Deirdre's suicide. The suspense
is skilfully built up, the poetry sensuous and sinister. This is
the story of a quarrel which knows no mending, the legend of
"one woman and two men," and the circumstances of Yeats's
life gave it imaginative intensity. Naoise plays a self-conscious
rôle, but Deirdre triumphs finally over Conchubar; theirs are
"contrasted sorrows." The attention of the audience, indeed,
is meant to centre upon her and her situation. Though the
play departs from the simplicity of its sources it has a strange,
lofty dignity about it.

Though Yeats returned to the Cuchulain theme in his next
play, his treatment of the heroic Gaelic material was very
different. The Golden Helmet (1908), rewritten in verse as
The Green Helmet (1910), founded on an old Irish tale "The
Feast of Bricriu," was an ironical farce, a farce being for Yeats
"a moment of intense life." Though the play reflects quarrels
and controversies it praises Cuchulain's joyful fighting and
powers of reconciliation:

> And I choose the laughing life
> That shall not turn from laughing, whatever rise or fall;
> The heart the grows no bitterer although betrayed by all;
> The hand that loves to scatter; the life like a gambler's
>   throw . . .[23]

[22] Cf. W. B. Yeats, Wheels and Butterflies (1934), p. 102.
[23] W. B. Yeats, The Green Helmet, Collected Plays (1952),
p. 243. The Golden Helmet was first performed on 19 March 1908;
The Green Helmet on 10 February 1910, both at the Abbey Theatre, Dublin.

The Unicorn from the Stars (1908) was a rewriting of *Where There is Nothing*: it replaces the unsatisfactory episodic activities of the hero of the earlier play with a new concentrated action and a more convincing hero, Martin Hearne. This young coachbuilder has a vision of the unicorns which will destroy the existing order of things; he collects beggars, initiates a drunken revel, and finally realises, before he is shot, that he has been mistaken in giving way to the attraction of destructive violence.

Yeats's concern with the end of one era and the beginning of a new, symbolised by the iron-clawed beast of *Where There is Nothing* and the unicorns of *The Unicorn from the Stars*, was taken up yet again in the unicorn of *The Player Queen* (1922), the genesis of which is described in a note:

> I began in, I think, 1907, a verse tragedy, but at that time the thought I have set forth in *Per Amica Silentia Lunae* was coming into my head, and I found examples of it everywhere. I wasted the best working months of several years in an attempt to write a poetical play where every character became an example of the finding or not finding of what I have called the Antithetical Self; and because passion and not thought makes tragedy, what I made had neither simplicity nor life. I knew precisely what was wrong and yet could neither escape from thought nor give up my play. At last it came into my head all of a sudden that I could get rid of the play if I turned it into a farce; and never did I do anything so easily, for I think I wrote the present play in about a month . . .[24]

This "wild comedy" (first performed in 1919) is extremely effective on the stage. It can be enjoyed as a prose farce as well as an extension of the theory of the mask which finds expression in *Per Amica Silentia Lunae* (1918).[25] There are other, obscurer elements of Yeats's "system" in the play.

[24] W. B. Yeats, *Plays in Prose and Verse* (1922), p. 428.
[25] See W. B. Yeats, "Ego Dominus Tuus," *Collected Poems*, p. 180; "The Phases of the Moon," *ibid.*, p. 183, is a similar exposition of Yeats's "system."

Decima, according to Professor Ure, is both harlot and artist seeking her anti-self, and she can be explained in terms of Yeats's story *The Adoration of the Magi* (1897; 1925). F. A. C. Wilson sees the unicorn as the form in which divinity is to descend to Decima[26] (as the swan descends to Leda), but Professor Ure argues against this (since Decima does not marry a unicorn but the Prime Minister) and suggests that beneath the farce lies the tragedy, that Decima finds, instead of death, her anti-self and happiness, but, as a condition of this, has to unite with a buffoon.[27]

There had been much difficulty in getting the right actress for the initial production of *Deirdre*. Miss Darragh (Letitia Marion Dallas) was chosen; this appointment displeased the Abbey actors; and the part was subsequently played by Mrs. Campbell. For the part of Decima, Yeats had Mrs. Patrick Campbell in mind when he began to write the play that became *The Player Queen*. A possible reason for this move from tragedy to the farce of *The Golden Helmet* and *The Player Queen* may have been a desire to provide plays which would suit the Abbey actors. What he wanted, however, was an audience and actors to suit himself, and this situation was achieved in Lady Cunard's drawing-room on 2 April 1916. Here was performed *At the Hawk's Well* (1917),[28] the first of the four *Plays for Dancers* (1921). These were plays written out of his interest in the Japanese Noh drama, to which Ezra Pound had introduced him. This offered him a new, simple technique. He could do without an orthodox theatre—an unpopular one was better since he wanted a mysterious art, a ritual helped into being by music and dancing. This would allow him to make credible strange events and elaborate words.

At the Hawk's Well sums up some personal disillusion and uncertainty. It symbolises man's search for the unobtainable, the hawk suggesting the persecution of the abstract, and

26 F. A. C. Wilson, *Yeats and Tradition* (1958), p. 182.
27 P. Ure, *Yeats the Playwright* (1963), p. 144.
28 First published in *Harper's Bazaar*, March 1917.

Cuchulain the contradictory nature of carnage. *The Only Jealousy of Emer* (1919)[29] is more complicated in structure, and its account of Emer's renunciation of Cuchulain, a solitary act of sacrifice which is unknown to her husband, is encumbered by the ambiguous temptation offered by Fand, the woman of the Sidhe. *The Dreaming of the Bones* (1919)[30] is more successful in its mixture of the supernatural and the political. A revolutionary soldier meets the ghosts of Dermot and Devorgilla who were responsible for bringing Strongbow and the Normans into Ireland in the twelfth century. They reveal their identity; their anguished separation can be ended if someone of their own race forgives them. But the soldier cannot bring himself to do this, and their remorseful dance of longing ends the play.

Calvary (1921)[31] possesses the musicians' songs, the dance and masked actors, the grouped images of the other Noh-style plays. Its subject, however, marks it off as different, and it requires some knowledge of *A Vision* for its understanding. Christ, himself a victim of intellectual despair, can help neither the Roman soldiers, who are a form of objectivity, nor Lazarus, nor Judas, nor the heron, eagle, and swan, who are content with solitude. The play consists in Professor Ure's words, of "four variations on the theme of Christ's powerlessness to save those who can live without salvation."

Yeats wrote *The Cat and the Moon* (1926),[32] a brief, curiously Synge-like exercise,[33] and followed it with his two translations Sophocles' "*King Oedipus*" (1928) and Sophocles' "*Oedipus at Colonus*" (1934). *The Resurrection* (1931)[34] occupied him from 1925 to 1930; it develops the static atti-

[29] First published in *Poetry* (Chicago), January 1919.

[30] In *Two Plays for Dancers* (1919).

[31] In *Four Plays for Dancers* (1921).

[32] First published in *The Criterion*, July 1924, and in *The Dial*, July 1924.

[33] The play describes the friendship of George Moore and Edward Martyn. Cf. W. B. Yeats, *Autobiographies* (1956), p. 482.

[34] First published in *Adelphi*, June 1927; then in *Stories of Michael Robartes and His Friends* (1931).

tudes of *Calvary* into a far livelier, more effective play which
has structure and development. The plot rests upon Yeats's
view of history as antithetical; he thought Christianity brought
radical thought into the world and with it a new historical
period. He makes his abstract system live, first through ex-
planatory dialogue, then through the explosive tension gen-
erated out of the situation, an undercurrent of Dionysiac
irrational force, beating through the play, contrasting ironically
with the talk of the two main characters, the Greek and the
Hebrew. This is a masterpiece of dramatic intensity and econ-
omy. The stage-craft has a confidence, the dialogue an assur-
ance that reflects the effect that writing *A Vision*, "getting
it all in order," had on Yeats's poetry.

The same superb dramatic skill is at work in *The Words
upon the Window-Pane* (1934). Yeats's sense of dialogue
and of construction allow him to vary the tension of the play,
to make realistic use of a séance to communicate the terror in
his sense of Swift's agony of spirit:

> . . . beating on his breast in sibylline frenzy blind
> Because the heart in his blood-sodden breast had dragged
>   him down into mankind.[35]

The King of the Great Clock Tower (1934) was "the most
popular of my dance plays," and *A Full Moon in March*
(1935) was a second version of the idea based on Oscar
Wilde's *Salomé*. The characters are not convincing as people;
they are in fact parts of a ritual. *The Herne's Egg* (1938)—
"the strangest wildest thing I have ever written"—seemed to
Yeats to have more tragedy and philosophic depth than *The
Player Queen*. The hero, Congal, is at war with the bird-god,
the Great Herne: but he does not fully understand what he
fights. He is obtuse, he falls into a state of mind where he
decides the rape of Attracta will restore the state of disorder
which existed before he stole the herne's egg and so began the
quarrel which led to his killing of Aedh. The "first bout"

[35] W. B. Yeats, "Blood and the Moon," *Collected Poems*, p. 267.

with the God led to disorder, the second to the violation of Attracta, which Congal fails to understand in its fullest meaning. The third bout leads to his death in terms of the curse at the hands of a fool, and his reincarnation as a donkey. Congal is a tragic hero of the Othello or Coriolanus kind, limited because his virtues are also his flaws; he makes mistakes, and misunderstands the situation into which his mistakes lead him. The Great Herne has an impersonality and mystery which perhaps reinforce the unimportance of Congal's heroic activity, his inability to realise the difference between fighting against men and against the God.

Purgatory (1939)[36] dramatises some elements of a ghost story Yeats told earlier about Castle Dargan, near Sligo; in the play the protagonist is an old pedlar, who tells his bastard son the history of the ruined house and its inhabitants. The ghosts of the house appear to the old man—and then, finally, to the boy, as he and his father grapple together, fighting for the pedlar's money. The murder of the son, however, fails to arrest the haunting of the place, centred upon the pedlar's mother's dream. This is a play, on an Oresteia-like theme, upon the problem of the possible purification of a family and of the sexual act which began it. The irony of the repeated pattern of the murders adds to the horror of the play; the circle cannot be broken by mankind, and the old man prays, finally, to God to appease the misery of the living as well as the remains of the dead.

Yeats wrote *The Death of Cuchulain* (1939)[37] shortly before his death. Here he again returned to the material of Lady Gregory's *Cuchulain of Muirthemne*; he also weighted the play with the intimations of the system of *A Vision*. Cuchulain is given a false message by his mistress Eithne, who is under the spell of the goddess of war, which will lead him into hopeless battle; he faces the prospect of death with his usual bravery, forgiving Eithne with a magnanimity which is ironic. He is mortally wounded, and, though Aoife is about to re-

---

[36] In *Last Poems and Two Plays* (1939).
[37] *Ibid.*

venge upon him the death of their son Conlaech, the actual
death is ironically administered by a blind man for a paltry
reward. This is the Cuchulain, blinded by heroism, butchered
by a clown, who is envisaged in the final song of the play as
resuming his place in the folk memory of Irish tradition with
the occurrence of the Easter Rising of 1916:

> What stood in the Post Office
> With Pearse and Connolly?
> What comes out of the mountain
> Where men first shed their blood?
> Who thought Cuchulain till it seemed
> He stood where they had stood?
>
> No body like his body
> Has modern woman borne,
> But an old man looking on life
> Imagines it in scorn.
> A statue's there to mark the place,
> By Oliver Sheppard done.

Yeats had aimed to "make the old stories as familiar to Irish-
men at any rate as are the stories of King Arthur and his
Knights to all readers of books." In doing so he had helped to
bring a regenerated nation into being, and it was fitting that
his hero met death with the proud disdain he sought to
achieve himself.

NOTE ON THE TEXT

THE copy-text used is that of *Collected Plays* (1952). As the
dates given in that edition (in the list of contents and under
the title of each play) for the first published versions are not
always correct they have been omitted from the body of this
text. The notes of this edition attempt to establish where
possible the dates of the first publication and production of
each play included in the selection. The order of the plays
in *Collected Plays* (1952) is followed, with one exception.
The text of *Cathleen ni Hoolihan* is taken from *Samhain*,
1902, in which it first appeared, in view of the play's imme-
diate effect upon its audience. It is, therefore, placed after
those plays which are taken from *Collected Plays* (1952).
I am greatly indebted to Mrs. W. B. Yeats for her aid in
correcting the text of *Collected Plays* (1952) and for other
assistance in annotation. Professor David Greene and Mr.
Brendan Kennelly have also helped me greatly with the iden-
tification of Gaelic material.

ON BAILE'S STRAND

On Baile's Strand

PERSONS IN THE PLAY

A Fool
A Blind Man
Cuchulain, *King of Muirthemne*
Conchubar, *High King of Uladh*
A Young Man, *son of Cuchulain*
Kings and Singing Women

A great hall at Dundealgan, not "Cuchulain's great ancient house" but an assembly-house nearer to the sea. A big door at the back, and through the door misty light as of sea-mist. There are many chairs and one long bench. One of these chairs, which is towards the front of the stage, is bigger than the others. Somewhere at the back there is a table with flagons of ale upon it and drinking-horns. There is a small door at one side of the hall. A Fool and Blind Man, both ragged, and their features made grotesque and extravagant by masks, come in through the door at the back. The Blind Man leans upon a staff.

Fool. What a clever man you are though you are blind! There's nobody with two eyes in his head that is as clever as you are. Who but you could have thought that the hen-wife sleeps every day a little at noon? I would never be able to steal anything if you didn't tell me where to look for it. And what a good cook you are! You take the fowl out of my hands after I have stolen it and plucked it, and you put it into the big pot at the fire there, and I can go out and run races with the witches at the edge of the waves and get an appetite, and when I've got it, there's the hen waiting inside for me, done to the turn.

Blind Man [*who is feeling about with his stick*]. Done to the turn.

Fool [*putting his arm round Blind Man's neck*]. Come now, I'll have a leg and you'll have a leg, and we'll draw lots for the wish-bone. I'll be praising you, I'll be praising you while we're eating it, for your good plans and for your good cooking. There's nobody in the world like you, Blind Man. Come, come. Wait a minute. I shouldn't have closed the door. There are some that look for me, and I wouldn't like them not to find me. Don't tell it to anybody, Blind Man. There are some that follow me. Boann herself out of the river and Fand out of the deep sea. Witches they are, and they come by in the wind, and they cry, "Give a kiss, Fool, give a kiss," that's what they cry. That's wide enough. All the witches can come in now. I wouldn't have them beat at the door and say, "Where is the Fool? Why has he put a lock on the door?" Maybe they'll hear the bubbling of the pot and come in and sit on the ground. But we won't give them any of the fowl. Let them go back to the sea, let them go back to the sea.

Blind Man [*feeling legs of big chair with his hands*]. Ah! [*Then, in a louder voice as he feels the back of it.*] Ah—ah—

Fool. Why do you say "Ah-ah"?

Blind Man. I know the big chair. It is to-day the High King Conchubar is coming. They have brought out his chair. He is going to be Cuchulain's master in earnest from this day out. It is that he's coming for.

Fool. He must be a great man to be Cuchulain's master.

Blind Man. So he is. He is a great man. He is over all the rest of the kings of Ireland.

Fool. Cuchulain's master! I thought Cuchulain could do anything he liked.

Blind Man. So he did, so he did. But he ran too wild, and Conchubar is coming to-day to put an oath upon him that will stop his rambling and make him as biddable as a house-dog and keep him always at his hand. He will sit in this chair and put the oath upon him.

Fool. How will he do that?

Blind Man. You have no wits to understand such things. [*The Blind Man has got into the chair.*] He will sit up in this chair and he'll say: "Take the oath, Cuchulain. I bid you take the oath. Do as I tell you. What are your wits compared with mine, and what are your riches compared with mine? And what sons have you to pay your debts and to put a stone over you when you die? Take the oath, I tell you. Take a strong oath."

Fool [*crumpling himself up and whining*]. I will not. I'll take no oath. I want my dinner.

Blind Man. Hush, hush! It is not done yet.

Fool. You said it was done to a turn.

Blind Man. Did I, now? Well, it might be done, and not done. The wings might be white, but the legs might be red. The flesh might stick hard to the bones and not come away in the teeth. But, believe me, Fool, it will be well done before you put your teeth in it.

Fool. My teeth are growing long with the hunger.

Blind Man. I'll tell you a story—the kings have story-tellers while they are waiting for their dinner—I will tell you a story with a fight in it, a story with a champion in it, and a ship and a queen's son that has his mind set on killing somebody that you and I know.

Fool. Who is that? Who is he coming to kill?

Blind Man. Wait, now, till you hear. When you were stealing the fowl, I was lying in a hole in the sand, and I heard three men coming with a shuffling sort of noise. They were wounded and groaning.

Fool. Go on. Tell me about the fight.

Blind Man. There had been a fight, a great fight, a tremendous great fight. A young man had landed on the shore, the guardians of the shore had asked his name, and he had refused to tell it, and he had killed one, and others had run away.

Fool. That's enough. Come on now to the fowl. I wish it was bigger. I wish it was as big as a goose.

Blind Man. Hush! I haven't told you all. I know who that

young man is. I heard the men who were running away
say he had red hair, that he had come from Aoife's country,
that he was coming to kill Cuchulain.

Fool. Nobody can do that.

[*To a tune*]
Cuchulain has killed kings,
Kings and sons of kings,
Dragons out of the water,
And witches out of the air,

Banachas and Bonachas and people of the woods.

Blind Man. Hush! hush!

Fool [*still singing*].

Witches that steal the milk,
Fomor that steal the children,
Hags that have heads like hares,
Hares that have claws like witches,
All riding a-cock-horse

[*Spoken*]

Out of the very bottom of the bitter black North.

Blind Man. Hush, I say!

Fool. Does Cuchulain know that he is coming to kill him?

Blind Man. How would he know that with his head in the
clouds? He doesn't care for common fighting. Why would
he put himself out, and nobody in it but that young man?
Now if it were a white fawn that might turn into a queen
before morning—

Fool. Come to the fowl. I wish it was as big as a pig; a fowl
with goose grease and pig's crackling.

Blind Man. No hurry, no hurry. I know whose son it is. I
wouldn't tell anybody else, but I will tell you,—a secret is
better to you than your dinner. You like being told secrets.

Fool. Tell me the secret.

Blind Man. That young man is Aoife's son. I am sure it is
Aoife's son, it flows in upon me that it is Aoife's son. You
have often heard me talking of Aoife, the great woman-
fighter Cuchulain got the mastery over in the North?

Fool. I know, I know. She is one of those cross queens that live in hungry Scotland.

Blind Man. I am sure it is her son. I was in Aoife's country for a long time.

Fool. That was before you were blinded for putting a curse upon the wind.

Blind Man. There was a boy in her house that had her own red colour on him, and everybody said he was to be brought up to kill Cuchulain, that she hated Cuchulain. She used to put a helmet on a pillar-stone and call it Cuchulain and set him casting at it. There is a step outside—Cuchulain's step.

[*Cuchulain passes by in the mist outside the big door.*

Fool. Where is Cuchulain going?

Blind Man. He is going to meet Conchubar that has bidden him to take the oath.

Fool. Ah, an oath, Blind Man. How can I remember so many things at once? Who is going to take an oath?

Blind Man. Cuchulain is going to take an oath to Conchubar who is High King.

Fool. What a mix-up you make of everything, Blind Man! You were telling me one story, and now you are telling me another story. . . . How can I get the hang of it at the end if you mix everything at the beginning? Wait till I settle it out. There now, there's Cuchulain [*he points to one foot*], and there is the young man [*he points to the other foot*] that is coming to kill him, and Cuchulain doesn't know. But where's Conchubar? [*Takes bag from side.*] That's Conchubar with all his riches—Cuchulain, young man, Conchubar.—And where's Aoife? [*Throws up cap.*] There is Aoife, high up on the mountains in high hungry Scotland. Maybe it is not true after all. Maybe it was your own making up. It's many a time you cheated me before with your lies. Come to the cooking-pot, my stomach is pinched and rusty. Would you have it to be creaking like a gate?

Blind Man. I tell you it's true. And more than that is true. If you listen to what I say, you'll forget your stomach.

Fool. I won't.

Blind Man. Listen. I know who the young man's father is,
but I won't say. I would be afraid to say. Ah, Fool, you
would forget everything if you could know who the young
man's father is.

Fool. Who is it? Tell me now quick, or I'll shake you. Come,
out with it, or I'll shake you.

> [*A murmur of voices in the distance.*

Blind Man. Wait, wait. There's somebody coming. . . . It is
Cuchulain is coming. He's coming back with the High
King. Go and ask Cuchulain. He'll tell you. It's little you'll
care about the cooking-pot when you have asked Cuchulain,
that . . .

> [*Blind Man goes out by side door.*

Fool. I'll ask him. Cuchulain will know. He was in Aoife's
country. [*Goes up stage.*] I'll ask him. [*Turns and goes down
stage.*] But, no, I won't ask him, I would be afraid. [*Going
up again.*] Yes, I will ask him. What harm in asking? The
Blind Man said I was to ask him. [*Going down.*] No, no.
I'll not ask him. He might kill me. I have but killed hens
and geese and pigs. He has killed kings. [*Goes up again
almost to big door.*] Who says I'm afraid? I'm not afraid.
I'm no coward. I'll ask him. No, no, Cuchulain, I'm not
going to ask you.

> He has killed kings,
> Kings and the sons of kings,
> Dragons out of the water,
> And witches out of the air,

Banachas and Bonachas and people of the woods.

> [*Fool goes out by side door, the last words being heard
> outside. Cuchulain and Conchubar enter through the
> big door at the back. While they are still outside,
> Cuchulain's voice is heard raised in anger. He is a dark
> man, something over forty years of age. Conchubar is
> much older and carries a long staff, elaborately carved
> or with an elaborate gold handle.*

Cuchulain. Because I have killed men without your bidding
And have rewarded others at my own pleasure,
Because of half a score of trifling things,

You'd lay this oath upon me, and now—and now
You add another pebble to the heap,
And I must be your man, well-nigh your bondsman,
Because a youngster out of Aoife's country
Has found the shore ill-guarded.

Conchubar.   He came to land
While you were somewhere out of sight and hearing,
Hunting or dancing with your wild companions.

Cuchulain. He can be driven out. I'll not be bound.
I'll dance or hunt, or quarrel or make love,
Wherever and whenever I've a mind to.
If time had not put water in your blood,
You never would have thought it.

Conchubar.   I would leave
A strong and settled country to my children.

Cuchulain. And I must be obedient in all things;
Give up my will to yours; go where you please;
Come when you call; sit at the council-board
Among the unshapely bodies of old men;
I whose mere name has kept this country safe,
I that in early days have driven out
Macvc of Cruachan and the northern pirates,
The hundred kings of Sorcha, and the kings
Out of the Garden in the East of the World.
Must I, that held you on the throne when all
Had pulled you from it, swear obedience
As if I were some cattle-raising king?
Are my shins speckled with the heat of the fire,
Or have my hands no skill but to make figures
Upon the ashes with a stick? Am I
So slack and idle that I need a whip
Before I serve you?

Conchubar.   No, no whip, Cuchulain,
But every day my children come and say:
"This man is growing harder to endure.
How can we be at safety with this man
That nobody can buy or bid or bind?
We shall be at his mercy when you are gone;

He burns the earth as if he were a fire,
And time can never touch him."

Cuchulain.   And so the tale
Grows finer yet; and I am to obey
Whatever child you set upon the throne,
As if it were yourself!

Conchubar.   Most certainly.
I am High King, my son shall be High King;
And you for all the wildness of your blood,
And though your father came out of the sun,
Are but a little king and weigh but light
In anything that touches government,
If put into the balance with my children.

Cuchulain. It's well that we should speak our minds out
      plainly,
For when we die we shall be spoken of
In many countries. We in our young days
Have seen the heavens like a burning cloud
Brooding upon the world, and being more
Than men can be now that cloud's lifted up,
We should be the more truthful. Conchubar,
I do not like your children—they have no pith,
No marrow in their bones, and will lie soft
Where you and I lie hard.

Conchubar.   You rail at them
Because you have no children of your own.

Cuchulain. I think myself most lucky that I leave
No pallid ghost or mockery of a man
To drift and mutter in the corridors
Where I have laughed and sung.

Conchubar.   That is not true,
For all your boasting of the truth between us;
For there is no man having house and lands,
That have been in the one family, called
By that one family's name for centuries,
But is made miserable if he know
They are to pass into a stranger's keeping,
As yours will pass.

Cuchulain.   The most of men feel that,
  But you and I leave names upon the harp.
Conchubar. You play with arguments as lawyers do,
  And put no heart in them. I know your thoughts,
  For we have slept under the one cloak and drunk
  From the one wine-cup. I know you to the bone,
  I have heard you cry, aye, in your very sleep,
  "I have no son," and with such bitterness
  That I have gone upon my knees and prayed
  That it might be amended.
Cuchulain.   For you thought
  That I should be as biddable as others
  Had I their reason for it; but that's not true;
  For I would need a weightier argument
  Than one that marred me in the copying,
  As I have that clean hawk out of the air
  That, as men say, begot this body of mine
  Upon a mortal woman.
Conchubar.   Now as ever
  You mock at every reasonable hope,
  And would have nothing, or impossible things.
  What eye has ever looked upon the child
  Would satisfy a mind like that?
Cuchulain.   I would leave
  My house and name to none that would not face
  Even myself in battle.
Conchubar.   Being swift of foot,
  And making light of every common chance,
  You should have overtaken on the hills.
  Some daughter of the air, or on the shore
  A daughter of the Country-under-Wave.
Cuchulain. I am not blasphemous.
Conchubar.   Yet you despise
  Our queens, and would not call a child your own,
  If one of them had borne him.
Cuchulain   I have not said it.
Conchubar. Ah! I remember I have heard you boast,
  When the ale was in your blood, that there was one

In Scotland, where you had learnt the trade of war,
That had a stone-pale cheek and red-brown hair;
And that although you had loved other women,
You'd sooner that fierce woman of the camp
Bore you a son than any queen among them.

Cuchulain. You call her a "fierce woman of the camp,"
For, having lived among the spinning-wheels,
You'd have no woman near that would not say,
"Ah! how wise!" "What will you have for supper?"
"What shall I wear that I may please you, sir?"
And keep that humming through the day and night
For ever. A fierce woman of the camp!
But I am getting angry about nothing.
You have never seen her. Ah! Conchubar, had you seen
   her
With that high, laughing, turbulent head of hers
Thrown backward, and the bowstring at her ear,
Or sitting at the fire with those grave eyes
Full of good counsel as it were with wine,
Or when love ran through all the lineaments
Of her wild body—although she had no child,
None other had all beauty, queen or lover,
Or was so fitted to give birth to kings.

Conchubar. There's nothing I can say but drifts you farther
From the one weighty matter. That very woman—
For I know well that you are praising Aoife—
Now hates you and will leave no subtlety
Unknotted that might run into a noose
About your throat, no army in idleness
That might bring ruin on this land you serve.

Cuchulain. No wonder in that, no wonder at all in that.
I never have known love but as a kiss
In the mid-battle, and a difficult truce
Of oil and water, candles and dark night,
Hillside and hollow, the hot-footed sun
And the cold, sliding, slippery-footed moon—
A brief forgiveness between opposites

That have been hatreds for three times the age
Of this long-'stablished ground.

Conchubar. Listen to me.
Aoife makes war on us, and every day
Our enemies grow greater and beat the walls
More bitterly, and you within the walls
Are every day more turbulent; and yet,
When I would speak about these things, your fancy
Runs as it were a swallow on the wind.

[*Outside the door in the blue light of the sea-mist are
many old and young Kings; among them are three
Women, two of whom carry a bowl of fire. The third,
in what follows, puts from time to time fragrant herbs
into the fire so that it flickers up into brighter flame.*

Look at the door and what men gather there—
Old counsellors that steer the land with me,
And younger kings, the dancers and harp-players
That follow in your tumults, and all these
Are held there by the one anxiety.
Will you be bound into obedience
And so make this land safe for them and theirs?
You are but half a king and I but half;
I need your might of hand and burning heart,
And you my wisdom.

Cuchulain [*going near to door*]. Nestlings of a high nest,
Hawks that have followed me into the air
And looked upon the sun, we'll out of this
And sail upon the wind once more. This king
Would have me take an oath to do his will,
And having listened to his tune from morning,
I will no more of it. Run to the stable
And set the horses to the chariot-pole,
And send a messenger to the harp-players.
We'll find a level place among the woods,
And dance awhile.

A Young King. Cuchulain, take the oath.
There is none here that would not have you take it.

Cuchulain. You'd have me take it? Are you of one mind?
The Kings. All, all, all, all!
A Young King.   Do what the High King bids you.
Conchubar. There is not one but dreads this turbulence
  Now that they're settled men.
Cuchulain.   Are you so changed,
  Or have I grown more dangerous of late?
  But that's not it. I understand it all.
  It's you that have changed. You've wives and children now,
  And for that reason cannot follow one
  That lives like a bird's flight from tree to tree.—
  It's time the years put water in my blood
  And drowned the wildness of it, for all's changed,
  But that unchanged.—I'll take what oath you will:
  The moon, the sun, the water, light, or air,
  I do not care how binding.
Conchubar.   On this fire
  That has been lighted from your hearth and mine;
  The older men shall be my witnesses,
  The younger, yours. The holders of the fire
  Shall purify the thresholds of the house
  With waving fire, and shut the outer door,
  According to the custom; and sing rhyme.
  That has come down from the old law-makers
  To blow the witches out. Considering
  That the wild will of man could be oath-bound,
  But that a woman's could not, they bid us sing
  Against the will of woman at its wildest
  In the Shape-Changers that run upon the wind.
                    [*Conchubar has gone on to his throne.*
The Women. [*They sing in a very low voice after the first few
    words so that the others all but drown their words.*
            May this fire have driven out
            The Shape-Changers that can put
            Ruin on a great king's house
            Until all be ruinous.
            Names whereby a man has known
            The threshold and the hearthstone,

Gather on the wind and drive
The women none can kiss and thrive,
For they are but whirling wind,
Out of memory and mind.
They would make a prince decay
With light images of clay
Planted in the running wave;
Or, for many shapes they have,
They would change them into hounds
Until he had died of his wounds,
Though the change were but a whim;
Or they'd hurl a spell at him,
That he follow with desire
Bodies that can never tire
Or grow kind, for they anoint
All their bodies, joint by joint,
With a miracle-working juice
That is made out of the grease
Of the ungoverned unicorn.
But the man is thrice forlorn,
Emptied, ruined, wracked, and lost,
That they follow, for at most
They will give him kiss for kiss
While they murmur, "After this
Hatred may be sweet to the taste."
Those wild hands that have embraced
All his body can but shove
At the burning wheel of love
Till the side of hate comes up.
Therefore in this ancient cup
May the sword-blades drink their fill
Of the home-brew there, until
They will have for masters none
But the threshold and hearthstone.

Cuchulain [*speaking, while they are singing*]. I'll take and
    keep this oath, and from this day
  I shall be what you please, my chicks, my nestlings.
  Yet I had thought you were of those that praised

Whatever life could make the pulse run quickly,
Even though it were brief, and that you held
That a free gift was better than a forced.—
But that's all over.—I will keep it, too;
I never gave a gift and took it again.
If the wild horse should break the chariot-pole,
It would be punished. Should that be in the oath?
> [*Two of the Women, still singing, crouch in front of him
> holding the bowl over their heads. He spreads his
> hands over the flame.*

I swear to be obedient in all things
To Conchubar, and to uphold his children.

Conchubar. We are one being, as these flames are one:
I give my wisdom, and I take your strength.
Now thrust the swords into the flame, and pray
That they may serve the threshold and the hearthstone
With faithful service.
> [*The Kings kneel in a semicircle before the two Women
> and Cuchulain, who thrusts his sword into the flame.
> They all put the points of their swords into the flame.
> The third Woman is at the back near the big door.*

Cuchulain.   O pure, glittering ones
That should be more than wife or friend or mistress,
Give us the enduring will, the unquenchable hope,
The friendliness of the sword!—
> [*The song grows louder, and the last words ring out
> clearly. There is a loud knocking at the door, and a
> cry of "Open! open!"*

Conchubar. Some king that has been loitering on the way.
Open the door, for I would have all know
That the oath's finished and Cuchulain bound,
And that the swords are drinking up the flame.
> [*The door is opened by the third Woman, and a Young
> Man with a drawn sword enters.*

Young Man. I am of Aoife's country.
> [*The Kings rush towards him. Cuchulain throws himself
> between.*

Cuchulain.   Put up your swords.
  He is but one. Aoife is far away.
Young Man. I have come alone into the midst of you
  To weigh this sword against Cuchulain's sword.
Conchubar. And are you noble? for if of common seed,
  You cannot weigh your sword against his sword
  But in mixed battle.
Young Man.   I am under bonds
  To tell my name to no man; but it's noble.
Conchubar. But I would know your name and not your bonds.
  You cannot speak in the Assembly House,
  If you are not noble.
First Old King.   Answer the High King!
Young Man. I will give no other proof than the hawk gives
  That it's no sparrow!

          [*He is silent for a moment, then speaks to all.*

                    Yet look upon me, kings.
  I, too, am of that ancient seed, and carry
  The signs about this body and in these bones.
Cuchulain. To have shown the hawk's grey feather is enough,
  And you speak highly, too. Give me that helmet.
  I'd thought they had grown weary sending champions.
  That sword and belt will do. This fighting's welcome.
  The High King there has promised me his wisdom;
  But the hawk's sleepy till its well-beloved
  Cries out amid the acorns, or it has seen
  Its enemy like a speck upon the sun.
  What's wisdom to the hawk, when that clear eye
  Is burning nearer up in the high air?

      [*Looks hard at Young Man; then comes down steps and
          grasps Young Man by shoulder.*

  Hither into the light.
  [*To Conchubar.*]   The very tint
  Of her that I was speaking of but now.

Not a pin's difference.
[*To Young Man.*]   You are from the North,
Where there are many that have that tint of hair—
Red-brown, the light red-brown. Come nearer, boy,
For I would have another look at you.
There's more likeness—a pale, a stone-pale cheek.
What brought you, boy? Have you no fear of death?
Young Man. Whether I live or die is in the gods' hands.
Cuchulain. That is all words, all words; a young man's talk.
  I am their plough, their harrow, their very strength;
  For he that's in the sun begot this body
  Upon a mortal woman, and I have heard tell
  It seemed as if he had outrun the moon
  That he must follow always through waste heaven,
  He loved so happily. He'll be but slow
  To break a tree that was so sweetly planted.
  Let's see that arm. I'll see it if I choose.
  That arm had a good father and a good mother,
  But it is not like this.
Young Man.   You are mocking me;
  You think I am not worthy to be fought.
  But I'll not wrangle but with this talkative knife.
Cuchulain. Put up your sword; I am not mocking you.
  I'd have you for my friend, but if it's not
  Because you have a hot heart and a cold eye,
  I cannot tell the reason.
  [*To Conchubar.*]   He has got her fierceness,
  And nobody is as fierce as those pale women.
  But I will keep him with me, Conchubar,
  That he may set my memory upon her
  When the day's fading.—You will stop with us,
  And we will hunt the deer and the wild bulls;
  And, when we have grown weary, light our fires
  Between the wood and water, or on some mountain
  Where the Shape-Changers of the morning come.
  The High King there would make a mock of me
  Because I did not take a wife among them.
  Why do you hang your head? It's a good life:

The head grows prouder in the light of the dawn,
And friendship thickens in the murmuring dark
Where the spare hazels meet the wool-white foam.
But I can see there's no more need for words
And that you'll be my friend from this day out.

Conchubar. He has come hither not in his own name
But in Queen Aoife's, and has challenged us
In challenging the foremost man of us all.

Cuchulain. Well, well, what matter?

Conchubar.   You think it does not matter,
And that a fancy lighter than the air,
A whim of the moment, has more matter in it.
For, having none that shall reign after you,
You cannot think as I do, who would leave
A throne too high for insult.

Cuchulain.   Let your children
Re-mortar their inheritance, as we have,
And put more muscle on.—I'll give you gifts,
But I'd have something too—that arm-ring, boy.
We'll have this quarrel out when you are older.

Young Man. There is no man I'd sooner have my friend
Than you, whose name has gone about the world
As if it had been the wind; but Aoife'd say
I had turned coward.

Cuchulain.   I will give you gifts
That Aoife'll know, and all her people know,
To have come from me.   [*Showing cloak.*
                    My father gave me this.
He came to try me, rising up at dawn
Out of the cold dark of the rich sea.
He challenged me to battle, but before
My sword had touched his sword, told me his name,
Gave me this cloak, and vanished. It was woven
By women of the Country-under-Wave
Out of the fleeces of the sea. O! tell her
I was afraid, or tell her what you will.
No; tell her that I heard a raven croak
On the north side of the house, and was afraid.

Conchubar. Some witch of the air has troubled Cuchulain's
    mind.
Cuchulain. No witchcraft. His head is like a woman's head
    I had a fancy for.
Conchubar.   A witch of the air
    Can make a leaf confound us with memories.
    They run upon the wind and hurl the spells
    That make us nothing, out of the invisible wind.
    They have gone to school to learn the trick of it.
Cuchulain. No, no—there's nothing out of common here;
    The winds are innocent.—That arm-ring, boy.
A King. If I've your leave I'll take this challenge up.
Another King. No, give it me, High King, for this wild Aoife
    Has carried off my slaves.
Another King.   No, give it me,
    For she has harried me in house and herd.
Another King. I claim this fight.
Other Kings [*together*].   And I! And I! And I!
Cuchulain. Back! back! Put up your swords! Put up your
    swords!
    There's none alive that shall accept a challenge
    I have refused. Laegaire, put up your sword!
Young Man. No, let them come. If they've a mind for it,
    I'll try it out with any two together.
Cuchulain. That's spoken as I'd have spoken it at your age.
    But you are in my house. Whatever man
    Would fight with you shall fight it out with me.
    They're dumb, they're dumb. How many of you would
        meet   [*Draws sword*.
    This mutterer, this old whistler, this sand-piper,
    This edge that's greyer than the tide, this mouse
    That's gnawing at the timbers of the world,
    This, this—Boy, I would meet them all in arms
    If I'd a son like you. He would avenge me
    When I have withstood for the last time the men
    Whose fathers, brothers, sons, and friends I have killed
    Upholding Conchubar, when the four provinces
    Have gathered with the ravens over them.

But I'd need no avenger. You and I
Would scatter them like water from a dish.
Young Man. We'll stand by one another from this out.
  Here is the ring.
Cuchulain.   No, turn and turn about.
  But my turn's first because I am the older.
                        [*Spreading out cloak.*
  Nine queens out of the Country-under-Wave
  Have woven it with the fleeces of the sea
  And they were long embroidering at it.—Boy,
  If I had fought my father, he'd have killed me,
  As certainly as if I had a son.
  And fought with him, I should be deadly to him;
  For the old fiery fountains are far off
  And every day there is less heat o' the blood.
Conchubar [*in a loud voice*]. No more of this. I will not have
  this friendship.
  Cuchulain is my man, and I forbid it.
  He shall not go unfought, for I myself—
Cuchulain. I will not have it.
Conchubar.   You lay commands on me?
Cuchulain [*seizing Conchubar*]. You shall not stir, High King.
  I'll hold you there.
Conchubar. Witchcraft has maddened you.
The Kings [*shouting*].   Yes, witchcraft! witchcraft!
First Old King. Some witch has worked upon your mind,
  Cuchulain.
  The head of that young man seemed like a woman's
  You'd had a fancy for. Then of a sudden
  You laid your hands on the High King himself!
Cuchulain. And laid my hands on the High King himself?
Conchubar. Some witch is floating in the air above us.
Cuchulain. Yes, witchcraft! witchcraft! Witches of the air!
  [*To Young Man.*] Why did you? Who was it set you to this
  work?
  Out, out! I say, for now it's sword on sword!
Young Man. But . . . but I did not.
Cuchulain.   Out, I say, out, out!

    [*Young Man goes out followed by Cuchulain. The Kings*
    follow them out with confused cries, and words one
    can hardly hear because of the noise. Some cry,
    "Quicker, quicker!" "Why are you so long at the
    door?" "We'll be too late!" "Have they begun to
    fight?" "Can you see if they are fighting?" and so on.
    Their voices drown each other. The three Women are
    left alone.

First Woman. I have seen, I have seen!
Second Woman.   What do you cry aloud?
First Woman. The Ever-living have shown me what's to come.
Third Woman. How? Where?
First Woman.   In the ashes of the bowl.
Second Woman. While you were holding it between your
   hands?
Third Woman. Speak quickly!
First Woman.   I have seen Cuchulain's roof-tree
  Leap into fire, and the walls split and blacken.
Second Woman. Cuchulain has gone out to die.
Third Woman.   O! O!
Second Woman. Who could have thought that one so great
   as he
  Should meet his end at this unnoted sword!
First Woman. Life drifts between a fool and a blind man
  To the end, and nobody can know his end.
Second Woman. Come, look upon the quenching of this
   greatness.

    [*The other two go to the door, but they stop for a mo-*
    ment upon the threshold and wail.

First Woman. No crying out, for there'll be need of cries
  And rending of the hair when it's all finished.

    [*The Women go out. There is the sound of clashing*
    swords from time to time during what follows.
    Enter the Fool, dragging the Blind Man.

Fool. You have eaten it, you have eaten it! You have left me nothing but the bones.

[*He throws Blind Man down by big chair.*

Blind Man. O, that I should have to endure such a plague! O, I ache all over! O, I am pulled to pieces! This is the way you pay me all the good I have done you.

Fool. You have eaten it! You have told me lies. I might have known you had eaten it when I saw your slow, sleepy walk. Lie there till the kings come. O, I will tell Conchubar and Cuchulain and all the kings about you!

Blind Man. What would have happened to you but for me, and you without your wits? If I did not take care of you, what would you do for food and warmth?

Fool. You take care of me? You stay safe, and send me into every kind of danger. You sent me down the cliff for gulls' eggs while you warmed your blind eyes in the sun; and then you ate all that were good for food. You left me the eggs that were neither egg nor bird. [*Blind Man tries to rise; Fool makes him lie down again.*] Keep quiet now, till I shut the door. There is some noise outside—a high vexing noise, so that I can't be listening to myself. [*Shuts the big door.*] Why can't they be quiet? Why can't they be quiet? [*Blind Man tries to get away.*] Ah! you would get away, would you? [*Follows Blind Man and brings him back.*] Lie there! lie there! No, you won't get away! Lie there till the kings come. I'll tell them all about you. I will tell it all. How you sit warming yourself, when you have made me light a fire of sticks, while I sit blowing it with my mouth. Do you not always make me take the windy side of the bush when it blows, and the rainy side when it rains?

Blind Man. O, good Fool! listen to me. Think of the care I have taken of you. I have brought you to many a warm hearth, where there was a good welcome for you, but you would not stay there; you were always wandering about.

Fool. The last time you brought me in, it was not I who wandered away, but you that got put out because you took the crubeen out of the pot when nobody was looking. Keep quiet, now!

Cuchulain [*rushing in*]. Witchcraft! There is no witchcraft on the earth, or among the witches of the air, that these hands cannot break.

Fool. Listen to me, Cuchulain. I left him turning the fowl at the fire. He ate it all, though I had stolen it. He left me nothing but the feathers.

Cuchulain. Fill me a horn of ale!

Blind Man. I gave him what he likes best. You do not know how vain this Fool is. He likes nothing so well as a feather.

Fool. He left me nothing but the bones and feathers. Nothing but the feathers, though I had stolen it.

Cuchulain. Give me that horn. Quarrels here, too! [*Drinks.*] What is there between you two that is worth a quarrel? Out with it!

Blind Man. Where would he be but for me? I must be always thinking—thinking to get food for the two of us, and when we've got it, if the moon is at the full or the tide on the turn, he'll leave the rabbit in the snare till it is full of maggots, or let the trout slip back through his hands into the stream.

[*The Fool has begun singing while the Blind Man is speaking.*

Fool [*singing*].

> When you were an acorn on the tree-top,
>   Then was I an eagle-cock;
> Now that you are a withered old block,
>   Still am I an eagle-cock.

Blind Man. Listen to him, now. That's the sort of talk I have to put up with day out, day in.

[*The Fool is putting the feathers into his hair. Cuchulain takes a handful of feathers out of a heap the Fool has on the bench beside him, and out of the Fool's hair, and begins to wipe the blood from his sword with them.*

Fool. He has taken my feathers to wipe his sword. It is blood that he is wiping from his sword.

Cuchulain [*goes up to door at back and throws away feathers*]. They are standing about his body. They will not awaken him, for all his witchcraft.

Blind Man. It is that young champion that he has killed. He that came out of Aoife's country.

Cuchulain. He thought to have saved himself with witchcraft.

Fool. That Blind Man there said he would kill you. He came from Aoife's country to kill you. That Blind Man said they had taught him every kind of weapon that he might do it. But I always knew that you would kill him.

Cuchulain [*to the Blind Man*]. You knew him, then?

Blind Man. I saw him, when I had my eyes, in Aoife's country.

Cuchulain. You were in Aoife's country?

Blind Man. I knew him and his mother there.

Cuchulain. He was about to speak of her when he died.

Blind Man. He was a queen's son.

Cuchulain. What queen? what queen? [*Seizes Blind Man, who is now sitting upon the bench.*] Was it Scathach? There were many queens. All the rulers there were queens.

Blind Man. No, not Scathach.

Cuchulain. It was Uathach, then? Speak! speak!

Blind Man. I cannot speak; you are clutching me too tightly. [*Cuchulain lets him go.*] I cannot remember who it was. I am not certain. It was some queen.

Fool. He said a while ago that the young man was Aoife's son.

Cuchulain. She? No, no! She had no son when I was there.

Fool. That Blind Man there said that she owned him for her son.

Cuchulain. I had rather he had been some other woman's son. What father had he? A soldier out of Alba? She was an amorous woman—a proud, pale, amorous woman.

Blind Man. None knew whose son he was.

Cuchulain. None knew! Did you know, old listener at doors?

Blind Man. No, no; I knew nothing.

Fool. He said a while ago that he heard Aoife boast that she'd never but the one lover, and he the only man that had overcome her in battle. [*Pause.*

Blind Man. Somebody is trembling, Fool! The bench is

shaking. Why are you trembling? Is Cuchulain going to hurt us? It was not I who told you, Cuchulain.

Fool. It is Cuchulain who is trembling. It is Cuchulain who is shaking the bench.

Blind Man. It is his own son he has slain.

Cuchulain. 'Twas they that did it, the pale windy people.
　Where? where? where? My sword against the thunder!
　But no, for they have always been my friends;
　And though they love to blow a smoking coal
　Till it's all flame, the wars they blow aflame
　Are full of glory, and heart-uplifting pride,
　And not like this. The wars they love awaken
　Old fingers and the sleepy strings of harps.
　Who did it then? Are you afraid? Speak out!
　For I have put you under my protection,
　And will reward you well. Dubthach the Chafer?
　He'd an old grudge. No, for he is with Maeve.
　Laegaire did it! Why do you not speak?
　What is this house? [*Pause.*] Now I remember all.

　　　[*Comes before Conchubar's chair, and strikes out with
　　　　his sword, as if Conchubar was sitting upon it.*

　'Twas you who did it—you who sat up there
　With your old rod of kingship, like a magpie
　Nursing a stolen spoon. No, not a magpie,
　A maggot that is eating up the earth!
　Yes, but a magpie, for he's flown away.
　Where did he fly to?

Blind Man.　　　　　　He is outside the door.

Cuchulain. Outside the door?

Blind Man.　　　　　　　　Between the door and the sea.

Cuchulain. Conchubar, Conchubar! the sword into your heart!
　　　[*He rushes out. Pause. Fool creeps up to the big door
　　　　and looks after him.*

Fool. He is going up to King Conchubar. They are all about the young man. No, no, he is standing still. There is a great wave going to break, and he is looking at it. Ah! now he is running down to the sea, but he is holding up his sword as if he were going into a fight. [*Pause.*] Well struck! well struck!

Blind Man. What is he doing now?

Fool. O! he is fighting the waves!

Blind Man. He sees King Conchubar's crown on every one of them.

Fool. There, he has struck at a big one! He has struck the crown off it; he has made the foam fly. There again, another big one!

Blind Man. Where are the kings? What are the kings doing?

Fool. They are shouting and running down to the shore, and the people are running out of the houses. They are all running.

Blind Man. You say they are running out of the houses? There will be nobody left in the houses. Listen, Fool!

Fool. There, he is down! He is up again. He is going out in the deep water. There is a big wave. It has gone over him. I cannot see him now. He has killed kings and giants, but the waves have mastered him, the waves have mastered him! *life has overpowered him.*

Blind Man. Come here, Fool!

Fool. The waves have mastered him.

Blind Man. Come here!

Fool. The waves have mastered him.

Blind Man. Come here, I say.

Fool [*coming towards him, but looking backwards towards the door*]. What is it?

Blind Man. There will be nobody in the houses. Come this way; come quickly! The ovens will be full. We will put our hands into the ovens.   [*They go out.*

Steal while houses empty.

THE END

Life still goes on, despite the heroes.

DEIRDRE

Deirdre

PERSONS IN THE PLAY

Musicians

Fergus, *an old man*

Naoise (*pronounced Neesh-e*), *a young king*

Deirdre, *his queen*

A Dark-faced Messenger

Conchubar (*pronounced Conohar*), *the old King of Uladh, who is still strong and vigorous*

A Dark-faced Executioner

A Guest-house in a wood. It is a rough house of timber; through the doors and some of the windows one can see the great spaces of the wood, the sky dimming, night closing in. But a window to the left shows the thick leaves of a coppice; the landscape suggests silence and loneliness. There is a door to right and left, and through the side windows one can see anybody who approaches either door, a moment before he enters. In the centre, a part of the house is curtained off; the curtains are drawn. There are unlighted torches in brackets on the walls. There is, at one side, a small table with a chess- board and chessmen upon it. At the other side of the room there is a brazier with a fire; two women, with musical instru- ments beside them, crouch about the brazier: they are comely women of about forty. Another woman, who carries a stringed instrument, enters hurriedly; she speaks, at first standing in the doorway.

First Musician. I have a story right, my wanderers,
   That has so mixed with fable in our songs
   That all seemed fabulous. We are come, by chance,
   Into King Conchubar's country, and this house
   Is an old guest-house built for travellers

From the seashore to Conchubar's royal house,
And there are certain hills among these woods
And there Queen Deirdre grew.

Second Musician.   That famous queen
Who has been wandering with her lover Naoise
Somewhere beyond the edges of the world?

First Musician [*going nearer to the brazier*]. Some dozen years
    ago, King Conchubar found
A house upon a hillside in this wood,
And there a child with an old witch to nurse her,
And nobody to say if she were human,
Or of the gods, or anything at all
Of who she was or why she was hidden there,
But that she'd too much beauty for good luck.
He went up thither daily, till at last
She put on womanhood, and he lost peace,
And Deirdre's tale began. The King was old.
A month or so before the marriage-day,
A young man, in the laughing scorn of his youth,
Naoise, the son of Usna, climbed up there,
And having wooed, or, as some say, been wooed,
Carried her off.

Second Musician.   The tale were well enough
Had it a finish.

First Musician.   Hush! I have more to tell;
But gather close about that I may whisper
The secrets of a king.

Second Musician   There's none to hear!

First Musician. I have been to Conchubar's house and fol-
    lowed up
A crowd of servants going out and in
With loads upon their heads: embroideries
To hang upon the walls, or new-mown rushes
To strew upon the floors, and came at length
To a great room.

Second Musician.   Be silent; there are steps!
    *Enter Fergus, an old man, who moves about from
    door to window excitedly through what follows.*

Fergus. I thought to find a message from the King.
  You are musicians by these instruments,
  And if as seems—for you are comely women—
  You can praise love, you'll have the best of luck,
  For there'll be two, before the night is in,
  That bargained for their love, and paid for it.
  All that men value. You have but the time
  To weigh a happy music with a sad,
  To find what is most pleasing to a lover,
  Before the son of Usna and his queen
  Have passed this threshold.

First Musician.   Deirdre and her man!

Fergus. I was to have found a message in this house,
  And ran to meet it. Is there no messenger
  From Conchubar to Fergus, son of Rogh?

First Musician. Are Deirdre and her lover tired of life?

Fergus. You are not of this country, or you'd know
  That they are in my charge and all forgiven.

First Musician. We have no country but the roads of the world.

Fergus. Then you should know that all things change in the world,
  And hatred turns to love and love to hate,
  And even kings forgive.

First Musician.   An old man's love
  Who casts no second line is hard to cure;
  His jealousy is like his love.

Fergus.   And that's but true.
  You have learned something in your wanderings.
  He was so hard to cure that the whole court,
  But I alone, thought it impossible;
  Yet after I had urged it at all seasons,
  I had my way, and all's forgiven now;
  And you shall speak the welcome and the joy
  That I lack tongue for.

First Musician.   Yet old men are jealous.

Fergus [*going to door*]. I am Conchubar's near friend, and that
  weighed somewhat,

And it was policy to pardon them.
The need of some young, famous, popular man
To lead the troops, the murmur of the crowd,
And his own natural impulse, urged him to it.
They have been wandering half a dozen years.
First Musician. And yet old men are jealous.
Fergus [*coming from door*].   Sing the more sweetly
Because, though age is arid as a bone,
This man has flowered. I've need of music, too;
If this grey head would suffer no reproach,
I'd dance and sing—
  [*Dark-faced men with strange, barbaric dress and arms
     begin to pass by the doors and windows. They pass one
     by one and in silence.*
                              and dance till the hour ran out,
Because I have accomplished this good deed.
First Musician. Look there—there at the window, those dark
    men,
With murderous and outlandish-looking arms—
They've been about the house all day.
Fergus [*looking after them*].   What are you?
Where do you come from, who is it sent you here?
First Musician. They will not answer you.
Fergus.   They do not hear.
First Musician. Forgive my open speech, but to these eyes
That have seen many lands they are such men
As kings will gather for a murderous task
That neither bribes, commands, nor promises
Can bring their people to.
Fergus.   And that is why
You harped upon an old man's jealousy.
A trifle sets you quaking. Conchubar's fame
Brings merchandise on every wind that blows.
They may have brought him Libyan dragon-skin,
Or the ivory of the fierce unicorn.
First Musician. If these be merchants, I have seen the goods
They have brought to Conchubar, and understood
His murderous purpose.

Fergus.   Murderous, you say?
   Why, what new gossip of the roads is this?
   But I'll not hear.
First Musician.   It may be life or death.
   There is a room in Conchubar's house, and there—
Fergus. Be silent, or I'll drive you from the door.
   There's many a one that would do more than that,
   And make it prison, or death, or banishment
   To slander the High King.
          [*Suddenly restraining himself and speaking gently.*
                     He is my friend;
   I have his oath, and I am well content.
   I have known his mind as if it were my own
   These many years, and there is none alive
   Shall buzz against him, and I there to stop it.
   I know myself, and him, and your wild thought
   Fed on extravagant poetry, and lit
   By such a dazzle of old fabulous tales
   That common things are lost, and all that's strange
   Is true because 'twere pity if it were not.
                     [*Going to the door again.*
   Quick! quick! your instruments! they are coming now.
   I hear the hoofs a-clatter. Begin that song!
   But what is it to be? I'd have them hear
   A music foaming up out of the house
   Like wine out of a cup. Come now, a verse
   Of some old time not worth remembering,
   And all the lovelier because a bubble.
   Begin, begin, of some old king and queen,
   Of Lugaidh Redstripe or another; no, not him,
   He and his lady perished wretchedly.

             First Musician [*singing*]
          "Why is it," Queen Edain said,
             "If I do but climb the stair . . ."
Fergus. Ah! that is better. . . . They are alighted now.
   Shake all your cockscombs, children; these are lovers.
                     [*Fergus goes out.*

First Musician
"Why is it," Queen Edain said,
  "If I do but climb the stair
To the tower overhead,
  When the winds are calling there,
Or the gannets calling out
  In waste places of the sky,
There's so much to think about
  That I cry, that I cry?"
Second Musician
But her goodman answered her:
  "Love would be a thing of naught
Had not all his limbs a stir
  Born out of immoderate thought;
Were he anything by half,
  Were his measure running dry.
Lovers, if they may not laugh,
  Have to cry, have to cry."

[*Deirdre, Naoise, and Fergus have been seen for a moment through the windows, but now they have entered.*

The Three Musicians [*together*]
But is Edain worth a song
  Now the hunt begins anew?
Praise the beautiful and strong;
  Praise the redness of the yew;
Praise the blossoming apple-stem.
  But our silence had been wise.
What is all our praise to them
  That have one another's eyes?

Deirdre. Silence your music, though I thank you for it;
  But the wind's blown upon my hair, and I
  Must set the jewels on my neck and head
  For one that's coming.

Naoise.   Your colour has all gone
  As 'twere with fear, and there's no cause for that.

Deirdre. These women have the raddle that they use
  To make them brave and confident, although
  Dread, toil, or cold may chill the blood o' their cheeks.

You'll help me, women. It is my husband's will
I show my trust in one that may be here
Before the mind can call the colour up.
My husband took these rubies from a king
Of Surracha that was so murderous
He seemed all glittering dragon. Now wearing them
Myself wars on myself, for I myself—
That do my husband's will, yet fear to do it—
Grow dragonish to myself.

> [*The women have gathered about her. Naoise has stood*
> *looking at her, but Fergus brings him to the chess-*
> *table.*

Naoise.   No messenger!
It's strange that there is none to welcome us.
Fergus. King Conchubar has sent no messenger
That he may come himself.
Naoise.   And being himself,
Being High King, he cannot break his faith.
I have his word and I must take that word,
Or prove myself unworthy of my nurture
Under a great man's roof.
Fergus.   We'll play at chess
Till the King comes. It is but natural
That she should doubt him, for her house has been
The hole of the badger and the den of the fox.
Naoise. If I had not King Conchubar's word I'd think
That chess-board ominous.
Fergus.   How can a board
That has been lying there these many years
Be lucky or unlucky?
Naoise.   It is the board
Where Lugaidh Redstripe and that wife of his,
Who had a seamew's body half the year,
Played at the chess upon the night they died.
Fergus. I can remember now, a tale of treachery,
A broken promise and a journey's end—
But it were best forgot.

[*Deirdre has been standing with the women about her.
They have been helping her to put on her jewels and
to put the pigment on her cheeks and arrange her hair.
She has gradually grown attentive to what Fergus is
saying.*

Naoise.   If the tale's true,
When it was plain that they had been betrayed,
They moved the men and waited for the end
As it were bedtime, and had so quiet minds
They hardly winked their eyes when the sword flashed.
Fergus. She never could have played so, being a woman,
If she had not the cold sea's blood in her.
Deirdre. The gods turn clouds and casual accidents
Into omens.
Naoise.   It would but ill become us,
Now that King Conchubar has pledged his word,
Should we be startled by a cloud or a shadow.
Deirdre. There's none to welcome us.
Naoise.   Being his guest,
Words that would wrong him can but wrong ourselves.
Deirdre. An empty house upon the journey's end!
Is that the way a king that means no mischief
Honours a guest?
Fergus.   He is but making ready
A welcome in his house, arranging where
The moorhen and the mallard go, and where
The speckled heathcock on a golden dish.
Deirdre. Had he no messenger?
Naoise.   Such words and fears
Wrong this old man who's pledged his word to us.
We must not speak or think as women do,
That when the house is all abed sit up
Marking among the ashes with a stick
Till they are terrified.—Being what we are
We must meet all things with an equal mind.
[*To Fergus.*] Come, let us look if there's a messenger
From Conchubar. We cannot see from this
Because we are blinded by the leaves and twigs,

But it may be the wood will thin again.
It is but kind that when the lips we love
Speak words that are unfitting for kings' ears
Our ears be deaf.

Fergus.   But now I had to threaten
These wanderers because they would have weighed
Some crazy fantasy of their own brain
Or gossip of the road with Conchubar's word.
If I had thought so little of mankind
I never could have moved him to this pardon.
I have believed the best of every man,
And find that to believe it is enough
To make a bad man show him at his best,
Or even a good man swing his lantern higher.

  [*Naoise and Fergus go out. The last words are spoken as
  they go through the door. One can see them through
  part of what follows, either through door or window.
  They move about, talking or looking along the road
  towards Conchubar's house.*

First Musician. If anything lies heavy on your heart,
Speak freely of it, knowing it is certain
That you will never see my face again.

Deirdre. You've been in love?

First Musician.   If you would speak of love
Speak freely. There is nothing in the world
That has been friendly to us but the kisses
That were upon our lips, and when we are old
Their memory will be all the life we have.

Deirdre. There was a man that loved me. He was old;
I could not love him. Now I can but fear.
He has made promises, and brought me home;
But though I turn it over in my thoughts,
I cannot tell if they are sound and wholesome,
Or hackles on the hook.

First Musician.   I have heard he loved you
As some old miser loves the dragon-stone
He hides among the cobwebs near the roof.

Deirdre. You mean that when a man who has loved like that
  Is after crossed, love drowns in its own flood,
  And that love drowned and floating is but hate;
  And that a king who hates sleeps ill at night
  Till he has killed; and that, though the day laughs,
  We shall be dead at cock-crow.
First Musician.   You've not my thought.
  When I lost one I loved distractedly,
  I blamed my crafty rival and not him,
  And fancied, till my passion had run out,
  That could I carry him away with me,
  And tell him all my love, I'd keep him yet.
Deirdre. Ah! now I catch your meaning, that this king
  Will murder Naoise, and keep me alive.
First Musician. 'Tis you that put that meaning upon words
  Spoken at random.
Deirdre.   Wanderers like you,
  Who have their wit alone to keep their lives,
  Speak nothing that is bitter to the ear
  At random; if they hint at it at all
  Their eyes and ears have gathered it so lately
  That it is crying out in them for speech.
First Musician. We have little that is certain.
Deirdre.   Certain or not,
  Speak it out quickly, I beseech you to it;
  I never have met any of your kind
  But that I gave them money, food, and fire.
First Musician. There are strange, miracle-working, wicked
      stones,
  Men tear out of the heart and the hot brain
  Of Libyan dragons.
Deirdre.   The hot Istain stone,
  And the cold stone of Fanes, that have power
  To stir even those at enmity to love.
First Musician. They have so great an influence, if but sewn
  In the embroideries that curtain in
  The bridal bed.

Deirdre.   O Mover of the stars
    That made this delicate house of ivory,
    And made my soul its mistress, keep it safe!
First Musician. I have seen a bridal bed, so curtained in,
    So decked for miracle in Conchubar's house,
    And learned that a bride's coming.
Deirdre.   And I the bride?
    Here is worse treachery than the seamew suffered,
    For she but died and mixed into the dust
    Of her dear comrade, but I am to live
    And lie in the one bed with him I hate.
    Where is Naoise? I was not alone like this
    When Conchubar first chose me for his wife;
    I cried in sleeping or waking and he came,
    But now there is worse need.
Naoise [entering with Fergus].   Why have you called?
    I was but standing there, without the door.
Deirdre. I have heard terrible mysterious things,
    Magical horrors and the spells of wizards.
Fergus. Why, that's no wonder. You have been listening
    To singers of the roads that gather up
    The stories of the world.
Deirdre.   But I have one
    To make the stories of the world but nothing.
Naoise. Be silent if it is against the King
    Whose guest you are.
Fergus.   No, let her speak it out.
    I know the High King's heart as it were my own,
    And can refute a slander, but already
    I have warned these women that it may be death.
Naoise. I will not weigh the gossip of the roads
    With the King's word. I ask your pardon for her:
    She has the heart of the wild birds that fear
    The net of the fowler or the wicker cage.
Deirdre. Am I to see the fowler and the cage
    And speak no word at all?
Naoise.   You would have known,
    Had they not bred you in that mountainous place,

That when we give a word and take a word
    Sorrow is put away, past wrong forgotten.
Deirdre. Though death may come of it?
Naoise.   Though death may come.
Deirdre. When first we came into this empty house
    You had foreknowledge of our death, and even
    When speaking of the paleness of my cheek
    Your own cheek blanched.
Naoise.   Listen to this old man.
    He can remember all the promises
    We trusted to.
Deirdre.   You speak from the lips out,
    And I am pleading for your life and mine.
Naoise. Listen to this old man, for many think
    He has a golden tongue.
Deirdre.   Then I will say
    What it were best to carry to the grave.
    Look at my face where the leaf raddled it
    And at these rubies on my hair and breast.
    It was for him, to stir him to desire,
    I put on beauty; yes, for Conchubar.
Naoise. What frenzy put these words into your mouth?
Deirdre. No frenzy, for what need is there for frenzy
    To change what shifts with every change of the wind,
    Or else there is no truth in men's old sayings?
    Was I not born a woman?
Naoise.   You're mocking me.
Deirdre. And is there mockery in this face and eyes,
    Or in this body, in these limbs that brought
    So many mischiefs? Look at me and say
    If that that shakes my limbs be mockery.
Naoise. What woman is there that a man can trust
    But at the moment when he kisses her
    At the first midnight?
Deirdre.   Were it not most strange
    That women should put evil in men's hearts
    And lack it in themselves? And yet I think

That being half good I might change round again
Were we aboard our ship and on the sea.
Naoise. We'll to the horses and take ship again.
Fergus. Fool, she but seeks to rouse your jealousy
  With crafty words.
Deirdre.   Were we not born to wander?
  These jewels have been reaped by the innocent sword
  Upon a mountain, and a mountain bred me;
  But who can tell what change can come to love
  Among the valleys? I speak no falsehood now.
  Away to windy summits, and there mock
  The night-jar and the valley-keeping bird!
Fergus. Men blamed you that you stirred a quarrel up
  That has brought death to many. I have made peace,
  Poured water on the fire, but if you fly
  King Conchubar may think that he is mocked
  And the house blaze again: and in what quarter,
  If Conchubar were the treacherous man you think,
  Would you find safety now that you have come
  Into the very middle of his power,
  Under his very eyes?
Deirdre.   Under his eyes
  And in the very middle of his power!
  Then there is but one way to make all safe:
  I'll spoil this beauty that brought misery
  And houseless wandering on the man I loved.
  These wanderers will show me how to do it;
  To clip this hair to baldness, blacken my skin
  With walnut juice, and tear my face with briars.
  O that the creatures of the woods had torn
  My body with their claws!
Fergus.   What, wilder yet!
Deirdre [*to Naoise*]. Whatever were to happen to my face
  I'd be myself, and there's not any way
  But this to bring all trouble to an end.
Naoise. Leave the gods' handiwork unblotched, and wait
  For their decision, our decision is past.

[*A Dark-faced Messenger comes to the threshold.*

Fergus. Peace, peace; the messenger is at the door;
   He stands upon the threshold; he stands there;
   He stands, King Conchubar's purpose on his lips.
Messenger. Supper is on the table. Conchubar
   Is waiting for his guests.
Fergus.   All's well again!
   All's well! All's well! You cried your doubts so loud
   That I had almost doubted.
Naoise.   We doubted him,
   And he the while but busy in his house
   For the more welcome.
Deirdre.   The message is not finished.
Fergus. Come quickly. Conchubar will laugh, that I—
   Although I held out boldly in my speech—
   That I, even I—
Deirdre.   Wait, wait! He is not done.
Messenger. Deirdre and Fergus, son of Rogh, are summoned;
   But not the traitor that bore off the Queen.
   It is enough that the King pardon her,
   And call her to his table and his bed.
Naoise. So, then, it's treachery.
Fergus.   I'll not believe it.
Naoise. Lead on and I will follow at your heels
   That I may challenge him before his court
   To match me there, or match me in some place
   Where none can come between us but our swords,
   For I have found no truth on any tongue
   That's not of iron.
Messenger.   I am Conchubar's man,
   I am content to serve an iron tongue:
   That Tongue commands that Fergus, son of Rogh,
   And Deirdre come this night into his house,
   And none but they.   [*He goes, followed by Naoise.*
Fergus.   Some rogue, some enemy,
   Has bribed him to embroil us with the King;
   I know that he has lied because I know

King Conchubar's mind as if it were my own,
But I'll find out the truth.

[*He is about to follow Naoise, but Deirdre stops him.*

Deirdre. No, no, old man.
You thought the best, and the worst came of it;
We listened to the counsel of the wise,
And so turned fools. But ride and bring your friends.
Go, and go quickly. Conchubar has not seen me;
It may be that his passion is asleep,
And that we may escape.
Fergus. But I'll go first,
And follow up that Libyan heel, and send
Such words to Conchubar that he may know
At how great peril he lays hands upon you.

Naoise enters

Naoise. The Libyan, knowing that a servant's life
Is safe from hands like mine, but turned and mocked.
Fergus. I'll call my friends, and call the reaping-hooks,
And carry you in safety to the ships.
My name has still some power. I will protect,
Or, if that is impossible, revenge.

[*Goes out by other door.*
Naoise [*who is calm, like a man who has passed beyond life*].
The crib has fallen and the birds are in it;
There is not one of the great oaks about us
But shades a hundred men.
Deirdre. Let's out and die,
Or break away, if the chance favour us.
Naoise. They would but drag you from me, stained with
blood.
Their barbarous weapons would but mar that beauty,
And I would have you die as a queen should—
In a death-chamber. You are in my charge.
We will wait here, and when they come upon us,
I'll hold them from the doors, and when that's over,
Give you a cleanly death with this grey edge.

Deirdre. I will stay here; but you go out and fight.
　Our way of life has brought no friends to us,
　And if we do not buy them leaving it,
　We shall be ever friendless.
Naoise.　　　　　　　　What do they say?
　That Lugaidh Redstripe and that wife of his
　Sat at this chess-board, waiting for their end.
　They knew that there was nothing that could save them,
　And so played chess as they had any night
　For years, and waited for the stroke of sword.
　I never heard a death so out of reach
　Of common hearts, a high and comely end.
　What need have I, that gave up all for love,
　To die like an old king out of a fable,
　Fighting and passionate? What need is there
　For all that ostentation at my setting?
　I have loved truly and betrayed no man.
　I need no lightning at the end, no beating
　In a vain fury at the cage's door.
　[*To Musicians.*] Had you been here when that man and his
　　queen
　Played at so high a game, could you have found
　An ancient poem for the praise of it?
　It should have set out plainly that those two,
　Because no man and woman have loved better,
　Might sit on there contentedly, and weigh
　The joy comes after. I have heard the seamew
　Sat there, with all the colour in her cheeks,
　As though she'd say: "There's nothing happening
　But that a king and queen are playing chess."
Deirdre. He's in the right, though I have not been born
　Of the cold, haughty waves, my veins being hot,
　And though I have loved better than that queen,
　I'll have as quiet fingers on the board.
　O, singing women, set it down in a book,
　That love is all we need, even though it is
　But the last drops we gather up like this;
　And though the drops are all we have known of life,

For we have been most friendless—praise us for it,
And praise the double sunset, for naught's lacking
But a good end to the long, cloudy day.
Naoise. Light torches there and drive the shadows out,
For day's grey end comes up.

> [*A Musician lights a torch in the fire and then crosses
> before the chess-players, and slowly lights the torches
> in the sconces. The light is almost gone from the wood,
> but there is a clear evening light in the sky, increasing
> the sense of solitude and loneliness.*

Deirdre.   Make no sad music.
What is it but a king and queen at chess?
They need a music that can mix itself
Into imagination, but not break
The steady thinking that the hard game needs.

> [*During the chess, the Musicians sing this song*]
>> Love is an immoderate thing
>>   And can never be content
>> Till it dip an ageing wing
>>   Where some laughing element
>> Leaps and Time's old lanthorn dims.
>>   What's the merit in love-play,
>> In the tumult of the limbs
>>   That dies out before 'tis day,
>> Heart on heart, or mouth on mouth,
>>   All that mingling of our breath,
>> When love-longing is but drouth
>>   For the things come after death?

> [*During the last verses Deirdre rises from the board and
> kneels at Naoise's feet.*

Deirdre. I cannot go on playing like that woman
That had but the cold blood of the sea in her veins.
Naoise. It is your move. Take up your man again.
Deirdre. Do you remember that first night in the woods
We lay all night on leaves, and looking up,
When the first grey of the dawn awoke the birds,

Saw leaves above us? You thought that I still slept,
And bending down to kiss me on the eyes,
Found they were open. Bend and kiss me now,
For it may be the last before our death.
And when that's over, we'll be different;
Imperishable things, a cloud or a fire.
And I know nothing but this body, nothing
But that old vehement, bewildering kiss.

> [Conchubar comes to the door

First Musician. Children, beware!
Naoise [laughing].   He has taken up my challenge;
  Whether I am a ghost or living man
  When day has broken, I'll forget the rest,
  And say that there is kingly stuff in him.

> [Turns to fetch spear and shield, and then sees that
> Conchubar has gone.

First Musician. He came to spy upon you, not to fight.
Naoise. A prudent hunter, therefore, but no king.
  He'd find if what has fallen in the pit
  Were worth the hunting, but has come too near,
  And I turn hunter. You're not man, but beast.
  Go scurry in the bushes, now, beast, beast,
  For now it's topsy-turvy, I upon you.

> [He rushes out after Conchubar.

Deirdre. You have a knife there, thrust into your girdle.
  I'd have you give it me.
First Musician.   No, but I dare not.
Deirdre. No, but you must.
First Musician.   If harm should come to you,
  They'd know I gave it.
Deirdre [snatching knife].   There is no mark on this
  To make it different from any other
  Out of a common forge.

> [Goes to the door and looks out.

First Musician. You have taken it,
  I did not give it you; but there are times
  When such a thing is all the friend one has.
Deirdre. The leaves hide all, and there's no way to find
  What path to follow. Why is there no sound?

  [*She goes from door to window.*

First Musician. Where would you go?
Deirdre. To strike a blow for Naoise,
  If Conchubar call the Libyans to his aid.
  But why is there no clash? They have met by this!
First Musician. Listen. I am called wise. If Conchubar win,
  You have a woman's wile that can do much,
  Even with men in pride of victory.
  He is in love and old. What were one knife
  Among a hundred?
Deirdre [*going towards them*]. Women, if I die,
  If Naoise die this night, how will you praise?
  What words seek out? for that will stand to you;
  For being but dead we shall have many friends.
  All through your wanderings, the doors of kings
  Shall be thrown wider open, the poor man's hearth
  Heaped with new turf, because you are wearing this

  [*Gives Musician a bracelet.*

  To show that you have Deirdre's story right.
First Musician. Have you not been paid servants in love's
    house
  To sweep the ashes out and keep the doors?
  And though you have suffered all for mere love's sake
  You'd live your lives again.
Deirdre. Even this last hour.
    Conchubar enters with dark-faced men
Conchubar. One woman and two men; that is the quarrel
  That knows no mending. Bring in the man she chose
  Because of his beauty and the strength of his youth.

       [The dark-faced men drag in Naoise entangled in a net.
Naoise. I have been taken like a bird or a fish.
Conchubar. He cried "Beast, beast!" and in a blind-beast rage
  He ran at me and fell into the nets,
  But we were careful for your sake, and took him
  With all the comeliness that woke desire
  Unbroken in him. I being old and lenient,
  I would not hurt a hair upon his head.
Deirdre. What do you say? Have you forgiven him?
Naoise. He is but mocking us. What's left to say
  Now that the seven years' hunt is at an end?
Deirdre. He never doubted you until I made him,
  And therefore all the blame for what he says
  Should fall on me.
Conchubar.   But his young blood is hot,
  And if we're of one mind, he shall go free,
  And I ask nothing for it, or, if something,
  Nothing I could not take. There is no king
  In the wide world that, being so greatly wronged,
  Could copy me, and give all vengeance up.
  Although her marriage-day had all but come,
  You carried her away; but I'll show mercy.
  Because you had the insolent strength of youth
  You carried her away; but I've had time
  To think it out through all these seven years.
  I will show mercy.
Naoise.   You have many words.
Conchubar. I will not make a bargain; I but ask
  What is already mine.
     [Deirdre moves slowly towards Conchubar while he is
       speaking, her eyes fixed upon him.
               You may go free
  If Deirdre will but walk into my house
  Before the people's eyes, that they may know,
  When I have put the crown upon her head,
  I have not taken her by force and guile.
  The doors are open, and the floors are strewed
  And in the bridal chamber curtains sewn

With all enchantments that give happiness
By races that are germane to the sun,
And nearest him, and have no blood in their veins—
For when they're wounded the wound drips with wine—
Nor speech but singing. At the bridal door
Two fair king's daughters carry in their hands
The crown and robe.

Deirdre.   O no! Not that, not that!
Ask any other thing but that one thing.
Leave me with Naoise. We will go away
Into some country at the ends of the earth.
We'll trouble you no more; and there is no one
That will not praise you if you pardon us.
"He is good, he is good," they'll say to one another;
"There's nobody like him, for he forgave
Deirdre and Naoise."

Conchubar.   Do you think that I
Shall let you go again, after seven years
Of longing and of planning here and there,
And trafficking with merchants for the stones
That make all sure, and watching my own face
That none might read it?

Deirdre [*to Naoise*].   It's better to go with him.
Why should you die when one can bear it all?
My life is over; it's better to obey.
Why should you die? I will not live long, Naoise.
I'd not have you believe I'd long stay living;
O no, no, no! You will go far away.
You will forget me. Speak, speak, Naoise, speak,
And say that it is better that I go.
I will not ask it. Do not speak a word,
For I will take it all upon myself.
Conchubar, I will go.

Naoise.   And do you think
That, were I given life at such a price,
I would not cast it from me? O my eagle!
Why do you beat vain wings upon the rock
When hollow night's above?

Deirdre.   It's better, Naoise.
It may be hard for you, but you'll forget.
For what am I, to be remembered always?
And there are other women. There was one,
The daughter of the King of Leodas;
I could not sleep because of her. Speak to him;
Tell it out plain, and make him understand.
And if it be he thinks I shall stay living,
Say that I will not.
Naoise.   Would I had lost life
Among those Scottish kings that sought it of me
Because you were my wife, or that the worst
Had taken you before this bargaining!
O eagle! If you were to do this thing,
And buy my life of Conchubar with your body,
Love's law being broken, I would stand alone
Upon the eternal summits, and call out,
And you could never come there, being banished.
Deirdre [*kneeling to Conchubar*]. I would obey, but cannot.
    Pardon us.
I know that you are good. I have heard you praised
For giving gifts; and you will pardon us,
Although I cannot go into your house.
It was my fault. I only should be punished.
                    [*Unseen by Deirdre, Naoise is gagged.*
The very moment these eyes fell on him,
I told him; I held out my hands to him;
How could he refuse? At first he would not—
I am not lying—he remembered you.
What do I say? My hands?—No, no, my lips—
For I had pressed my lips upon his lips—
I swear it is not false—my breast to his;
    [*Conchubar motions; Naoise, unseen by Deirdre, is taken
        behind the curtain.*
Until I woke the passion that's in all,
And how could he resist? I had my beauty.
You may have need of him, a brave, strong man,
Who is not foolish at the council-board,

Nor does he quarrel by the candle-light
And give hard blows to dogs. A cup of wine
Moves him to mirth, not madness.

[*She stands up.*
What am I saying?
You may have need of him, for you have none
Who is so good a sword, or so well loved
Among the common people. You may need him,
And what king knows when the hour of need may come?
You dream that you have men enough. You laugh.
Yes; you are laughing to yourself. You say,
"I am Conchubar—I have no need of him."
You will cry out for him some day and say,
"If Naoise were but living"—[*she misses Naoise*]. Where is
he?
Where have you sent him? Where is the son of Usna?
Where is he, O, where is he?
[*She staggers over to the Musicians. The Executioner
has come out with a sword on which there is blood;
Conchubar points to it. The Musicians give a wail.*
Conchubar. The traitor who has carried off my wife
No longer lives. Come to my house now, Deirdre,
For he that called himself your husband's dead.
Deirdre. O, do not touch me. Let me go to him.

[*Pause.*
King Conchubar is right. My husband's dead.
A single woman is of no account,
Lacking array of servants, linen cupboards,
The bacon hanging—and King Conchubar's house
All ready, too—I'll to King Conchubar's house.
It is but wisdom to do willingly
What has to be.
Conchubar. But why are you so calm?
I thought that you would curse me and cry out,
And fall upon the ground and tear your hair.
Deirdre [*laughing*]. You know too much of women to think so;
Though, if I were less worthy of desire,
I would pretend as much; but, being myself,

It is enough that you were master here.
Although we are so delicately made,
There's something brutal in us, and we are won
By those who can shed blood. It was some woman
That taught you how to woo: but do not touch me:
I shall do all you bid me, but not yet,
Because I have to do what's customary.
We lay the dead out, folding up the hands,
Closing the eyes, and stretching out the feet,
And push a pillow underneath the head,
Till all's in order; and all this I'll do
For Naoise, son of Usna.

Conchubar.   It is not fitting.
You are not now a wanderer, but a queen,
And there are plenty that can do these things.

Deirdre [*motioning Conchubar away*]. No, no. Not yet. I
cannot be your queen
Till the past's finished, and its debts are paid.
When a man dies, and there are debts unpaid,
He wanders by the debtor's bed and cries,
"There's so much owing."

Conchubar.   You are deceiving me.
You long to look upon his face again.
Why should I give you now to a dead man
That took you from a living?

                    [*He makes a step towards her.*
Deirdre.   In good time.
You'll stir me to more passion than he could,
And yet, if you are wise, you'll grant me this:
That I go look upon him that was once
So strong and comely and held his head so high
That women envied me. For I will see him
All blood-bedabbled and his beauty gone.
It's better, when you're beside me in your strength,
That the mind's eye should call up the soiled body,
And not the shape I loved. Look at him, women.
He heard me pleading to be given up,
Although my lover was still living, and yet

He doubts my purpose. I will have you tell him
How changeable all women are; how soon
Even the best of lovers is forgot
When his day's finished.

Conchubar. No; but I will trust
The strength that you have praised, and not your purpose.

Deirdre [*almost with a caress*]. It is so small a gift and you will
grant it
Because it is the first that I have asked.
He has refused. There is no sap in him;
Nothing but empty veins. I thought as much.
He has refused me the first thing I have asked—
Me, me, his wife. I understand him now;
I know the sort of life I'll have with him;
But he must drag me to his house by force.
If he refuses [*she laughs*], he shall be mocked of all.
They'll say to one another, "Look at him
That is so jealous that he lured a man
From over sea, and murdered him, and yet
He trembled at the thought of a dead face!"

[*She has her hand upon the curtain.*

Conchubar. How do I know that you have not some knife,
And go to die upon his body?

Deirdre. Have me searched,
If you would make so little of your queen.
It may be that I have a knife hid here
Under my dress. Bid one of these dark slaves
To search me for it. [*Pause.*

Conchubar. Go to your farewells, Queen.

Deirdre. Now strike the wire, and sing to it a while,
Knowing that all is happy, and that you know
Within what bride-bed I shall lie this night,
And by what man, and lie close up to him,
For the bed's narrow, and there outsleep the cockcrow.

[*She goes behind the curtain.*

First Musician. They are gone, they are gone. The proud may
lie by the proud.

Second Musician. Though we were bidden to sing, cry nothing
  loud.
First Musician. They are gone, they are gone.
Second Musician.   Whispering were enough.
First Musician. Into the secret wilderness of their love.
Second Musician. A high, grey cairn. What more is to be said?
First Musician. Eagles have gone into their cloudy bed.

[*Shouting outside. Fergus enters. Many men with scythes
    and sickles and torches gather about the doors. The
    house is lit with the glare of their torches.*

Fergus. Where's Naoise, son of Usna, and his queen?
  I and a thousand reaping-hooks and scythes
  Demand him of you.
Conchubar.   You have come too late.
  I have accomplished all. Deirdre is mine;
  She is my queen, and no man now can rob me.
  I had to climb the topmost bough, and pull
  This apple among the winds. Open the curtain
  That Fergus learn my triumph from her lips.

[*The curtain is drawn back. The Musicians begin to keen
    with low voices.*

  No, no; I'll not believe it. She is not dead—
  She cannot have escaped a second time!
Fergus. King, she is dead; but lay no hand upon her.
  What's this but empty cage and tangled wire,
  Now the bird's gone? But I'll not have you touch it.
Conchubar. You are all traitors, all against me—all.
  And she has deceived me for a second time;
  And every common man can keep his wife,
  But not the King.

[*Loud shouting outside*: "Death to Conchubar!" "Where
    is Naoise?" etc. *The dark-faced men gather round
    Conchubar and draw their swords; but he motions
    them away.*

I have no need of weapons,
There's not a traitor that dare stop my way.
Howl, if you will; but I, being King, did right
In choosing her most fitting to be Queen,
And letting no boy lover take the sway.

THE END

THE PLAYER QUEEN

The Player Queen

Decima	The Stage Manager
Septimus	The Tapster
Nona	An Old Beggar
The Queen	Old Men, Old Women,
The Prime Minister	Citizens, Countrymen,
The Bishop.	Players, etc.

SCENE I: *An open space at the meeting of three streets*
SCENE II: *The Throne-Room*

SCENE I

An open space at the meeting of three streets. One can see for some way down one of these streets, and at some little distance it turns, showing a bare piece of wall lighted by a hanging lamp. Against this lighted wall are silhouetted the heads and shoulders of two Old Men. They are leaning from the upper windows, one on either side of the street. They wear grotesque masks. A little to one side of the stage is a great stone for mounting a horse from. The houses have knockers.

First Old Man. Can you see the Queen's castle? You have better sight than I.

Second Old Man. I can just see it rising over the tops of the houses yonder on its great rocky hill.

First Old Man. Is the dawn breaking? Is it touching the tower?

Second Old Man. It is beginning to break upon the tower, but these narrow streets will be dark for a long while. [*A pause.* Do you hear anything? You have better hearing than I.

First Old Man. No, all is quiet.

Second Old Man. At least fifty passed by an hour since, a crowd of fifty men walking rapidly.

First Old Man. Last night was very quiet, not a sound, not a breath.

Second Old Man. And not a thing to be seen till the Tapster's old dog came down the street upon this very hour from Cooper Malachi's ash-pit.

First Old Man. Hush, I hear feet, many feet. Perhaps they are coming this way. [*Pause.*] No, they are going the other way, they are gone now.

Second Old Man. The young are at some mischief,—the young and the middle-aged.

First Old Man. Why can't they stay in their beds, and they can sleep too—seven hours, eight hours? I mind the time when I could sleep ten hours. They will know the value of sleep when they are near upon ninety years.

Second Old Man. They will never live so long. They have not the health and strength that we had. They wear themselves out. They are always in a passion about something or other.

First Old Man. Hush! I hear a step now, and it is coming this way. We had best pull in our heads. The world has grown very wicked and there is no knowing what they might do to us or say to us.

Second Old Man. Yes, better shut the windows and pretend to be asleep.

　　　[*They pull in their heads. One hears a knocker being struck in the distance, then a pause, and a knocker is struck close at hand. Another pause, and Septimus, a handsome man of thirty-five, staggers on to the stage. He is very drunk.*

Septimus. An uncharitable place, and unchristian place. [*He begins banging at a knocker.*] Open there, open there. I want to come in and sleep.

　　　[*A third Old Man puts his head from an upper window.*
Third Old Man. Who are you? What do you want?

Septimus. I am Septimus. I have a bad wife. I want to come in and sleep.

Third Old Man. You are drunk.

Septimus. Drunk! So would you be if you had as bad a wife.

Third Old Man. Go away.   [*He shuts the window.*

Septimus. Is there not one Christian in this town? [*He begins hammering the knocker of First Old Man, but there is no answer.*] No one there? All dead or drunk maybe—bad wives! There must be one Christian man.

   [*He hammers a knocker at the other side of the stage. An Old Woman puts her head out of the window above.*

Old Woman [*in a shrill voice*]. Who's there? What do you want? Has something happened?

Septimus. Yes, that's it. Something has happened. My wife has hid herself, has run away, or has drowned herself.

Old Woman. What do I care about your wife? You are drunk.

Septimus. Not care about my wife! But I tell you that my wife has to play by order of the Prime Minister before all the people in the great hall of the Castle precisely at noon, and she cannot be found.

Old Woman. Go away, go away! I tell you, go away.

                [*She shuts the window.*

Septimus. Treat Septimus, who has played before Kubla Khan, like this! Septimus, dramatist and poet! [*The Old Woman opens the window again and empties a jug of water over him.*] Water! drenched to the skin—must sleep in the street. [*Lies down.*] Bad wife—others have had bad wives, but others were not left to lie down in the open street under the stars, drenched with cold water, a whole jug of cold water, shivering in the pale light of the dawn, to be run over, to be trampled upon, to be eaten by dogs, and all because their wives have hidden themselves.

   [*Enter two Men a little older than Septimus. They stand still and gaze into the sky.*

First Man. Ah, my friend, the little fair-haired one is a minx.

Second Man. Never trust fair hair—I will have nothing but brown hair.

First Man. They have kept us too long—brown or fair.

Second Man. What are you staring at?

First Man. At the first streak of the dawn on the Castle tower.

Second Man. I would not have my wife find out for the world.

Septimus [*sitting up*]. Carry me, support me, drag me, roll me, pull me, or sidle me along, but bring me where I may sleep in comfort. Bring me to a stable—my Saviour was content with a stable.

First Man. Who are you? I don't know your face.

Septimus. I am Septimus, a player, a playwright, and the most famous poet in the world.

Second Man. That name, sir, is unknown to me.

Septimus. Unknown?

Second Man. But my name will not be unknown to you. I am called Peter of the Purple Pelican, after the best known of my poems, and my friend is called Happy Tom. He also is a poet.

Septimus. Bad, popular poets.

Second Man. You would be a popular poet if you could.

Septimus. Bad, popular poets.

First Man. Lie where you are if you can't be civil.

Septimus. What do I care for any one now except Venus and Adonis and the other planets of heaven?

Second Man. You can enjoy their company by yourself.

[*The two Men go out.*

Septimus. Robbed, so to speak; naked, so to speak—bleeding, so to speak—and they pass by on the other side of the street.

[*A crowd of Citizens and Countrymen enter. At first only a few, and then more and more till the stage is filled by an excited crowd.*

First Citizen. There is a man lying here.

Second Citizen. Roll him over.

First Citizen. He is one of those players who are housed at the Castle. They arrived yesterday.

Second Citizen. Drunk, I suppose. He'll be killed or maimed by the first milk-cart.

Third Citizen. Better roll him into the corner. If we are in for

a bloody day's business, there is no need for him to be killed—an unnecessary death might bring a curse upon us.
First Citizen. Give me a hand here.

[*They begin rolling Septimus.*

Septimus [*muttering*]. Not allowed to sleep! Rolled off the street! Shoved into a stony place! Unchristian town!

[*He is left lying at the foot of the wall to one side of the stage.*

Third Citizen. Are we all friends here, are we all agreed?
First Citizen. These men are from the country. They came in last night. They know little of the business. They won't be against the people, but they want to know more.
First Countryman. Yes, that is it. We are with the people, but we want to know more.
Second Countryman. We want to know all, but we are with the people.

[*Other voices take up the words,* "We want to know all, but we are with the people," *etc. There is a murmur of voices together.*

Third Citizen. Have you ever seen the Queen, countryman?
First Countryman. No.
Third Citizen. Our Queen is a witch, a bad evil-living witch, and we will have her no longer for Queen.
Third Countryman. I would be slow to believe her father's daughter a witch.
Third Citizen. Have you ever seen the Queen, countryman?
Third Countryman. No.
Third Citizen. Nor has any one else. Not a man here has set eyes on her. For seven years she has been shut up in that great black house on the great rocky hill. From the day her father died she has been there with the doors shut on her, but we know now why she has hidden herself. She has no good companions in the dark night.
Third Countryman. In my district they say that she is a holy woman and prays for us all.
Third Citizen. That story has been spread about by the Prime Minister. He has spies everywhere spreading stories. He is a crafty man.

First Countryman. It is true, they always deceive us country people. We are not educated like the people of the town.

A Big Countryman. The Bible says, Suffer not a witch to live. Last Candlemas twelvemonth I strangled a witch with my own hands.

Third Citizen. When she is dead we will make the Prime Minister King.

Second Citizen. No, no, he is not a king's son.

Second Countryman. I'd send a bellman through the world. There are many kings in Arabia, they say.

Third Countryman. The people must be talking. If you and I were to hide ourselves, or to be someway hard to understand, maybe they would put some bad name on us. I am not against the people, but I want testimony.

Third Citizen. Come, Tapster, stand up there on the stone and tell what you know.

[*The Tapster climbs up on the mounting-stone.*

Tapster. I live in the quarter where her Castle is. The garden of my house and the gardens of all the houses in my row run right up to the rocky hill that has her Castle on the top. There is a lad in my quarter that has a goat in his garden.

First Citizen. That's Strolling Michael—I know him.

Tapster. That goat is always going astray. Strolling Michael got out of his bed early one morning to go snaring birds, and nowhere could he see that goat. So he began climbing up the rock, and up and up he went, till he was close under the wall, and there he found the goat and it shaking and sweating as though something had scared it. Presently he heard a thing neigh like a horse, and after that a something like a white horse ran by, but it was no horse, but a unicorn. He had his pistol, for he had thought to bring down a rabbit, and seeing it rushing at him as he imagined, he fired at the unicorn. It vanished all in a moment, but there was blood on a great stone.

Third Citizen. Seeing what company she keeps in the small hours, what wonder that she never sets foot out of doors!

Third Countryman. I wouldn't believe all that night rambler says—boys are liars. All that we have against her for certain is that she won't put her foot out of doors. I knew a man once that when he was five-and-twenty refused to get out of his bed. He wasn't ill—no, not he, but he said life was a vale of tears, and for forty and four years till they carried him out to the churchyard he never left that bed. All tried him—parson tried him, priest tried him, doctor tried him, and all he'd say was, "Life is a vale of tears." It's too snug he was in his bed, and believe me, that ever since she has had no father to rout her out of a morning she has been in her bed, and small blame to her maybe.

The Big Countryman. But that's the very sort that are witches. They know where to find their own friends in the lonely hours of the night. There was a witch in my own district that I strangled last Candlemas twelvemonth. She had an imp in the shape of a red cat, that sucked three drops of blood from her poll every night a little before the cock crew. It's with their blood they feed them; until they have been fed with the blood they are images and shadows; but when they have it drunk they can be for a while stronger than you or me.

Third Countryman. The man I knew was no witch, he was no way active. "Life is a vale of tears," he said. Parson tried him, doctor tried him, priest tried him—but that was all he'd say.

First Citizen. We'd have no man go beyond evidence and reason, but hear the Tapster out, and when you have you'll say that we cannot leave her alive this day—no, not for one day longer.

Tapster. It's not a story that I like to be telling, but you are all married men. Another night that boy climbed up after his goat, and it was an hour earlier by his clock and no light in the sky, and when he came to the Castle wall he clambered along the wall among the rocks and bushes till he saw a light from a little window over his head. It was an old wall full of holes, where mortar had fallen out, and he climbed up, putting his toes into the holes, till he could look in through the window; and when he looked in, what did he see but the Queen!

First Countryman. And did he say what she was like?

Tapster. He saw more than that. He saw her coupling with a great white unicorn.

[*Murmurs among the crowd*

Second Countryman. I will not have the son of the unicorn to reign over us, although you will tell me he would be no more than half a unicorn.

First Countryman. I'll not go against the people, but I'd let her live if the Prime Minister promised to rout her out of bed in the morning and to set a guard to drive off the unicorn.

The Big Countryman. I have strangled an old witch with these two hands, and to-day I will strangle a young witch.

Septimus [*who has slowly got up and climbed up on to the mounting-stone which the Tapster has left*]. Did I hear somebody say that the Unicorn is not chaste? It is a most noble beast, a most religious beast. It has a milk-white skin and a milk-white horn, and milk-white hooves, but a mild blue eye, and it dances in the sun. I will have no one speak against it, not while I am still upon the earth. It is written in "The Great Beastery of Paris" that it is chaste, that it is the most chaste of all the beasts in the world.

The Big Countryman. Pull him out of that, he's drunk.

Septimus. Yes, I am drunk, I am very drunk, but that is no reason why I should permit any one to speak against the Unicorn.

Second Citizen. Let's hear him out. We can do nothing till the sun's up.

Septimus. Nobody shall speak against the Unicorn. No, my friends and poets, nobody. I will hunt it if you will, though it is a dangerous and cross-grained beast. Much virtue has made it cross-grained. I will go with you to the high table-lands of Africa where it lives, and we will there shoot it through the head, but I will not speak against its character, and if any man declares it is not chaste I will fight him, for I affirm that its chastity is equal to its beauty.

The Big Countryman. He is most monstrously drunk.

Septimus. No longer drunk, but inspired.

Second Citizen. Go on, go on, we'll never hear the like again.

The Big Countryman. Come away. I've enough of this—we have work to do.

Septimus. Go away, did you say, and my breast-feathers thrust out and my white wings buoyed up with divinity? Ah! but I can see it now—you are bent upon going to some lonely place where uninterrupted you can speak against the character of the Unicorn, but you shall not, I tell you that you shall not. [*He comes down off the stone and squares up at the crowd which tries to pass him.*] In the midst of this uncharitable town I will protect that noble, milk-white, flighty beast.

The Big Countryman. Let me pass.

Septimus. No, I will not let you pass.

First Countryman. Leave him alone.

Second Countryman. No violence—it might bring ill-luck upon us.

[*They try to hold back the Big Countryman.*

Septimus. I will oppose your passing to the death. For I will not have it said that there is a smirch, or a blot, upon the most milky whiteness of an heroic brute that bathes by the sound of tabors at the rising of the sun and the rising of the moon, and the rising of the Great Bear, and above all, it shall not be said, whispered, or in any wise published abroad by you that stand there, so to speak, between two washings; for you were doubtless washed when you were born, and, it may be, shall be washed again after you are dead. [*The Big Countryman knocks him down.*

First Citizen. You have killed him.

The Big Countryman. Maybe I have, maybe I have not—let him lie there. A witch I strangled last Candlemas twelve-month, a witch I will strangle to-day. What do I care for the likes of him?

Third Citizen. Come round to the east quarter of the town. The basket-makers and the sieve-makers will be out by this.

Fourth Citizen. It is a short march from there to the Castle
   gate.
   [*They go up one of the side streets, but return quickly in
      confusion and fear.*
First Citizen. Are you sure that you saw him?
Second Citizen. Who could mistake that horrible old man?
Third Citizen. I was standing by him when the ghost spoke
   out of him seven years ago.
First Countryman. I never saw him before. He has never been
   in my district. I don't rightly know what sort he is, but I
   have heard of him, many a time I have heard of him.
First Citizen. His eyes become glassy, and that is the trance
   growing upon him, and when he is in the trance his soul
   slips away and a ghost takes its place and speaks out of him
   —a strange ghost.
Third Citizen. I was standing by him the last time. "Get me
   straw," said that old man, "my back itches." Then all of a
   sudden he lay down, with his eyes wide open and glassy,
   and he brayed like a donkey. At that moment the King died
   and the King's daughter was Queen.
First Countryman. They say it is the donkey that carried
   Christ into Jerusalem, and that is why it knows its rightful
   sovereign. He goes begging about the country and there is
   no man dare refuse him what he asks.
The Big Countryman. Then it is certain nobody will take
   my hand off her throat. I will make my grip tighter. He
   will be lying down on the straw and he will bray, and when
   he brays she will be dead.
First Countryman. Look! There he is coming over the top of
   the hill, and the mad look upon him.
Second Countryman. I wouldn't face him for the world this
   night. Come round to the market-place, we'll be less afraid
   in a big place.
The Big Countryman. I'm not afraid, but I'll go with you till
   I get my hand on her throat.
   [*They all go out but Septimus. Presently Septimus sits
      up; his head is bleeding. He rubs with his fingers his
      broken head and looks at the blood on his fingers.*

Septimus. Unchristian town! First I am, so to speak, thrown
out into the street, and then I am all but murdered; and I
drunk, and therefore in need of protection. All creatures
are in need of protection at some time or other. Even my
wife was once a frail child in need of milk, of smiles, of
love, as if in the midst of a flood, in danger of drowning,
so to speak.

[*An Old Beggar with long matted hair and beard and in
ragged clothes comes in.*

The Old Beggar. I want straw.

Septimus. Happy Tom and Peter of the Purple Pelican have
done it all. They are bad, popular poets, and being jealous
of my fame, they have stirred up the people. [*He catches
sight of the Old Beggar.*] There is a certain medicine which
is made by distilling camphor, Peruvian bark, spurge and
mandrake, and mixing all with twelve ounces of dissolved
pearls and four ounces of the oil of gold; and this medicine
is infallible to stop the flow of blood. Have you any of it,
old man?

The Old Beggar. I want straw.

Septimus. I can see that you have not got it, but no matter,
we shall be friends.

The Old Beggar. I want straw to lie down on.

Septimus. It is no doubt better that I should bleed to death.
For that way, my friend, I shall disgrace Happy Tom and
Peter of the Purple Pelican, but it is necessary that I shall
die somewhere where my last words can be taken down. I
am therefore in need of your support.

[*Having got up he now staggers over to the Old Beggar
and leans upon him.*

The Old Beggar. Don't you know who I am—aren't you
afraid? When something comes inside me, my back itches.
Then I must lie down and roll, and then I bray and the
crown changes.

Septimus. Ah! you are inspired. Then we are indeed brothers.
Come, I will rest upon your shoulder and we will mount
the hill side by side. I will sleep in the Castle of the Queen.

The Old Beggar. You will give me straw to lie upon?

Septimus. Asphodels! Yet, indeed, the asphodel is a flower
   much overrated by the classic authors. Still if a man has a
   preference, I say, for the asphodel—
      [*They go out and one hears the voice of Septimus mur-
      muring in the distance about asphodels.*
      [*The First Old Man opens his window and taps with his
      crutch at the opposite window. The Second Old Man
      opens his window.*
First Old Man. It is all right now. They are all gone. We can
   have our talk out.
Second Old Man. The whole Castle is lit by the dawn now,
   and it will begin to grow brighter in the street.
First Old Man. It's time for the Tapster's old dog to come
   down the street.
Second Old Man. Yesterday he had a bone in his mouth.

Scene II

*The Throne-Room in the Castle. Between pillars are gilded
openwork doors, except at one side, where there is a large
window. The morning light is slanting through the window,
making dark shadows among the pillars. As the scene goes on,
the light, at first feeble, becomes strong and suffused, and the
shadows disappear. Through the openwork doors one can see
down long passages, and one of these passages plainly leads
into the open air. One can see daylight at the end of it. There
is a throne in the centre of the room and a flight of steps that
leads to it.*

*The Prime Minister, an elderly man with an impatient
manner and voice, is talking to a group of Players, among
whom is Nona, a fair, comely, comfortable-looking young
woman of perhaps thirty-five; she seems to take the lead.*

Prime Minister. I will not be trifled with. I chose the play
   myself; I chose "The Tragical History of Noah's Deluge"
   because when Noah beats his wife to make her go into the
   Ark everybody understands, everybody is pleased, every-

body recognises the mulish obstinacy of their own wives, sweethearts, sisters. And now, when it is of the greatest importance to the State that everybody should be pleased, the play cannot be given. The leading lady is lost, you say, and there is some unintelligible reason why nobody can take her place; but I know what you are all driving at— you object to the play I have chosen. You want some dull, poetical thing, full of long speeches. I will have that play and no other. The rehearsal must begin at once and the performance take place at noon punctually.

Nona. We have searched all night, sir, and we cannot find her anywhere. She was heard to say that she would drown rather than play a woman older than thirty. Seeing that Noah's wife is a very old woman, we are afraid that she has drowned herself indeed.

[*Decima, a very pretty woman, puts her head out from under the throne where she has been lying hidden.*

Prime Minister. Nonsense! It is all a conspiracy. Your manager should be here. He is responsible. You can tell him when he does come that if the play is not performed, I will clap him into gaol for a year and pitch the rest of you over the border.

Nona. O, sir, he couldn't help it. She does whatever she likes.

Prime Minister. Does whatever she likes—I know her sort; would pull the world to pieces to spite her husband or her lover. I know her—a bladder full of dried peas for a brain, a brazen, bragging baggage. Of course he couldn't help it, but what do I care? [*Decima pulls in her head.*] To gaol he goes—somebody has got to go to gaol. Go and cry her name everywhere. Away with you! Let me hear you cry it out. Call the baggage. Louder. Louder. [*The Players go out crying,* "Where are you, Decima?"] O, Adam! why did you fall asleep in the garden? You might have known that, while you were lying there helpless, the Old Man in the Sky would play some prank upon you.

[*The Queen, who is young, with an ascetic timid face, enters in a badly fitting state dress.*

Ah!

Queen. I will show myself to the angry people as you have
bidden me. I am almost certain that I am ready for martyr-
dom. I have prayed all night. Yes, I am almost certain.

Prime Minister. Ah!

Queen. I have now attained to the age of my patroness, Holy
Saint Octema, when she was martyred at Antioch. You will
remember that her unicorn was so pleased at the spectacle
of her austerity that he caracoled in his excitement. There-
upon she dropped out of the saddle and was trampled to
death under the feet of the mob. Indeed, but for the
unicorn, the mob would have killed her long before.

Prime Minister. No, you will not be martyred. I have a plan
to settle that. I wil stop their anger with a word. Who
made that dress?

Queen. It was my mother's dress. She wore it at her corona-
tion. I would not have a new one made. I do not deserve
new clothes. I am always committing sin.

Prime Minister. Is there sin in an egg that has never been
hatched, that has never been warmed, in a chalk egg?

Queen. I wish I could resemble Holy Saint Octema in every
thing.

Prime Minister. What a dress! It is too late now. Nothing can
be done. It may appear right to those on the edge of the
crowd. The others must be conquered by charm, dignity,
royal manner. As for the dress, I must think of some excuse,
some explanation. Remember that they have never seen
your face, and you will put them in a bad humour if you
hang your head in that dumbfounded way.

Queen. I wish I could return to my prayers.

Prime Minister. Walk! Permit me to see your Majesty walk.
No, no, no. Be more majestic. Ah! If you had known the
queens I have known—they had a way with them. Morals
of a dragoon, but a way, a way! Put on a kind of eagle look,
a vulture look.

Queen. There are cobble-stones—if I might go barefoot it
would be a blessed penance. It was especially the bleeding
feet of Saint Octema that gave pleasure to the unicorn.

Prime Minister. Sleep of Adam! Barefoot—barefoot, did you say? [*A pause.*] There is not time to take off your shoes and stockings. If you were to look out of the window there, you would see the crowd becoming wickeder every minute. Come! [*He gives his arm to the Queen.*]

Queen. You have a plan to stop their anger so that I shall not be martyred?

Prime Minister. My plan will be disclosed before the face of the people and there alone. [*They go out.*

[*Nona comes in with a bottle of wine and a boiled lobster and lays them on the middle of the floor. She puts her finger on her lip and stands in the doorway towards the back of the stage.*

Decima [*comes cautiously out of her hiding-place singing*].

"IIe went away," my mother sang,
"When I was brought to bed."
And all the while her needle pulled
The gold and silver thread.

She pulled the thread and bit the thread
And made a golden gown,
She wept because she had dreamt that I
Was born to wear a crown.

[*She is just reaching her hand for the lobster when Nona comes forward holding out towards her the dress and mask of Noah's wife which she has been carrying over her left arm.*

Nona. Thank God you are found! [*Getting between her and the lobster.*] No, not until you have put on this dress and mask. I have caught you now, and you are not going to hide again.

Decima. Very well, when I have had my breakfast.

Nona. Not a mouthful till you arc drcsscd rcady for the rehearsal.

Decima. Do you know what song I was singing just now?

Nona. It is that song you're always singing. Septimus made it up.

Decima. It is the song of the mad singing daughter of a harlot.
The only song she had. Her father was a drunken sailor
waiting for the full tide, and yet she thought her mother
had foretold that she would marry a prince and become a
great queen. [*Singing.*]

"When she was got," my mother sang,
"I heard a seamew cry,
I saw a flake of yellow foam
That dropped upon my thigh."

How therefore could she help but braid
The gold upon my hair,
And dream that I should carry
The golden top of care?

The moment ago as I lay here I thought I could play a
queen's part, a great queen's part; the only part in the world
I can play is a great queen's part.

Nona. You play a queen's part? You that were born in a ditch
between two towns and wrapped in a sheet that was stolen
from a hedge.

Decima. The Queen cannot play at all, but I could play so
well. I could bow with my whole body down to my ankles
and could be stern when hard looks were in season. O, I
would know how to put all summer in a look and after that
all winter in a voice.

Nona. Low comedy is what you are fit for.

Decima. I understood all this in a wink of the eye, and then
just when I am saying to myself that I was born to sit up
there with soldiers and courtiers, you come shaking in front
of me that mask and that dress. I am not to eat my breakfast
unless I play an old peaky-chinned, drop-nosed harridan
that a foul husband beats with a stick because she won't
clamber among the other brutes into his cattle-boat. [*She
makes a dart at the lobster.*]

Nona. No, no, not a drop, not a mouthful till you have put
these on. Remember that if there is no play Septimus must
go to prison.

Decima. Would they give him dry bread to eat?

Nona. They would.

Decima. And water to drink and nothing in the water?

Nona. They would.

Decima. And a straw bed?

Nona. They would, and only a little straw maybe.

Decima. And iron chains that clanked.

Nona. They would.

Decima. And keep him there for a whole week?

Nona. A month maybe.

Decima. And he would say to the turnkey, "I am here because of my beautiful cruel wife, my beautiful flighty wife"?

Nona. He might not, he'd be sober.

Decima. But he'd think it, and every time he was hungry, every time he was thirsty, every time he felt the hardness of the stone floor, every time he heard the chains clank, he would think it, and every time he thought it I would become more beautiful in his eyes.

Nona. No, he would hate you.

Decima. Little do you know what the love of man is. If that Holy Image of the church where you put all those candles at Easter was pleasant and affable, why did you come home with the skin worn off your two knees?

Nona [*in tears*]. I understand—you cruel, bad woman!—you won't play the part at all, and all that Septimus may go to prison, and he a great genius that can't take care of himself.

[*Seeing Nona distracted with tears Decima makes a dart and almost gets the lobster.*

Nona. No, no! Not a mouthful, not a drop. I will break the bottle if you go near it. There is not another woman in the world would treat a man like that, and you were sworn to him in church—yes, you were, there is no good denying it. [*Decima makes another dart, but Nona, who is still in tears, puts the lobster in her pocket.*] Leave the food alone; not one mouthful will you get. I have never sworn to a man in church, but if I did swear, I would not treat him like a tinker's donkey—before God I would not—I was properly brought up; my mother always told me it was no light thing to take a man in church.

Decima. You are in love with my husband.

Nona. Because I don't want to see him gaoled you say I am in love with him. Only a woman with no heart would think one can't be sorry for a man without being in love with him—a woman who has never been sorry for anybody! But I won't have him gaoled; if you won't play the part I'll play it myself.

Decima. When I married him, I made him swear never to play with anybody but me, and well you know it.

Nona. Only this once, and in a part nobody can do anything with.

Decima. That is the way it begins, and all the time you would be saying things the audience couldn't hear.

Nona. Septimus will break his oath, and I have learnt the part. Every line of it.

Decima. Septimus would not break his oath for anybody in the world.

Nona. There is one person in the world for whom he will break his oath.

Decima. What have you in your head now?

Nona. He will break it for me.

Decima. You are crazy.

Nona. Maybe I have my secrets.

Decima. What are you keeping back? Have you been sitting in corners with Septimus? giving him sympathy because of the bad wife he has, and all the while he has sat there to have the pleasure of talking about me?

Nona. You think that you have his every thought because you are a devil.

Decima. Because I am a devil I have his every thought.

You know how his own song runs. The man speaks first—[*singing*]

> Put off that mask of burning gold
> With emerald eyes,

and then the woman answers—

> O no, my dear, you make so bold
> To find if hearts be wild and wise
> And yet not cold.

Nona. His every thought—that is a lie. He forgets all about you the moment you're out of his sight.

Decima. Then look what I carry under my bodice. This is a poem praising me, all my beauties one after the other—eyes, hair, complexion, shape, disposition, mind—everything. And there are a great many verses to it. And here is a little one he gave me yesterday morning. I had turned him out of bed and he had to lie alone by himself.

Nona. Alone by himself!

Decima. And as he lay there alone, unable to sleep, he made it up, wishing that he were blind so as not to be troubled by looking at my beauty. Hear how it goes!

[*sings again*]

> O would that I were an old beggar
> Without a friend on this earth
> But a thieving rascally cur,
> A beggar blind from his birth;
> Or anything else but a man
> Lying alone on a bed
> Remembering a woman's beauty,
> Alone with a crazy head.

Nona. Alone in his bed indeed. I know that long poem, that one with all the verses; I know it to my hurt, though I haven't read a word of it. Four lines in every verse, four beats in every line, and fourteen verses—my curse upon it!

Decima [*taking out a manuscript from her bodice*]. Yes, fourteen verses. There are numbers to them.

Nona. You have another there—ten verses all in fours and threes.

Decima [*looking at another manuscript*]. Yes, the verses are in fours and threes. But how do you know all this? I carry them here. They are a secret between him and me, and nobody can see them till they have lain a long while upon my heart.

Nona. They have lain upon your heart, but they were made upon my shoulder. Ay, and down along my spine in the small hours of the morning; so many beats a line, and for every beat a tap of the fingers.

Decima. My God!

Nona. That one with the fourteen verses kept me from my sleep two hours, and when the lines were finished he lay upon his back another hour waving one arm in the air, making up the music. I liked him well enough to seem to be asleep through it all, and many another poem too—but when he made up that short one you sang he was so pleased that he muttered the words all about his lying alone in his bed thinking of you, and that made me mad. So I said to him, "Am I not beautiful? Turn round and look." O, I cut it short, for even I can please a man when there is but one candle. [*She takes a pair of scissors that are hanging round her neck and begins snipping at the dress for Noah's wife.*] And now you know why I can play the part in spite of you and not be driven out. Work upon Septimus if you have a mind for it. Little need I care. I will clip this a trifle and re-stitch it again—I have a needle and thread ready.

> [*The Stage Manager comes in ringing a bell. He is followed by various players all dressed up in the likeness of various beasts.*

Stage Manager. Put on that mask—get into your clothes. Why are you standing there as if in a trance?

Nona. Decima and I have talked the matter over and we have settled that I am to play the part.

Stage Manager. Do as you please. Thank God it's a part that anybody can play. All you have got to do is to copy an old woman's squeaky voice. We are all here now but Septimus, and we cannot wait for him. I will read the part of Noah. He will be here before we are finished, I daresay. We will suppose that the audience is upon this side, and that the Ark is over there with a gangway for the beasts to climb. All you beasts are to crowd up on the prompt side. Lay down Noah's hat and cloak there till Septimus comes. As the first scene is between Noah and the beasts, you can go on with your sewing.

Decima. No, I must first be heard. My husband has been spending his nights with Nona, and that is why she sits clipping and stitching with that vainglorious air.

Nona. She made him miserable, she knows every trick of breaking a man's heart—he came to me with his troubles —I seemed to be a comfort to him, and now—why should I deny it?—he is my lover.

Decima. I will take the vainglory out of her. I have been a plague to him. O, I have been a badger and a weasel and a hedgehog and pole-cat, and all because I was dead sick of him. And, thank God!, she has got him and I am free. I threw away a part and I threw away a man—she has picked both up.

Stage Manager. It seems to me that it all concerns you two. It's your business and not ours. I don't see why we should delay the rehearsal.

Decima. I will have no rehearsal yet. I'm too happy now that I am free. I must find somebody who will dance with me for a while. Come, we must have music. [*She picks up a lute which has been laid down amongst some properties.*] You can't all be claws and hoofs.

Stage Manager. We've only an hour and the whole play to go through.

Nona. O, she has taken my scissors, she is only pretending not to care. Look at her! She is mad! Take them away from her! Hold her hand! She is going to kill me or to kill herself. [*To Stage Manager.*] Why don't you interfere? My God! She is going to kill me.

Decima. Here, Peter.

[*She begins cutting through the breast-feathers of the Swan.*

Nona. She is doing it all to stop the rehearsal, out of vengeance; and you stand there and do nothing.

Stage Manager. If you have taken her husband, why didn't you keep the news till the play was over? She is going to make them all mad now, I can see that much in her eyes.

Decima. Now that I have thrown Septimus into her lap, I will choose a new man, Shall it be you, Turkey-cock? or you, Bullhead?

Stage Manager. There is nothing to be done. It is all your

fault. If Septimus can't manage his wife, it's certain that I
can't.   [*He sits down helplessly.*

Decima. Dance, Bullhead, dance—no—no—stop. I will not
have you for my man, slow on the feet and heavy of build,
and that means jealousy, and there is a sort of melancholy
in your voice. What a folly that I should find love nothing,
and yet through sympathy with that voice should stretch
and yawn as if I loved! Dance, Turkey-cock, dance—no,
stop. I cannot have you, for my man must be lively on his
feet and have a quick eye. I will not have that round eye
fixed upon me now that I have sent my mind asleep. Yet
what do I care who it is, so that I choose and get done
with it? Dance, all dance, and I will choose the best dancer
among you. Quick, quick, begin to dance.

[*All dance round Decima.*

Decima [*singing*].

        Shall I fancy beast or fowl?
        Queen Pasiphae chose a bull,
        While a passion for a swan
        Made Queen Leda stretch and yawn,
        Wherefore spin ye, whirl ye, dance ye,
        Till Queen Decima's found her fancy.
              Chorus
        Wherefore spin ye, whirl ye, dance ye,
        Till Queen Decima's found her fancy.

Decima.

        Spring and straddle, stride and strut,
        Shall I chose a bird or brute?
        Name the feather or the fur
        For my single comforter?
              Chorus
        Wherefore spin ye, whirl ye, dance ye,
        Till Queen Decima's found her fancy.

Decima.

        None has found, that found out love,
        Single bird or brute enough;
        Any bird or brute may rest
        An empty head upon my breast.

Chorus
Wherefore spin ye, whirl ye, dance ye,
Till Queen Decima's found her fancy.

Stage Manager. Stop, stop, here is Septimus.

Septimus [*the blood still upon his face, and but little soberer*] Gather about me, for I announce the end of the Christian Era, the coming of a New Dispensation, that of the New Adam, that of the Unicorn; but alas, he is chaste, he hesitates, he hesitates.

Stage Manager. This is not a time for making up speeches for your new play.

Septimus. His unborn children are but images; we merely play with images.

Stage Manager. Let us get on with the rehearsal.

Septimus. No; let us prepare to die. The mob is climbing up the hill with pitchforks to stick into our vitals and burning wisps to set the roof on fire.

First Player [*who has gone to the window*]. My God, it's true. There is a great crowd at the bottom of the hill.

Second Player. But why should they attack us?

Septimus. Because we are the servants of the Unicorn.

Third Player [*at window*]. My God, they have dung-forks and scythes set on poles and they are coming this way.

[*Many Players gather round the window.*]

Septimus [*who has found the bottle and is drinking*]. Some will die like Cato, some like Cicero, some like Demosthenes, triumphing over death in sonorous eloquence, or, like Petronius Arbiter, will tell witty, scandalous tales; but I will speak, no, I will sing, as if the mob did not exist. I will rail upon the Unicorn for his chastity. I will bid him trample mankind to death and beget a new race. I will even put my railing into rhyme, and all shall run sweetly, sweetly, for, even if they blow up the floor with gunpowder, they are merely the mob.

Upon the round blue eye I rail,
Damnation on the milk-white horn.

A telling sound, a sound to linger in the ear—hale, tale, bale, gale—my God, I am even too sober to find a rhyme!

[*He drinks and then picks up a lute*]—a tune that my murderers may remember my last words and croon them to their grandchildren.

[*For the next few speeches he is busy making his tune.*

First Player. The players of this town are jealous. Have we not been chosen before them all, because we are the most famous players in the world? It is they who have stirred up the mob.

Second Player. It is of me they are jealous. They know what happened at Xanadu. At the end of that old play "The Fall of Troy" Kubla Khan sent for me and said that he would give his kingdom for such a voice, and for such a presence. I stood before him dressed as Agamemnon just as when in a great scene at the end I had reproached Helen for all the misery she had wrought.

First Player. My God, listen to him! Is it not always the comedian who draws the crowd? Am I dreaming, or was it not I who was called six times before the curtain? Answer me that—

Second Player. What if you were called six dozen times? The players of this town are not jealous because of the crowd's applause. They have that themselves. The unendurable thought, the thought that wrenches their hearts, the thought that puts murder into their minds is that I alone, alone of all the world's players, have looked as an equal into the eyes of Kubla Khan.

Stage Manager. Stop quarrelling with one another and listen to what is happening out there. There is a man making a speech, and the crowd is getting angrier and angrier, and which of you they are jealous of I don't know, but they are all coming this way and maybe they will burn the place down as if it were Troy, and if you will do what I say you will get out of this.

First Player. Must we go dressed like this?

Second Player. There is not time to change, and besides, should the hill be surrounded, we can gather in some cleft of the rocks where we can be seen only from a distance.

They will suppose we are a drove of cattle or a flock of birds.

[*All go out except Septimus, Decima, and Nona. Nona is making a bundle of Noah's hat and cloak and other properties. Decima is watching Septimus.*

Septimus [*while the Players are going out*]. Leave me to die alone? I do not blame you. There is courage in red wine, in white wine, in beer, even in thin beer sold by a blear-eyed pot-boy in a bankrupt tavern, but there is none in the human heart. When my master the Unicorn bathes by the light of the Great Bear, and to the sound of tabors, even the sweet river-water makes him drunk; but it is cold, it is cold, alas! it is cold.

Nona. I'll pile these upon your back. I shall carry the rest myself and so shall save all.

[*She begins trying a great bundle of properties on Septimus' back.*

Septimus. You are right. I accept the reproach. It is necessary that we who are the last artists—all the rest have gone over to the mob—shall save the images and implements of our art. We must carry into safety the cloak of Noah, the high-crowned hat of Noah, and the mask of the sister of Noah. She was drowned because she thought her brother was telling lies; certainly we must save her rosy cheeks and rosy mouth, that drowned, wicked mouth.

Nona. Thank God you can still stand upright on your legs.

Septimus. Tie all upon my back and I will tell you the great secret that came to me at the second mouthful of the bottle. Man is nothing till he is united to an image. Now the Unicorn is both an image and beast; that is why he alone can be the new Adam. When we have put all in safety we will go to the high tablelands of Africa and find where the Unicorn is stabled and sing a marriage song. I will stand before the terrible blue eye.

Nona. There, now, I have tied them on.

[*She begins making another bundle for herself, but forgets the mask of the sister of Noah. It lies near the throne.*

Septimus. You will make Ionian music—music with its eyes upon that voluptuous Asia—the Dorian scale would but confirm him in his chastity. One Dorian note might undo us, and above all we must be careful not to speak of Delphi. The oracle is chaste.

Nona. Come, let us go.

Septimus. If we cannot fill him with desire he will deserve death. Even unicorns can be killed. What they dread most in the world is a blow from a knife that has been dipped in the blood of a serpent that died gazing upon an emerald.

[*Nona and Septimus are about to go out, Nona leading Septimus.*

Decima. Stand back, do not dare to move a step.

Septimus. Beautiful as the Unicorn, but fierce.

Decima. I have locked the gates that we may have a talk.

[*Nona lets the hat of Noah fall in her alarm.*

Septimus. That is well, very well. You would talk with me because to-day I am extraordinarily wise.

Decima. I will not unlock the gate till I have a promise that I will drive her from the company.

Nona. Do not listen to her; take the key from her.

Septimus. If I were not her husband I would take the key, but because I am her husband she is terrible. The Unicorn will be terrible when it loves.

Nona. You are afraid.

Septimus. Could not you yourself take it? She does not love you, therefore she will not be terrible.

Nona. If you are a man at all you will take it.

Septimus. I am more than a man, I am extraordinarily wise. I will take the key.

Decima. If you come a step nearer I will shove the key through the grating of the door.

Nona [*pulling him back*]. Don't go near her; if she shoves it through the door we shall not be able to escape. The crowd will find us and murder us.

Decima. I will unlock this gate when you have taken an oath to drive her from the company, an oath never to speak with her or look at her again, a terrible oath.

Septimus. You are jealous; it is very wrong to be jealous. An ordinary man would be lost even I am not yet wise enough. [*Drinks again.*] Now all is plain.

Decima. You have been unfaithful to me.

Septimus. I am only unfaithful when I am sober. Never trust a sober man. All the world over they are unfaithful. Never trust a man who has not bathed by the light of the Great Bear. I warn you against all sober men from the bottom of my heart. I am extraordinarily wise.

Nona. Promise, if it is only an oath she wants. Take whatever oath she bids you. If you delay we shall all be murdered.

Septimus. I can see your meaning. You would explain to me that an oath can be broken, more especially an oath under compulsion, but no, I say to you, no, I say to you, certainly not. Am I a rascally sober man, such a man as I have warned you against? Shall I be forsworn before the very eyes of Delphi, so to speak, before the very eyes of that cold, rocky oracle? What I promise I perform, therefore, my little darling, I will not promise anything at all.

Decima. Then we shall wait here. They will come in through this door, they will carry dung-forks with burning wisps. They will put the burning wisps into the roof and we shall be burnt.

Septimus. I shall die railing upon that beast. The Christian era has come to an end, but because of the machinations of Delphi he will not become the new Adam.

Decima. I shall be avenged. She starved me, but I shall have killed her.

Nona [*who has crept behind Decima and snatched the key*]. I have it, I have it!

[*Decima tries to take the key again, but Septimus holds her.*

Septimus. Because I am an unforsworn man I am strong: a violent virginal creature, that is how it is put in "The Great Beastery of Paris."

Decima. Go, then, I shall stay here and die.

Nona. Let us go. A half hour since she offered herself to every man in the company.

Decima. If you would be faithful to me, Septimus, I would not let a man of them touch me.

Septimus. Flighty, but beautiful.

Nona. She is a bad woman.   [*Nona runs out.*

Septimus. A beautiful, bad, flighty woman I will follow, but follow slowly. I will take with me this noble hat. [*He picks up Noah's hat with difficulty.*] No, it may lie there, what have I to do with that drowned, wicked mouth—beautiful, drowned, flighty mouth? I will have nothing to do with it, but I will save the noble, high-crowned hat of Noah. I will carry it thus with dignity. I will go slowly that they may see I am not afraid.   [*Singing.*

> Upon the round blue eye I rail,
> Damnation on the milk-white horn.

But not one word of Delphi. I am extraordinarily wise.

[*He goes.*

Decima. Betrayed, betrayed, and for a nobody. For a woman that a man can shake and twist like so much tallow. A woman that till now never looked higher than a prompter or a property man. [*The Old Beggar comes in.*] Have you come to kill me, old man?

Old Beggar. I am looking for straw. I must soon lie down and roll, and where will I get straw to roll on? I went round to the kitchen, and "Go away," they said. They made the sign of the cross as if it were a devil that puts me rolling.

Decima. When will the mob come to kill me?

Old Beggar. Kill you? It is not you they are going to kill. It's the itching in my back that drags them hither, for when I bray like a donkey, the crown changes.

Decima. The crown? So it is the Queen they are going to kill.

Old Beggar. But, my dear, she can't die till I roll and bray, and I will whisper to you what it is that rolls. It is the donkey that carried Christ into Jerusalem, and that is why he is so proud; and that is why he knows the hour when there is to be a new King or a new Queen.

Decima. Are you weary of the world, old man?

Old Beggar. Yes, yes, because when I roll and bray I am asleep. I know nothing about it, and that is a great pity. I remember nothing but the itching in my back. But I must stop talking and find some straw.

Decima [*picking up the scissors*]. Old man, I am going to drive this into my heart.

Old Beggar. No, no; don't do that. You don't know what you will be put to when you are dead, into whose gullet you will be put to sing or to bray. You have a look of a foretelling sort. Who knows you might be put to foretell the death of kings; and bear in mind I will have no rivals, I could not endure a rival.

Decima. I have been betrayed by a man, I have been made a mockery of. Do those who are dead, old man, make love and do they find good lovers?

Old Beggar. I will whisper you another secret. People talk, but I have never known of anything to come from there but an old jackass. Maybe there is nothing else. Who knows but he has the whole place to himself? But there, my back is beginning to itch, and I have not yet found any straw.

[*He goes out. Decima leans the scissors upon the arm of the throne and is about to press herself upon them when the Queen enters.*

Queen [*stopping her*]. No, no—that would be a great sin.

Decima. Your Majesty!

Queen. I thought I would like to die a martyr, but that would be different, that would be to die for God's glory. The Holy Saint Octema was a martyr.

Decima. I am very unhappy.

Queen. I, too, am very unhappy. When I saw the great angry crowd and knew that they wished to kill me, though I had wanted to be a martyr, I was afraid and ran away.

Decima. I would not have run away, O no; but it is hard to drive a knife into one's own flesh.

Queen. In a moment they will have come and they will beat in the door, and how shall I escape them?

Decima. If they could mistake me for you, you would escape.

Queen. I could not let another die instead of me. That would be very wrong.

Decima. O, your Majesty, I shall die whatever you do, and if only I could wear that gold brocade and those gold slippers for one moment, it would not be so hard to die.

Queen. They say that those who die to save a rightful sovereign show great virtue.

Decima. Quick! the dress.

Queen. If you killed yourself your soul would be lost, and now you will be sure of Heaven.

Decima. Quick, I hear them coming.

[*Decima puts on the Queen's robe of state and her slippers. Underneath her robe of state the Queen wears some kind of nun-like dress.*

The following speech is spoken by the Queen while she is helping Decima to fasten the dress and the slippers.

Queen. Was it love? [*Decima nods.*] O, that is a great sin. I have never known love. Of all things, that is what I have had most fear of. Saint Octema shut herself up in a tower on a mountain because she was loved by a beautiful prince. I was afraid it would come in at the eye and seize upon me in a moment. I am not naturally good, and they say people will do anything for love, there is so much sweetness in it. Even Saint Octema was afraid of it. But you will escape all that and go up to God as a pure virgin. [*The change is now complete.*] Good-bye, I know how I can slip away. There is a convent that will take me in. It is not a tower, it is only a convent, but I have long wanted to go there to lose my name and disappear. Sit down upon the throne and turn your face away. If you do not turn your face away, you will be afraid. [*The Queen goes out.*

[*Decima is seated upon the throne. A great crowd gathers outside the gates. A Bishop enters.*

Bishop. Your loyal people, your Majesty, offer you their homage. I bow before you in their name. Your royal will has spoken by the mouth of the Prime Minister—has filled them with gratitude. All misunderstandings are at an end, all has been settled by your condescension in bestowing your royal hand upon the Prime Minister. [*To crowd.*] Her Majesty, who has hitherto shut herself away from all men's eyes that she might pray for this kingdom undisturbed, will henceforth show herself to her people. [*To Player Queen.*] So beautiful a Queen need never fear the disobedience of her people [*shouts from crowd of "Never"*].

Prime Minister [*entering hurriedly*]. I will explain all, your Majesty—there was nothing else to be done—this Bishop has been summoned to unite us [*seeing the Queen*]; but, sleep of Adam!—this—who is this?

Decima. Your emotion is too great for words. Do not try to speak.

Prime Minister. This—this . . . !

Decima [*standing up*]. I am Queen. I know what it is to be Queen. If I were to say to you I had an enemy you would kill him—you would tear him in pieces, would you not? [*Shouts: "We would kill him," "We would tear him in pieces," etc.*] But I do not bid you kill any one—I bid you obey my husband when I have raised him to the throne. He is not of royal blood, but I choose to raise him to the throne. That is my will. Show me that you will obey him so long as I bid you to obey.   [*Great cheering.*

[*Septimus, who has been standing among the crowd, comes forward and takes the Prime Minister by the sleeve. Various persons kiss the hand of the supposed Queen.*

Septimus. My lord, that is not the Queen; that is my bad wife.
                    [*Decima looks at them.*

Prime Minister. Did you see that? Did you see the devil in her eye? They are mad after her pretty face, and she knows it. They would not believe a word I say; there is nothing to be done till they cool.

Decima. Are all here my faithful servants?

Bishop. All, your Majesty.

Decima. All?

Prime Minister [*bowing low*]. All your Majesty.

Decima [*singing*].

> She pulled the thread, and bit the thread
> And made a golden gown.

Hand me that plate. While I am eating I will have a good look at my new man.

[*The plate and a bottle of wine are handed to her. The bray of a donkey is heard and the Old Beggar is dragged in.*

Bishop. At last we have found this impostor out. He has been accepted by the whole nation as if he were the Voice of God. As if the crown could not be settled firmly on any head without his help. It's plain that he has been in league with the conspirators, and believed that your Majesty had been killed. He is keeping it up still. Look at his glassy eye. But his madman airs won't help him now.

Prime Minister. Carry him to prison, we will hang him in the morning. [*Shaking Septimus.*] Do you understand that there has been a miracle, that God or the Fiend has spoken, and that the crown is on her head for good, that fate has brayed on that man's lips? [*Aloud.*] We will hang him in the morning.

Septimus. She is my wife.

Prime Minister. The crown has changed and there is no help for it. Sleep of Adam, I must have that woman for wife. The Oracle has settled that.

Septimus. She is my wife, she is my bad, flighty wife.

Prime Minister. Seize this man. He has been whispering slanders against Her Majesty. Cast him beyond the borders of the kingdom, and his players after him.

Decima. He must not return upon pain of death. He has wronged me, and I will never look upon his face again.

Prime Minister. Away with him.

Decima. My good name is dearer than my life, but I will see the players before they go.

Prime Minister. Sleep of Adam! What has she got into her head? Fetch the players.

Decima [*picking up the mask of the sister of Noah*]. My loyal subjects must forgive me if I hide my face—it is not yet used to the light of day, it is a modest face. I will be much happier if His Holiness will help me to tie the mask.

Prime Minister. The players come.

Enter Players, who all bow to the new Queen

Decima. They had some play they were to perform, but I will make them dance instead, and after that they must be richly rewarded.

Prime Minister. It shall be as you will.

Decima. You are banished and must not return upon pain of death, and yet not one of you shall be poorer because banished. That I promise. But you have lost one thing that I will not restore. A woman player has left you. Do not mourn her. She was a bad, headstrong, cruel woman, and seeks destruction somewhere and with some man she knows nothing of; such a woman they tell me that this mask would well become, this foolish, smiling face! Come, dance.

> [*They dance, and at certain moments she cries* "Good-bye, good-bye" *or else* "Farewell." *And she throws them money.*]

THE END

THE ONLY JEALOUSY OF EMER

Báile's Strand = prose

vs. written in verse

The Only Jealousy of Emer

PERSONS IN THE PLAY

Three Musicians (*their faces made up to resemble masks*)
The Ghost of Cuchulain (*wearing a mask*)
The Figure of Cuchulain (*wearing a mask*)
Emer ⎱ (*masked, or their faces made up to resemble*
Eithne Inguba ⎰ *masks*)
Woman of the Sidhe (*wearing a mask*)

Enter Musicians, who are dressed and made up as in "At the Hawk's Well." They have the same musical instruments, which can either be already upon the stage or be brought in by the First Musician before he stands in the centre with the cloth between his hands, or by a player when the cloth has been unfolded. The stage as before can be against the wall of any room, and the same black cloth can be used as in "At the Hawk's Well."

[*Song for the folding and unfolding of the cloth*]
First Musician.   *Runs thru play*
        A woman's beauty is like a white
        Frail bird, like a white sea-bird alone
        At daybreak after stormy night
        Between two furrows upon the ploughed land:
        A sudden storm, and it was thrown
        Between dark furrows upon the ploughed land.
        How many centuries spent
        The sedentary soul
        In toils of measurement
        Beyond eagle or mole,
        Beyond hearing or seeing,
        Or Archimedes' guess,

113

To raise into being
That loveliness?

A strange, unserviceable thing,
A fragile, exquisite, pale shell,
That the vast troubled waters bring
To the loud sands before day has broken.
The storm arose and suddenly fell
Amid the dark before day had broken.
What death? what discipline?
What bonds no man could unbind,
Being imagined within
The labyrinth of the mind,
What pursuing or fleeing,
What wounds, what bloody press,
Dragged into being
This loveliness?

[*When the cloth is folded again the Musicians take their
place against the wall. The folding of the cloth shows
on one side of the stage the curtained bed or litter on
which lies a man in his grave-clothes. He wears an
heroic mask. Another man with exactly similar clothes
and mask crouches near the front. Emer is sitting
beside the bed.*

First Musician [*speaking*]. I call before the eyes a roof
With cross-beams darkened by smoke;
A fisher's net hangs from a beam,
A long oar lies against the wall.
I call up a poor fisher's house;
A man lies dead or swooning,
That amorous man,
That amorous, violent man, renowned Cuchulain,
Queen Emer at his side.
At her own bidding all the rest have gone;
But now one comes on hesitating feet,
Young Eithne Inguba, Cuchulain's mistress.
She stands a moment in the open door.

Beyond the open door the bitter sea,
The shining, bitter sea, is crying out,
[*singing*] White shell, white wing!
I will not choose for my friend
A frail, unserviceable thing
That drifts and dreams, and but knows
That waters are without end
And that wind blows.

Emer [*speaking*]. Come hither, come sit down beside the bed;
    You need not be afraid, for I myself
    Sent for you, Eithne Inguba.

Eithne Inguba.   No, Madam,
    I have too deeply wronged you to sit there.

Emer. Of all the people in the world we two,
    And we alone, may watch together here,
    Because we have loved him best.

Eithne Inguba.   And is he dead?

Emer. Although they have dressed him out in his grave-
    clothes
    And stretched his limbs, Cuchulain is not dead;
    The very heavens when that day's at hand,
    So that his death may not lack ceremony,
    Will throw out fires, and the earth grow red with blood.
    There shall not be a scullion but foreknows it
    Like the world's end.

Eithne Inguba.   How did he come to this?

Emer. Towards noon in the assembly of the kings
    He met with one who seemed a while most dear.
    The kings stood round; some quarrel was blown up;
    He drove him out and killed him on the shore
    At Baile's tree, and he who was so killed
    Was his own son begot on some wild woman
    When he was young, or so I have heard it said;
    And thereupon, knowing what man he had killed,
    And being mad with sorrow, he ran out;
    And after, to his middle in the foam,
    With shield before him and with sword in hand.

He fought the deathless sea. The kings looked on
And not a king dared stretch an arm, or even
Dared call his name, but all stood wondering
In that dumb stupor like cattle in a gale,
Until at last, as though he had fixed his eyes
On a new enemy, he waded out
Until the water had swept over him;
But the waves washed his senseless image up
And laid it at this door.

Eithne Inguba.　　　　　How pale he looks!

Emer. He is not dead.

Eithne Inguba.　　　　You have not kissed his lips
　　Nor laid his head upon your breast.

Emer.　　　　　　　　It may be
　　An image has been put into his place,
　　A sea-borne log bewitched into his likeness,
　　Or some stark horseman grown too old to ride
　　Among the troops of Manannan, Son of the Sea,
　　Now that his joints are stiff.

Eithne Inguba.　　　　　Cry out his name.
　　All that are taken from our sight, they say,
　　Loiter amid the scenery of their lives
　　For certain hours or days, and should he hear
　　He might, being angry, drive the changeling out.

Emer. It is hard to make them hear amid their darkness.
　　And it is long since I could call him home;
　　I am but his wife, but if you cry aloud
　　With the sweet voice that is so dear to him
　　He cannot help but listen.

Eithne Inguba.　　　　　He loves me best,
　　Being his newest love, but in the end
　　Will love the woman best who loved him first
　　And loved him through the years when love seemed lost.

Emer. I have that hope, the hope that some day somewhere
　　We'll sit together at the hearth again.

Eithne Inguba. Women like me, the violent hour passed over,
　　Are flung into some corner like old nut-shells.
　　Cuchulain, listen.

Emer.   No, not yet, for first
   I'll cover up his face to hide the sea;
   And throw new logs upon the hearth and stir
   The half-burnt logs until they break in flame.
   Old Manannan's unbridled horses come
   Out of the sea, and on their backs his horsemen;
   But all the enchantments of the dreaming foam
   Dread the hearth-fire.

   [*She pulls the curtains of the bed so as to hide the sick
   man's face, that the actor may change his mask unseen.
   She goes to one side of the platform and moves her
   hand as though putting logs on a fire and stirring it
   into a blaze. While she makes these movements the
   Musicians play, marking the movements with drum
   and flute perhaps.*

      *Having finished she stands beside the imaginary fire
      at a distance from Cuchulain and Eithne Inguba.*
                  Call on Cuchulain now.
Eithne Inguba. Can you not hear my voice?
Emer.   Bend over him;
   Call out dear secrets till you have touched his heart,
   If he lies there; and if he is not there,
   Till you have made him jealous.
Eithne Inguba.   Cuchulain, listen.
Emer. Those words sound timidly; to be afraid
   Because his wife is but three paces off,
   When there is so great need, were but to prove
   The man that chose you made but a poor choice:
   We're but two women struggling with the sea.
Eithne Inguba. O my beloved, pardon me, that I
   Have been ashamed. I thrust my shame away.
   I have never sent a message or called out,
   Scarce had a longing for your company
   But you have known and come; and if indeed
   You are lying there, stretch out your arms and speak;
   Open your mouth and speak, for to this hour
   My company has made you talkative.
   What ails your tongue, or what has closed your ears?

Our passion had not chilled when we were parted
On the pale shore under the breaking dawn.
He cannot speak: or else his ears are closed
And no sound reaches him.

Emer.   Then kiss that image;
  The pressure of your mouth upon his mouth
  May reach him where he is.

Eithne Inguba [*starting back*]. It is no man.
  I felt some evil thing that dried my heart
  When my lips touched it.

Emer.   No, his body stirs;
  The pressure of your mouth has called him home;
  He has thrown the changeling out.

Eithne Inguba [*going further off*]. Look at that arm;
  That arm is withered to the very socket.

Emer [*going up to the bed*]. What do you come for; and from
      where?

Figure of Cuchulain.   I have come
  From Manannan's court upon a bridleless horse.

Emer. What one among the Sidhe has dared to lie
  Upon Cuchulain's bed and take his image?

Figure of Cuchulain. I am named Bricriu—not the man—that
      Bricriu,
  Maker of discord among gods and men,
  Called Bricriu of the Sidhe.

Emer.   Come for what purpose?

Figure of Cuchulain [*sitting up, parting curtain and showing
      its distorted face, as Eithne Inguba goes out*]. I show my
      face, and everything he loves
  Must fly away.

Emer.   You people of the wind
  Are full of lying speech and mockery:
  I have not fled your face.

Figure of Cuchulain.   You are not loved.

Emer. And therefore have no dread to meet your eyes
  And to demand him of you.

Figure of Cuchulain.   For that I have come.
  You have but to pay the price and he is free.

Emer. Do the Sidhe bargain?

Figure of Cuchulain.   When they would free a captive
They take in ransom a less valued thing.
The fisher, when some knowledgeable man
Restores to him his wife, or son, or daughter,
Knows he must lose a boat or a net, or it may be
The cow that gives his children milk; and some
Have offered their own lives. I do not ask
Your life, or any valuable thing;
You spoke but now of the mere chance that some day
You'd be the apple of his eye again
When old and ailing, but renounce that chance
And he shall live again.

Emer.   I do not question
But you have brought ill-luck on all he loves;
And now, because I am thrown beyond your power
Unless your words are lies, you come to bargain.

Figure of Cuchulain. You loved your mastery, when but newly
    married,
And I love mine for all my withered arm;
You have but to put yourself into that power
And he shall live again.

Emer.   No, never, never.

Figure of Cuchulain. You dare not be accursed, yet he has
    dared.

Emer. I have but two joyous thoughts, two things I prize,
A hope, a memory, and now you claim that hope.

Figure of Cuchulain. He'll never sit beside you at the hearth
Or make old bones, but die of wounds and toil
On some far shore or mountain, a strange woman
Beside his mattress.

Emer.   You ask for my one hope
That you may bring your curse on all about him.

Figure of Cuchulain. You've watched his loves and you have
    not been jealous,
Knowing that he would tire, but do those tire
That love the Sidhe? Come closer to the bed
That I may touch your eyes and give them sight.

[*He touches her eyes with his left hand, the right being withered.*

Emer [*seeing the crouching Ghost of Cuchulain*]. My husband is there.

Figure of Cuchulain.   I have dissolved the dark
That hid him from your eyes, but not that other
That's hidden you from his.

Emer.   O husband, husband!

Figure of Cuchulain. He cannot hear—being shut off, a phantom
That can neither touch, nor hear, nor see;
The longing and the cries have drawn him hither.
He heard no sound, heard no articulate sound;
They could but banish rest, and make him dream,
And in that dream, as do all dreaming shades
Before they are accustomed to their freedom,
He has taken his familiar form; and yet
He crouches there not knowing where he is
Or at whose side he is crouched.

[*A Woman of the Sidhe has entered and stands a little inside the door.*

Emer.   Who is this woman?

Figure of Cuchulain. She has hurried from the Country-under-Wave
And dreamed herself into that shape that he
May glitter in her basket; for the Sidhe
Are dexterous fishers and they fish for men
With dreams upon the hook.

Emer.   And so that woman
Has hid herself in this disguise and made
Herself into a lie.

Figure of Cuchulain. A dream is body;
The dead move ever towards a dreamless youth
And when they dream no more return no more;
And those more holy shades that never lived
But visit you in dreams.

Emer.   I know her sort.
They find our men asleep, weary with war,

Lap them in cloudy hair or kiss their lips;
Our men awake in ignorance of it all,
But when we take them in our arms at night
We cannot break their solitude. = love for so much else

[*She draws a knife from her girdle.*

Figure of Cuchulain.   No knife
Can wound that body of air. Be silent; listen;
I have not given you eyes and ears for nothing.

[*The Woman of the Sidhe moves round the crouching
Ghost of Cuchulain at front of stage in a dance that
grows gradually quicker, as he slowly awakes. At mo-
ments she may drop her hair upon his head, but she
does not kiss him. She is accompanied by string and
flute and drum. Her mask and clothes must suggest
gold or bronze or brass or silver, so that she seems
more an idol than a human being. This suggestion may
be repeated in her movements. Her hair, too, must
keep the metallic suggestion.*

Ghost of Cuchulain. Who is it stands before me there
Shedding such light from limb and hair
As when the moon, complete at last
With every labouring crescent past,
And lonely with extreme delight,
Flings out upon the fifteenth night?

Woman of the Sidhe. Because I long I am not complete.
What pulled your hands about your feet,
Pulled down your head upon your knees,
And hid your face?

Ghost of Cuchulain. Old memories:
A woman in her happy youth
Before her man had broken troth,
Dead men and women. Memories
Have pulled my head upon my knees.

Woman of the Sidhe. Could you that have loved many a
    woman
That did not reach beyond the human,
Lacking a day to be complete,

Love one that, though her heart can beat,
Lacks it but by an hour or so?
Ghost of Cuchulain. I know you now, for long ago
I met you on a cloudy hill
Beside old thorn-trees and a well.
A woman danced and a hawk flew,
I held out arms and hands; but you,
That now seem friendly, fled away,
Half woman and half bird of prey.
Woman of the Sidhe. Hold out your arms and hands again;
You were not so dumbfounded when
I was that bird of prey, and yet
I am all woman now.
Ghost of Cuchulain.   I am not
The young and passionate man I was,
And though that brilliant light surpass
All crescent forms, my memories
Weigh down my hands, abash my eyes.
Woman of the Sidhe. Then kiss my mouth. Though memory
Be beauty's bitterest enemy
I have no dread, for at my kiss
Memory on the moment vanishes:
Nothing but beauty can remain.
Ghost of Cuchulain. And shall I never know again
Intricacies of blind remorse?
Woman of the Sidhe. Time shall seem to stay his course;
When your mouth and my mouth meet
All my round shall be complete
Imagining all its circles run;
And there shall be oblivion
Even to quench Cuchulain's drouth,
Even to still that heart.
Ghost of Cuchulain.   Your mouth!
                    [*They are about to kiss, he turns away.*

O Emer, Emer!
Woman of the Sidhe. So then it is she
Made you impure with memory.

Ghost of Cuchulain. O Emer, Emer, there we stand;
  Side by side and hand in hand
  Tread the threshold of the house
  As when our parents married us.
Woman of the Sidhe. Being among the dead you love her
  That valued every slut above her
  While you still lived.

notes

Ghost of Cuchulain.   O my lost Emer!
Woman of the Sidhe. And there is not a loose-tongued
    schemer
  But could draw you, if not dead,
  From her table and her bed.
  But what could make you fit to wive
  With flesh and blood, being born to live
  Where no one speaks of broken troth,
  For all have washed out of their eyes
  Wind-blown dirt of their memories
  To improve their sight?
Ghost of Cuchulain.   Your mouth, your mouth!
          [*She goes out followed by Ghost of Cuchulain.*
Figure of Cuchulain. Cry out that you renounce his love; make
    haste
  And cry that you renounce his love for ever.
Emer. No, never will I give that cry.
Figure of Cuchulain.   Fool, fool!
  I am Fand's enemy come to thwart her will,
  And you stand gaping there. There is still time.
  Hear how the horses trample on the shore,
  Hear how they trample! She has mounted up.
  Cuchulain's not beside her in the chariot.
  There is still a moment left; cry out, cry out!
  Renounce him, and her power is at an end.
  Cuchulain's foot is on the chariot-step.
  Cry—
Emer.   I renounce Cuchulain's love for ever.
      [*The Figure of Cuchulain sinks back upon the bed, half-
      drawing the curtain. Eithne Inguba comes in and
      kneels by bed.*

Eithne Inguba. Come to me, my beloved, it is I.
  I, Eithne Inguba. Look! He is there.
  He has come back and moved upon the bed.
  And it is I that won him from the sea,
  That brought him back to life.
Emer.   Cuchulain wakes.

   [*The figure turns round. It once more wears the heroic
     mask.*

Cuchulain. Your arms, your arms! O Eithne Inguba,
  I have been in some strange place and am afraid.

   [*The First Musician comes to the front of stage, the
     others from each side, and unfold the cloth singing.*
   [*Song for the unfolding and folding of the cloth*]

The Musicians.

            Why does your heart beat thus?
            Plain to be understood,
            I have met in a man's house
            A statue of solitude,
            Moving there and walking;
            Its strange heart beating fast
            For all our talking.
            O still that heart at last.

            O bitter reward
            Of many a tragic tomb!
            And we though astonished are dumb
            Or give but a sigh and a word,
            A passing word.

            Although the door be shut
            And all seem well enough,
            Although wide world hold not
            A man but will give you his love
            The moment he has looked at you,
            He that has loved the best
            May turn from a statue
            His too human breast.

O bitter reward
Of many a tragic tomb!
And we though astonished are dumb
Or give but a sigh and a word,
A passing word.

What makes your heart so beat?
What man is at your side?
When beauty is complete
Your own thought will have died
And danger not be diminished;
Dimmed a three-quarter light,
When moon's round is finished
The stars are out of sight.

O bitter reward
Of many a tragic tomb!
And we though astonished are dumb
Or give but a sigh and a word,
A passing word.
[*When the cloth is folded again the stage is bare.*

THE END

C's been reborn, because his
wife sacrificed her own
love for him.

THE RESURRECTION

The Resurrection

PERSONS IN THE PLAY

The Hebrew   The Syrian
The Greek   Christ

Three Musicians

Before I had finished this play I saw that its subject-matter might make it unsuited for the public stage in England or in Ireland. I had begun it with an ordinary stage scene in the mind's eye, curtained walls, a window and door at back, a curtained door at left. I now changed the stage directions and wrote songs for the unfolding and folding of the curtain that it might be played in a studio or a drawing-room like my dance plays, or at the Peacock Theatre before a specially chosen audience. If it is played at the Peacock Theatre the Musicians may sing the opening and closing songs, as they pull apart or pull together the proscenium curtain; the whole stage may be hung with curtains with an opening at the left. While the play is in progress the Musicians will sit towards the right of the audience; if at the Peacock, on the step which separates the stage from the audience, or one on either side of the proscenium.

[Song for the unfolding and folding of the curtain]

I

I saw a staring virgin stand
Where holy Dionysus died,
And tear the heart out of his side,
And lay the heart upon her hand
And bear that beating heart away;
And then did all the Muses sing

Of Magnus Annus at the spring,
As though God's death were but a play.

II

Another Troy must rise and set,
Another lineage feed the crow,
Another Argo's painted prow
Drive to a flashier bauble yet.
The Roman Empire stood appalled:
It dropped the reins of peace and war
When that fierce virgin and her Star
Out of the fabulous darkness called.

[*The Hebrew is discovered alone upon the stage; he has a sword or spear. The Musicians make faint drum-taps, or sound a rattle; the Greek enters through the audience from the left.*

The Hebrew. Did you find out what the noise was?

The Greek. Yes, I asked a Rabbi.

The Hebrew. Were you not afraid?

The Greek. How could he know that I am called a Christian? I wore the cap I brought from Alexandria. He said the followers of Dionysus were parading the streets with rattles and drums; that such a thing had never happened in this city before; that the Roman authorities were afraid to interfere. The followers of Dionysus have been out among the fields tearing a goat to pieces and drinking its blood, and are now wandering through the streets like a pack of wolves. The mob was so terrified of their frenzy that it left them alone, or, as seemed more likely, so busy hunting Christians it had time for nothing else. I turned to go, but he called me back and asked where I lived. When I said outside the gates, he asked if it was true that the dead had broken out of the cemeteries.

The Hebrew. We can keep the mob off for some minutes, long enough for the Eleven to escape over the roofs. I shall defend the narrow stair between this and the street until I

am killed, then you will take my place. Why is not the
Syrian here?

The Greek. I met him at the door and sent him on a message;
he will be back before long.

The Hebrew. The three of us will be few enough for the work
in hand.

The Greek [glancing towards the opening at the left]. What
are they doing now?

The Hebrew. While you were down below, James brought a
loaf out of a bag, and Nathanael found a skin of wine. They
put them on the table. It was a long time since they had
eaten anything. Then they began to speak in low voices,
and John spoke of the last time they had eaten in that
room.

The Greek. They were thirteen then.

The Hebrew. He said that Jesus divided bread and wine
among them. When John had spoken they sat still, nobody
eating or drinking. If you stand here you will see them.
That is Peter close to the window. He has been quite
motionless for a long time, his head upon his breast.

The Greek. Is it true that when the soldier asked him if he
were a follower of Jesus he denied it?

The Hebrew. Yes, it is true. James told me. Peter told the
others what he had done. But when the moment came
they were all afraid. I must not blame. I might have been
no braver. What are we all but dogs who have lost their
master?

The Greek. Yet you and I if the mob come will die rather
than let it up that stair.

The Hebrew. Ah! That is different. I am going to draw that
curtain; they must not hear what I am going to say. *[He
draws curtain.]*

The Greek. I know what is in your mind.

The Hebrew. They are afraid because they do not know what
to think. When Jesus was taken they could no longer believe him the Messiah. We can find consolation, but for the
Eleven it was always complete light or complete darkness.

The Greek. Because they are so much older.

The Hebrew. No, no. You have only to look into their faces to see they were intended to be saints. They are unfitted for anything else. What makes you laugh?

The Greek. Something I can see through the window. There, where I am pointing. There, at the end of the street. [*They stand together looking out over the heads of the audience.*]

The Hebrew. I cannot see anything.

The Greek. The hill.

The Hebrew. That is Calvary.

The Greek. And the three crosses on the top of it. [*He laughs again.*]

The Hebrew. Be quiet. You do not know what you are doing. You have gone out of your mind. You are laughing at Calvary.

The Greek. No, no. I am laughing because they thought they were nailing the hands of a living man upon the Cross, and all the time there was nothing there but a phantom.

The Hebrew. I saw him buried.

The Greek. We Greeks understand these things. No god has ever been buried; no god has ever suffered. Christ only seemed to be born, only seemed to eat, seemed to sleep, seemed to walk, seemed to die. I did not mean to tell you until I had proof.

The Hebrew. Proof?

The Greek. I shall have proof before nightfall.

The Hebrew. You talk wildly, but a masterless dog can bay the moon.

The Greek. No Jew can understand these things.

The Hebrew. It is you who do not understand. It is I and those men in there, perhaps, who begin to understand at last. He was nothing more than a man, the best man who ever lived. Nobody before him had so pitied human misery. He preached the coming of the Messiah because he thought the Messiah would take it all upon himself. Then some day when he was very tired, after a long journey perhaps, he thought that he himself was the Messiah. He thought it because of all destinies it seemed the most terrible.

The Greek. How could a man think himself the Messiah?

The Hebrew. It was always foretold that he would be born of a woman.

The Greek. To say that a god can be born of a woman, carried in her womb, fed upon her breast, washed as children are washed, is the most terrible blasphemy.

The Hebrew. If the Messiah were not born of a woman he could not take away the sins of man. Every sin starts a stream of suffering, but the Messiah takes it all away.

The Greek. Every man's sins are his property. Nobody else has a right to them.

The Hebrew. The Messiah is able to exhaust human suffering as though it were all gathered together in the spot of a burning-glass.

The Greek. That makes me shudder. The utmost possible suffering as an object of worship! You are morbid because your nation has no statues.

The Hebrew. What I have described is what I thought until three days ago.

The Greek. I say that there is nothing in the tomb.

The Hebrew. I saw him carried up the mountain and the tomb shut upon him.

The Greek. I have sent the Syrian to the tomb to prove that there is nothing there.

The Hebrew. You knew the danger we were all in and yet you weakened our guard?

The Greek. I have risked the apostles' lives and our own. What I have sent the Syrian to find out is more important.

The Hebrew. None of us are in our right mind to-day. I have got something in my own head that shocks me.

The Greek. Something you do not want to speak about?

The Hebrew. I am glad that he was not the Messiah; we might all have been deceived to our lives' end, or learnt the truth too late. One had to sacrifice everything that the divine suffering might, as it were, descend into one's mind and soul and make them pure. [*A sound of rattles and drums, at first in short bursts that come between sentences, but gradually growing continuous.*] One had to give up all worldly knowledge, all ambition, do nothing of one's own will. Only the divine could have any reality. God had to take complete possession. It must be a terrible thing when one is old, and the tomb round the corner, to think of all the ambitions one has put aside; to think, perhaps, a great deal about women. I want to marry and have children.

The Greek [*who is standing facing the audience, and looking out over their heads*]. It is the worshippers of Dionysus. They are under the window now. There is a group of women who carry upon their shoulders a bier with an image of the dead god upon it. No, they are not women. They are men dressed as women. I have seen something like it in Alexandria. They are all silent, as if something were going to happen. My God! What a spectacle! In Alexandria a few men paint their lips vermilion. They imitate women that they may attain in worship a woman's self-abandonment. No great harm comes of it—but here! Come and look for yourself.

The Hebrew. I will not look at such madmen.

The Greek. Though the music has stopped, some men are still dancing, and some of the dancers have gashed themselves with knives, imagining themselves, I suppose, at once the god and the Titans that murdered him. A little further off a man and woman are coupling in the middle of the street. She thinks the surrender to some man the dance threw into her arms may bring her god back to life. All are from the foreign quarter, to judge by face and costume, and are the most ignorant and excitable class of Asiatic Greeks, the dregs of the population. Such people suffer terribly and seek forgetfulness in monstrous ceremonies. Ah, that is what they were waiting for. The crowd has parted to make way for a singer. It is a girl. No, not a girl; a boy from the theatre. I know him. He acts girls' parts. He is dressed as a girl, but his finger-nails are gilded and his wig is made of gilded cords. He looks like a statue out of some temple. I remember something of the kind in Alexandria. Three days after the full moon, a full moon in March, they sing the death of the god and pray for his resurrection.

[*One of the Musicians sings the following song*]
Astrea's holy child!
A rattle in the wood
Where a Titan strode!
His rattle drew the child
Into that solitude.

Barrum, barrum, barrum [*Drum-taps accompany and follow the words*].

We wandering women,
Wives for all that come,
Tried to draw him home;
And every wandering woman
Beat upon a drum.

Barrum, barrum, barrum [*Drum-taps as before*].

But the murderous Titans
Where the woods grow dim
Stood and waited him.
The great hands of those Titans
Tore limb from limb.

Barrum, barrum, barrum [*Drum-taps as before*].

On virgin Astrea
That can succour all
Wandering women call;
Call out to Astrea
That the moon stood at the full.

Barrum, barrum, barrum [*Drum-taps as before*].

The Greek. I cannot think all that self-surrender and self-abasement is Greek, despite the Greek name of its god. When the goddess came to Achilles in the battle she did not interfere with his soul, she took him by his yellow hair. Lucretius thinks that the gods appear in the visions of the day and night but are indifferent to human fate; that, however, is the exaggeration of a Roman rhetorician. They can be discovered by contemplation, in their faces a high keen joy like the cry of a bat, and the man who lives heroically gives them the only earthly body that they covet. He, as it were, copies their gestures and their acts. What seems their indifference is but their eternal possession of themselves. Man, too, remains separate. He does not surrender his soul. He keeps his privacy.

[*Drum-taps to represent knocking at the door*]

The Hebrew. There is someone at the door, but I dare not open with that crowd in the street.

The Greek. You need not be afraid. The crowd has begun to move away. [*The Hebrew goes down into the audience towards the left.*] I deduce from our great philosophers that a god can overwhelm man with disaster, take health and wealth away, but man keeps his privacy. If that is the Syrian he may bring such confirmation that mankind will never forget his words.

The Hebrew [*from among the audience*]. It is the Syrian. There is something wrong. He is ill or drunk. [*He helps the Syrian on to the stage.*]

The Syrian. I am like a drunken man. I can hardly stand upon my feet. Something incredible has happened. I have run all the way.

The Hebrew. Well?

The Syrian. I must tell the Eleven at once. Are they still in there? Everybody must be told.

The Hebrew. What is it? Get your breath and speak.

The Syrian. I was on my way to the tomb. I met the Galilean women, Mary the mother of Jesus, Mary the mother of James, and the other women. The younger women were pale with excitement and began to speak all together. I did not know what they were saying; but Mary the mother of James said that they had been to the tomb at daybreak and found that it was empty.

The Greek. Ah!

The Hebrew. The tomb cannot be empty. I will not believe it.

The Syrian. At the door stood a man all shining, and cried out that Christ had arisen. [*Faint drum-taps and the faint sound of a rattle.*] As they came down the mountain a man stood suddenly at their side; that man was Christ himself. They stooped down and kissed his feet. Now stand out of my way that I may tell Peter and James and John.

The Hebrew [*standing before the curtained entrance of the inner room*]. I will not stand out of the way.

The Syrian. Did you hear what I said? Our master has arisen.

The Hebrew. I will not have the Eleven disturbed for the dreams of women.

The Greek. The women were not dreaming. They told you the truth, and yet this man is in the right. He is in charge here. We must all be convinced before we speak to the Eleven.

The Syrian. The Eleven will be able to judge better than we.

The Greek. Though we are so much younger we know more of the world than they do.

The Hebrew. If you told your story they would no more believe it than I do, but Peter's misery would be increased. I know him longer than you do and I know what would happen. Peter would remember that the women did not flinch; that not one among them denied her master; that the dream proved their love and faith. Then he would remember that he had lacked both, and imagine that John was looking at him. He would turn away and bury his head in his hands.

The Greek. I said that we must all be convinced, but there is another reason why you must not tell them anything. Somebody else is coming. I am certain that Jesus never had a human body; that he is phantom and can pass through that wall; that he will so pass; that he will pass through this room; that he himself will speak to the apostles.

The Syrian. He is no phantom. We put a great stone over the mouth of the tomb, and the women say that it has been rolled back.

The Hebrew. The Romans heard yesterday that some of our people planned to steal the body, and to put abroad a story that Christ had arisen; and so escape the shame of our defeat. They probably stole it in the night.

The Syrian. The Romans put sentries at the tomb. The women found the sentries asleep. Christ had put them asleep that they might not see him move the stone.

The Greek. A hand without bones, without sinews, cannot move a stone.

The Syrian. What matter if it contradicts all human knowledge?—another Argo seeks another fleece, another Troy is sacked.

The Greek. Why are you laughing?

The Syrian. What is human knowledge?

The Greek. The knowledge that keeps the road from here to Persia free from robbers, that has built the beautiful humane cities, that has made the modern world, that stands between us and the barbarian.

The Syrian. But what if there is something it cannot explain, something more important than anything else?

The Greek. You talk as if you wanted the barbarian back.

The Syrian. What if there is always something that lies outside knowledge, outside order? What if at the moment when knowledge and order seem complete that something appears?   [*He has begun to laugh.*

The Hebrew. Stop laughing.

The Syrian. What if the irrational return? What if the circle begin again?

The Hebrew. Stop! He laughed when he saw Calvary through the window, and now you laugh.

The Greek. He too has lost control of himself.

The Hebrew. Stop, I tell you. [*Drums and rattles.*]

The Syrian. But I am not laughing. It is the people out there who are laughing.

The Hebrew. No, they are shaking rattles and beating drums.

The Syrian. I thought they were laughing. How horrible!

The Greek [*looking out over heads of audience*]. The worshippers of Dionysus are coming this way again. They have hidden their image of the dead god, and have begun their lunatic cry, "God has arisen! God has arisen!"

[*The Musicians who have been saying* "God has arisen!" *fall silent.*

They will cry "God has arisen!" through all the streets of the city. They can make their god live and die at their pleasure; but why are they silent? They are dancing silently.

They are coming nearer and nearer, dancing all the while, using some kind of ancient step unlike anything I have seen in Alexandria. They are almost under the window now.

The Hebrew. They have come back to mock us, because their god arises every year, whereas our god is dead for ever.

The Greek. How they roll their painted eyes as the dance grows quicker and quicker! They are under the window. Why are they all suddenly motionless? Why are all those unseeing eyes turned upon this house? Is there anything strange about this house?

The Hebrew. Somebody has come into the room.

The Greek. Where?

The Hebrew. I do not know; but I thought I heard a step.

The Greek. I knew that he would come.

The Hebrew. There is no one here. I shut the door at the foot of the steps.

The Greek. The curtain over there is moving.

The Hebrew. No, it is quite still, and besides there is nothing behind it but a blank wall.

The Greek. Look, look!

The Hebrew. Yes, it has begun to move. [*During what follows he backs in terror towards the left-hand corner of the stage.*]

The Greek. There is someone coming through it.

  [*The figure of Christ wearing a recognisable but stylistic mask enters through the curtain. The Syrian slowly draws back the curtain that shuts off the inner room where the apostles are. The three young men are towards the left of the stage, the figure of Christ is at the back towards the right.*

The Greek. It is the phantom of our master. Why are you afraid? He has been crucified and buried, but only in semblance, and is among us once more. [*The Hebrew kneels.*] There is nothing here but a phantom, it has no flesh and blood. Because I know the truth I am not afraid. Look, I will touch it. It may be hard under my hand like a statue— I have heard of such things—or my hand may pass through it—but there is no flesh and blood. [*He goes slowly up to the figure and passes his hand over its side.*] The heart of a

phantom is beating! The heart of a phantom is beating!
[*He screams. The figure of Christ crosses the stage and
passes into the inner room.*]

The Syrian. He is standing in the midst of them. Some are
afraid. He looks at Peter and James and John. He smiles.
He has parted the clothes at his side. He shows them his
side. There is a great wound there. Thomas has put his hand
into the wound. He has put his hand where the heart is.

The Greek. O Athens, Alexandria, Rome, something has come
to destroy you. The heart of a phantom is beating. Man has
begun to die. Your words are clear at last, O Heraclitus.
God and man die each other's life, live each other's death.
[*The Musicians rise, one or more singing the following
words. If the performance is in a private room or
studio, they unfold and fold a curtain as in my dance
plays; if at the Peacock Theatre, they draw the proscenium curtain across.*

I

In pity for man's darkening thought
He walked that room and issued thence
In Galilean turbulence;
The Babylonian starlight brought
A fabulous, formless darkness in;
Odour of blood when Christ was slain
Made all Platonic tolerance vain
And vain all Doric discipline.

II

Everything that man esteems
Endures a moment or a day:
Love's pleasure drives his love away,
The painter's brush consumes his dreams;
The herald's cry, the soldier's tread
Exhaust his glory and his might:
Whatever flames upon the night
Man's own resinous heart has fed.

THE END

THE WORDS UPON
THE WINDOW-PANE

The Words Upon
the Window-Pane

PERSONS IN THE PLAY

Dr. Trench	Cornelius Patterson
Miss Mackenna	Abraham Johnson
John Corbet	Mrs. Mallet
	Mrs. Henderson

A lodging-house room, an armchair, a little table in front of it, chairs on either side. A fireplace and window. A kettle on the hob and some tea-things on a dresser. A door to back and towards the right. Through the door one can see an entrance hall. The sound of a knocker. Miss Mackenna passes through and then she re-enters hall together with John Corbet, a man of twenty-two or twenty-three, and Dr. Trench, a man of between sixty and seventy.

Dr. Trench [*in hall*]. May I introduce John Corbet, one of the Corbets of Ballymoney, but at present a Cambridge student? This is Miss Mackenna, our energetic secretary.

      [*They come into room, take off their coats.*
Miss Mackenna. I thought it better to let you in myself. This country is still sufficiently medieval to make spiritualism an undesirable theme for gossip. Give me your coats and hats. I will put them in my own room. It is just across the hall. Better sit down; your watches must be fast. Mrs. Henderson is lying down, as she always does before a séance. We won't begin for ten minutes yet. [*She goes out with hats and coats.*]
Dr. Trench. Miss Mackenna does all the real work of the Dublin Spiritualists' Association. She did all the corre-

spondence with Mrs. Henderson, and persuaded the land-
lady to let her this big room and a small room upstairs. We
are a poor society and could not guarantee anything in
advance. Mrs. Henderson has come from London at her
own risk. She was born in Dublin and wants to spread the
movement here. She lives very economically and does not
expect a great deal. We all give what we can. A poor
woman with the soul of an apostle.

John Corbet. Have there been many séances?

Dr. Trench. Only three so far.

John Corbet. I hope she will not mind my scepticism. I have
looked into Myers' *Human Personality* and a wild book by
Conan Doyle, but am unconvinced.

Dr. Trench. We all have to find the truth for ourselves. Lord
Dunraven, then Lord Adare, introduced my father to the
famous David Home. My father often told me that he saw
David Home floating in the air in broad daylight, but I did
not believe a word of it. I had to investigate for myself,
and I was very hard to convince. Mrs. Piper, an American
trance medium, not unlike Mrs. Henderson, convinced me.

John Corbet. A state of somnambulism and voices coming
through her lips that purport to be those of dead persons?

Dr. Trench. Exactly: quite the best kind of mediumship if
you want to establish the identity of a spirit. But do not
expect too much. There has been a hostile influence.

John Corbet. You mean an evil spirit?

Dr. Trench. The poet Blake said that he never knew a bad
man that had not something very good about him. I say a
hostile influence, an influence that disturbed the last séance
very seriously. I cannot tell you what happened, for I have
not been at any of Mrs. Henderson's séances. Trance
mediumship has nothing new to show me—I told the
young people when they made me their President that I
would probably stay at home, that I could get more out of
Emanuel Swedenborg than out of any séance. [A *knock.*]
That is probably old Cornelius Patterson; he thinks they
race horses and whippets in the other world, and is, so they
tell me, so anxious to find out if he is right that he is always

punctual. Miss Mackenna will keep him to herself for some minutes. He gives her tips for Harold's Cross.

[*Miss Mackenna crosses to hall door and admits Cornelius Patterson. She brings him to her room across the hall.*

John Corbet [*who has been wandering about*]. This is a wonderful room for a lodging-house.

Dr. Trench. It was a private house until about fifty years ago. It was not so near the town in those days, and there are large stables at the back. Quite a number of notable people lived here. Grattan was born upstairs; no, not Grattan, Curran perhaps—I forget—but I do know that this house in the early part of the eighteenth century belonged to friends of Jonathan Swift, or rather of Stella. Swift chaffed her in the *Journal to Stella* because of certain small sums of money she lost at cards probably in this very room. That was before Vanessa appeared upon the scene. It was a country-house in those days, surrounded by trees and gardens. Somebody cut some lines from a poem of hers upon the window-pane—tradition says Stella herself. [*A knock.*] Here they are, but you will hardly make them out in this light. [*They stand in the window. Corbet stoops down to see better. Miss Mackenna and Abraham Johnson enter and stand near door.*]

Abraham Johnson. Where is Mrs. Henderson?

Miss Mackenna. She is upstairs; she always rests before a séance.

Abraham Johnson. I must see her before the séance. I know exactly what to do to get rid of this evil influence.

Miss Mackenna. If you go up to see her there will be no séance at all. She says it is dangerous even to think, much less to speak, of an evil influence.

Abraham Johnson. Then I shall speak to the President.

Miss Mackenna. Better talk the whole thing over first in my room. Mrs. Henderson says that there must be perfect harmony.

Abraham Johnson. Something must be done. The last séance was completely spoiled. [*A knock.*]

Miss Mackenna. That may be Mrs. Mallet; she is a very experienced spiritualist. Come to my room, old Patterson and
some others are there already. [*She brings him to the other
room and later crosses to hall door to admit Mrs. Mallet.*]

John Corbet. I know those lines well—they are part of a poem
Stella wrote for Swift's fifty-fourth birthday. Only three
poems of hers—and some lines she added to a poem of
Swift's—have come down to us, but they are enough to
prove her a better poet than Swift. Even those few words
on the window make me think of a seventeenth-century
poet, Donne or Crashaw. [*He quotes*]

> "You taught how I might youth prolong
> By knowing what is right and wrong,
> How from my heart to bring supplies
> Of lustre to my fading eyes."

How strange that a celibate scholar, well on in life, should
keep the love of two such women! He met Vanessa in
London at the height of his political power. She followed
him to Dublin. She loved him for nine years, perhaps died
of love, but Stella loved him all her life.

Dr. Trench. I have shown that writing to several persons, and
you are the first who has recognised the lines.

John Corbet. I am writing an essay on Swift and Stella for my
doctorate at Cambridge. I hope to prove that in Swift's day
men of intellect reached the height of their power—the
greatest position they ever attained in society and the State,
that everything great in Ireland and in our character, in
what remains of our architecture, comes from that day; that
we have kept its seal longer than England.

Dr. Trench. A tragic life: Bolingbroke, Harley, Ormonde, all
those great Ministers that were his friends, banished and
broken.

John Corbet. I do not think you can explain him in that way—
his tragedy had deeper foundations. His ideal order was the
Roman Senate, his ideal men Brutus and Cato. Such an
order and such men had seemed possible once more, but
the movement passed and he foresaw the ruin to come,
Democracy, Rousseau, the French Revolution; that is why

he hated the common run of men,—"I hate lawyers, I hate doctors," he said, "though I love Dr. So-and-so and Judge So-and-so"—that is why he wrote *Gulliver*, that is why he wore out his brain, that is why he felt *saeva indignatio*, that is why he sleeps under the greatest epitaph in history. You remember how it goes? It is almost finer in English than in Latin: "He has gone where fierce indignation can lacerate his heart no more."

[*Abraham Johnson comes in, followed by Mrs. Mallet and Cornelius Patterson.*

Abraham Johnson. Something must be done, Dr. Trench, to drive away the influence that has destroyed our séances. I have come here week after week at considerable expense. I am from Belfast. I am by profession a minister of the Gospel, I do a great deal of work among the poor and ignorant. I produce considerable effect by singing and preaching, but I know that my effect should be much greater than it is. My hope is that I shall be able to communicate with the great Evangelist Moody. I want to ask him to stand invisible beside me when I speak or sing, and lay his hands upon my head and give me such a portion of his power that my work may be blessed as the work of Moody and Sankey was blessed.

Mrs. Mallet. What Mr. Johnson says about the hostile influence is quite true. The last two séances were completely spoilt. I am thinking of starting a tea-shop in Folkestone. I followed Mrs. Henderson to Dublin to get my husband's advice, but two spirits kept talking and would not let any other spirit say a word.

Dr. Trench. Did the spirits say the same thing and go through the same drama at both séances?

Mrs. Mallet. Yes—just as if they were characters in some kind of horrible play.

Dr. Trench. That is what I was afraid of.

Mrs. Mallet. My husband was drowned at sea ten years ago, but constantly speaks to me through Mrs. Henderson as if he were still alive. He advises me about everything I do, and I am utterly lost if I cannot question him.

Cornelius Patterson. I never did like the Heaven they talk about in churches: but when somebody told me that Mrs. Mallet's husband ate and drank and went about with his favourite dog, I said to myself, "That is the place for Corney Patterson." I came here to find out if it was true, and I declare to God I have not heard one word about it.

Abraham Johnson. I ask you, Dr. Trench, as President of the Dublin Spiritualists' Association, to permit me to read the ritual of exorcism appointed for such occasions. After the last séance I copied it out of an old book in the library of Belfast University. I have it here.

> [*He takes paper out of his pocket.*

Dr. Trench. The spirits are people like ourselves, we treat them as our guests and protect them from discourtesy and violence, and every exorcism is a curse or a threatened curse. We do not admit that there are evil spirits. Some spirits are earth-bound—they think they are still living and go over and over some action of their past lives, just as we go over and over some painful thought, except that where they are thought is reality. For instance, when a spirit which has died a violent death comes to a medium for the first time, it re-lives all the pains of death.

Mrs. Mallet. When my husband came for the first time the medium gasped and struggled as if she was drowning. It was terrible to watch.

Dr. Trench. Sometimes a spirit re-lives not the pain of death but some passionate or tragic moment of life. Swedenborg describes this and gives the reason for it. There is an incident of the kind in the *Odyssey*, and many in Eastern literature; the murderer repeats his murder, the robber his robbery, the lover his serenade, the soldier hears the trumpet once again. If I were a Catholic I would say that such spirits were in Purgatory. In vain do we write *requiescat in pace* upon the tomb, for they must suffer, and we in our turn must suffer until God gives peace. Such spirits do not often come to séances unless those séances are held in houses where those spirits lived, or where the event took place. This spirit which speaks those incomprehensible words and does not answer when spoken to is of such a nature. The more patient we are, the more quickly will it pass out of its passion and its remorse.

Abraham Johnson. I am still convinced that the spirit which disturbed the last séance is evil. If I may not exorcise it I will certainly pray for protection.

Dr. Trench. Mrs. Henderson's control, Lulu, is able and experienced and can protect both medium and sitters, but it may help Lulu if you pray that the spirit find rest.

[*Abraham Johnson sits down and prays silently, moving his lips. Mrs. Henderson comes in with Miss Mackenna and others. Miss Mackenna shuts the door.*

Dr. Trench. Mrs. Henderson, may I introduce to you Mr. Corbet, a young man from Cambridge and a sceptic, who hopes that you will be able to convince him?

Mrs. Henderson. We were all sceptics once. He must not expect too much from a first séance. He must persevere. [*She sits in the armchair, and the others begin to seat themselves. Miss Mackenna goes to John Corbet and they remain standing.*]

Miss Mackenna. I am glad that you are a sceptic.

John Corbet. I thought you were a spiritualist.

Miss Mackenna. I have seen a good many séances, and sometimes think it is all coincidence and thought-transference. [*She says this in a low voice.*] Then at other times I think as Dr. Trench does, and then I feel like Job—you know the quotation—the hair of my head stands up. A spirit passes before my face.

Mrs. Mallet. Turn the key, Dr. Trench, we don't want anybody blundering in here. [*Dr. Trench locks door.*] Come and sit here, Miss Mackenna.

Miss Mackenna. No, I am going to sit beside Mr. Corbet.
                    [*Corbet and Miss Mackenna sit down.*

John Corbet. You feel like Job to-night?

Miss Mackenna. I feel that something is going to happen, that is why I am glad that you are a sceptic.

John Corbet. You feel safer?

Miss Mackenna. Yes, safer.

Mrs. Henderson. I am glad to meet all my dear friends again
and to welcome Mr. Corbet among us. As he is a stranger
I must explain that we do not call up spirits, we make the
right conditions and they come. I do not know who is
going to come; sometimes there are a great many and the
guides choose between them. The guides try to send somebody for everybody but do not always succeed. If you want
to speak to some dear friend who has passed over, do not be
discouraged. If your friend cannot come this time, maybe
he can next time. My control is a dear little girl called Lulu
who died when she was five or six years old. She describes
the spirits present and tells us what spirit wants to speak.
Miss Mackenna, a verse of a hymn, please, the same we
had last time, and will everyone join in the singing.

[*They sing the following lines from Hymn 564, Irish
Church Hymnal.*

"Sun of my soul, Thou Saviour dear,
It is not night if Thou be near:
O may no earth-born cloud arise
To hide Thee from Thy servant's eyes."

[*Mrs. Henderson is leaning back in her chair asleep.*

Miss Mackenna [*to John Corbet*]. She always snores like that
when she is going off.

Mrs. Henderson [*in a child's voice*]. Lulu so glad to see all her
friends.

Mrs. Mallet. And we are glad you have come, Lulu.

Mrs. Henderson [*in a child's voice*]. Lulu glad to see new
friend.

Miss Mackenna [*to John Corbet*]. She is speaking to you.

John Corbet. Thank you, Lulu.

Mrs. Henderson [*in a child's voice*]. You mustn't laugh at the
way I talk.

John Corbet. I am not laughing, Lulu.

Mrs. Henderson [*in a child's voice*]. Nobody must laugh. Lulu
does her best but can't say big long words. Lulu sees a tall
man here, lots of hair on face [*Mrs. Henderson passes her
hands over her cheeks and chin*], not much on the top of

his head [*Mrs. Henderson passes her hand over the top of her head*], red necktie, and such a funny sort of pin.

Mrs. Mallet. Yes. . . . Yes. . . .

Mrs. Henderson [*in a child's voice*]. Pin like a horseshoe.

Mrs. Mallet. It's my husband.

Mrs. Henderson [*in a child's voice*]. He has a message.

Mrs. Mallet. Yes.

Mrs. Henderson [*in a child's voice*]. Lulu cannot hear. He is too far off. He has come near. Lulu can hear now. He says . . . he says, "Drive that man away!" He is pointing to somebody in the corner, that corner over there. He says it is the bad man who spoilt everything last time. If they won't drive him away, Lulu will scream.

Miss Mackenna. That horrible spirit again.

Abraham Johnson. Last time he monopolised the séance.

Mrs. Mallet. He would not let anybody speak but himself.

Mrs. Henderson [*in a child's voice*]. They have driven that bad man away. Lulu sees a young lady.

Mrs. Mallet. Is not my husband here?

Mrs. Henderson [*in a child's voice*]. Man with funny pin gone away. Young lady here—Lulu thinks she must be at a fancy dress party, such funny clothes, hair all in curls—all bent down on floor near that old man with glasses.

Dr. Trench. No, I do not recognize her.

Mrs. Henderson [*in a child's voice*]. That bad man, that bad old man in the corner, they have let him come back. Lulu is going to scream. O. . . . O. . . . [*In a man's voice.*] How dare you write to her? How dare you ask if we were married? How dare you question her?

Dr. Trench. A soul in its agony—it cannot see us or hear us.

Mrs. Henderson [*upright and rigid, only her lips moving, and still in a man's voice*]. You sit crouching there. Did you not hear what I said? How dared you question her? I found you an ignorant little girl without intellect, without moral ambition. How many times did I not stay away from great men's houses, how many times forsake the Lord Treasurer, how many times neglect the business of the State that we might read Plutarch together!

[*Abraham Johnson half rises. Dr. Trench motions him to remain seated.*

Dr. Trench. Silence!

Abraham Johnson. But, Dr. Trench . . .

Dr. Trench. Hush—we can do nothing.

Mrs. Henderson [*speaking as before*]. I taught you to think in every situation of life not as Hester Vanhomrigh would think in that situation, but as Cato or Brutus would, and now you behave like some common slut with her ear against the keyhole.

John Corbet [*to Miss Mackenna*]. It is Swift, Jonathan Swift, talking to the woman he called Vanessa. She was christened Hester Vanhomrigh.

Mrs. Henderson [*in Vanessa's voice*]. I questioned her, Jonathan, because I love. Why have you let me spend hours in your company if you did not want me to love you? [*In Swift's voice.*] When I rebuilt Rome in your mind it was as though I walked its streets. [*In Vanessa's voice.*] Was that all, Jonathan? Was I nothing but a painter's canvas? [*In Swift's voice.*] My God, do you think it was easy? I was a man of strong passions and I had sworn never to marry. [*In Vanessa's voice.*] If you and she are not married, why should we not marry like other men and women? I loved you from the first moment when you came to my mother's house and began to teach me. I thought it would be enough to look at you, to speak to you, to hear you speak. I followed you to Ireland five years ago and I can bear it no longer. It is not enough to look, to speak, to hear. Jonathan, Jonathan, I am a woman, the women Brutus and Cato loved were not different. [*In Swift's voice.*] I have something in my blood that no child must inherit. I have constant attacks of dizziness; I pretend they come from a surfeit of fruit when I was a child. I had them in London. . . . There was a great doctor there, Dr. Arbuthnot; I told him of those attacks of dizziness, I told him of worse things. It was he who explained. There is a line of Dryden's. . . . [*In Vanessa's voice.*] O, I know—"Great wits are sure to madness near allied." If you had children, Jonathan, my blood would make them healthy. I will take your hand, I will lay it upon my heart—upon the Vanhomrigh blood that has been healthy for generations. [*Mrs. Henderson slowly raises her left hand.*] That is the first time you have touched my body, Jonathan. [*Mrs. Henderson stands up and remains rigid. In Swift's voice.*] What do I care if it be healthy? What do I care if it could make mine healthy? Am I to add another to the healthy rascaldom and knavery of the world? [*In Vanessa's voice.*] Look at me, Jonathan. Your arrogant intellect separates us. Give me both your hands. I will put them upon my breast. [*Mrs. Henderson raises her right hand to the level of her left and then raises both to her breast.*] O, it is white—white as the gambler's dice—white ivory dice. Think of the uncertainty. Perhaps a mad child—perhaps a rascal—perhaps a knave—perhaps not, Jonathan. The dice of the intellect are loaded, but I am the common ivory dice. [*Her hands are stretched out as though drawing somebody towards her.*] It is not my hands that draw you back. My hands are weak, they could not draw you back if you did not love as I love. You said that you have strong passions; that is true, Jonathan—no man in Ireland is so passionate. That is why you need me, that is why you need children, nobody has greater need. You are growing old. An old man without children is very solitary. Even his friends, men as old as he, turn away, they turn towards the young, their children or their children's children. They cannot endure an old man like themselves. [*Mrs. Henderson moves away from the chair, her movements gradually growing convulsive.*] You are not too old for the dice, Jonathan, but a few years if you turn away will make you an old miserable childless man. [*In Swift's voice.*] O God, hear the prayer of Jonathan Swift, that afflicted man, and grant that he may leave to posterity nothing but his intellect that came to him from Heaven. [*In Vanessa's voice.*] Can you face solitude with that mind, Jonathan? [*Mrs. Henderson goes to the door, finds that it is closed.*] Dice, white ivory dice. [*In Swift's voice.*] My God, I am left alone with my enemy. Who locked the door, who locked me in with my enemy? [*Mrs. Henderson beats upon the door, sinks to the floor and then speaks as Lulu.*] Bad old man! Do not let him come back. Bad old man does not know he is dead. Lulu cannot find fathers, mothers, sons that have passed over. Power almost gone. [*Mrs. Mallet leads Mrs. Henderson, who seems very exhausted, back to her chair. She is still asleep. She speaks again as Lulu.*] Another verse of hymn. Everybody sing. Hymn will bring good influence.

[*They sing*]
"If some poor wandering child of Thine
Have spurned to-day the voice divine,
Now, Lord, the gracious work begin;
Let him no more lie down in sin."

[*During the hymn Mrs. Henderson has been murmuring "Stella," but the singing has almost drowned her voice. The singers draw one another's attention to the fact that she is speaking. The singing stops.*]

Dr. Trench. I thought she was speaking.

Mrs. Mallet. I saw her lips move.

Dr. Trench. She would be more comfortable with a cushion, but we might wake her.

Mrs. Mallet. Nothing can wake her out of a trance like that until she wakes up herself. [*She brings a cushion and she and Dr. Trench put Mrs. Henderson into a more comfortable position.*]

Mrs. Henderson [*in Swift's voice*]. Stella.

Miss Mackenna [*to John Corbet*]. Did you hear that? She said "Stella."

John Corbet. Vanessa has gone, Stella has taken her place.

Miss Mackenna. Did you notice the change while we were singing? The new influence in the room?

John Corbet. I thought I did, but it must have been fancy.

Mrs. Mallet. Hush!

Mrs. Henderson [*in Swift's voice*]. Have I wronged you, beloved Stella? Are you unhappy? You have no children, you have no lover, you have no husband. A cross and ageing man for friend—nothing but that. But no, do not answer—

you have answered already in that poem you wrote for my
last birthday. With what scorn you speak of the common
lot of women "with no endowments but a face—"

> "Before the thirtieth year of life
> A maid forlorn or hated wife."

It is the thought of the great Chrysostom who wrote in a
famous passage that women loved according to the soul,
loved as saints can love, keep their beauty longer, have
greater happiness than women loved according to the flesh.
That thought has comforted me, but it is a terrible thing
to be responsible for another's happiness. There are mo-
ments when I doubt, when I think Chrysostom may have
been wrong. But now I have your poem to drive doubt
away. You have addressed me in these noble words:

> "You taught how I might youth prolong
> By knowing what is right and wrong;
> How from my heart to bring supplies
> Of lustre to my fading eyes;
> How soon a beauteous mind repairs
> The loss of chang'd or falling hairs;
> How wit and virtue from within
> Can spread a smoothness o'er the skin."

John Corbet. The words upon the window-pane!

Mrs. Henderson [*in Swift's voice*]. Then, because you understand that I am afraid of solitude, afraid of outliving my
friends—and myself—you comfort me in that last verse—
you overpraise my moral nature when you attribute to it
a rich mantle, but O how touching those words which
describe your love:

> "Late dying may you cast a shred
> Of that rich mantle o'er my head;
> To bear with dignity my sorrow,
> One day alone, then die to-morrow."

Yes, you will close my eyes, Stella. O, you will live long
after me, dear Stella, for you are still a young woman, but
you will close my eyes. [*Mrs. Henderson sinks back in chair
and speaks as Lulu.*] Bad old man gone. Power all used up.
Lulu can do no more. Good-bye, friends. [*Mrs. Henderson,*

speaking in her own voice.] Go away, go away! [*She wakes.*]
I saw him a moment ago, has he spoilt the séance again?

Mrs. Mallet. Yes, Mrs. Henderson, my husband came, but he
was driven away.

Dr. Trench. Mrs. Henderson is very tired. We must leave her
to rest. [*To Mrs. Henderson.*] You did your best and nobody
can do more than that. [*He takes out money.*]

Mrs. Henderson. No. . . . No. . . . I cannot take any money,
not after a séance like that.

Dr. Trench. Of course you must take it, Mrs. Henderson. [*He
puts money on table, and Mrs. Henderson gives a furtive
glance to see how much it is. She does the same as each
sitter lays down his or her money.*]

Mrs. Mallet. A bad séance is just as exhausting as a good
séance, and you must be paid.

Mrs. Henderson. No. . . . No. . . . Please don't. It is very
wrong to take money for such a failure.

[*Mrs. Mallet lays down money.*

Cornelius Patterson. A jockey is paid whether he wins or not.
[*He lays down money.*]

Miss Mackenna. That spirit rather thrilled me. [*She lays down
money.*]

Mrs. Henderson. If you insist, I must take it.

Abraham Johnson. I shall pray for you to-night. I shall ask
God to bless and protect your séances. [*He lays down
money.*]

[*All go out except John Corbet and Mrs. Henderson.*

John Corbet. I know you are tired, Mrs. Henderson, but I
must speak to you. I have been deeply moved by what I
have heard. This is my contribution to prove that I am
satisfied, completely satisfied. [*He puts a note on the table.*]

Mrs. Henderson. A pound note—nobody ever gives me more
than ten shillings, and yet the séance was a failure.

John Corbet [*sitting down near Mrs. Henderson*]. When I
say I am satisfied I do not mean that I am convinced it
was the work of spirits. I prefer to think that you created
it all, that you are an accomplished actress and scholar. In
my essay for my Cambridge doctorate I examine all the

explanations of Swift's celibacy offered by his biographers and prove that the explanation you selected was the only plausible one. But there is something I must ask you. Swift was the chief representative of the intellect of his epoch, that arrogant intellect free at last from superstition. He foresaw its collapse. He foresaw Democracy, he must have dreaded the future. Did he refuse to beget children because of that dread? Was Swift mad? Or was it the intellect itself that was mad?

Mrs. Henderson. Who are you talking of, sir?

John Corbet. Swift, of course.

Mrs. Henderson. Swift? I do not know anybody called Swift.

John Corbet. Jonathan Swift, whose spirit seemed to be present to-night.

Mrs. Henderson. What? That dirty old man?

John Corbet. He was neither old nor dirty when Stella and Vanessa loved him.

Mrs. Henderson. I saw him very clearly just as I woke up. His clothes were dirty, his face covered with boils. Some disease had made one of his eyes swell up, it stood out from his face like a hen's egg.

John Corbet. He looked like that in his old age. Stella had been dead a long time. His brain had gone, his friends had deserted him. The man appointed to take care of him beat him to keep him quiet.

Mrs. Henderson. Now they are old, now they are young. They change all in a moment as their thought changes. It is sometimes a terrible thing to be out of the body, God help us all.

Dr. Trench [*at doorway*]. Come along, Corbet, Mrs. Henderson is tired out.

John Corbet. Good-bye, Mrs. Henderson. [*He goes out with Dr. Trench. All the sitters except Miss Mackenna, who has returned to her room, pass along the passage on their way to the front door. Mrs. Henderson counts the money, finds her purse, which is in a vase on the mantelpiece, and puts the money in it.*]

Mrs. Henderson. How tired I am! I'd be the better of a cup of tea. [*She finds the teapot and puts kettle on fire, and then as she crouches down by the hearth suddenly lifts up her hands and counts her fingers, speaking in Swift's voice.*] Five great Ministers that were my friends are gone, ten great Ministers that were my friends are gone. I have not fingers enough to count the great Ministers that were my friends and that are gone. [*She wakes with a start and speaks in her own voice.*] Where did I put that tea-caddy? Ah! there it is. And there should be a cup and saucer. [*She finds the saucer.*] But where's the cup? [*She moves aimlessly about the stage and then, letting the saucer fall and break, speaks in Swift's voice.*] Perish the day on which I was born!

THE END

A FULL MOON IN MARCH

A Full Moon in March

| First Attendant | The Queen |
| Second Attendant | The Swineherd |

The Swineherd wears a half-savage mask covering the upper part of his face. He is bearded. When the inner curtain rises for the second time the player who has hitherto taken the part of the Queen is replaced by a dancer.

When the stage curtain rises, two Attendants, an elderly woman and a young man, are discovered standing before an inner curtain.

First Attendant. What do we do?
  What part do we take?
  What did he say?
Second Attendant. Join when we like,
  Singing or speaking.
First Attendant. Before the curtain rises on the play?
Second Attendant. Before it rises.
First Attendant. What do we sing?
Second Attendant. "Sing anything, sing any old thing," said he.
First Attendant. Come then and sing about the dung of swine.
  [*They slowly part the inner curtain. The Second Attendant sings—the First Attendant may join in the singing at the end of the first or second verse. The First Attendant has a soprano, the Second a bass voice.*
Second Attendant.

> Every loutish lad in love
> Thinks his wisdom great enough,
> What cares love for this and that?

To make all his parish stare,
As though Pythagoras wandered there.
Crown of gold or dung of swine.

Should old Pythagoras fall in love
Little may he boast thereof.
What cares love for this and that?
Days go by in foolishness.
O how great their sweetness is!
Crown of gold or dung of swine.

Open wide those gleaming eyes,
That can make the loutish wise.
What cares love for this and that?
Make a leader of the schools
Thank the Lord, all men are fools.
Crown of gold or dung of swine.

[*They sit at one side of stage near audience. If they are
    musicians, they have beside them drum, flute, and
    zither. The Queen is discovered seated and veiled.*

The Queen [*stretching and yawning*]. What man is at the
door?

Second Attendant. Nobody, Queen.

The Queen. Some man has come, some terrifying man,
For I have yawned and stretched myself three times.
Admit him, Captain of the Guard. . . .

Second Attendant [*speaking as Captain of the Guard*]. He
comes.

Enter the Swineherd

The Swineherd. The beggars of my country say that he
That sings you best shall take you for a wife.

The Queen. He that best sings his passion.

The Swineherd.   And they say
The kingdom is added to the gift.

The Queen.   I swore it.

The Swineherd. But what if some blind aged cripple sing
Better than wholesome men?

The Queen.   Some I reject.
  Some I have punished for their impudence.
  None I abhor can sing.
The Swineherd.   So that's the catch.
  Queen, look at me, look long at these foul rags,
  At hair more foul and ragged than my rags;
  Look on my scratched foul flesh. Have I not come
  Through dust and mire? There in the dust and mire
  Beasts scratched my flesh; my memory too is gone,
  Because great solitudes have driven me mad.
  But when I look into a stream, the face
  That trembles upon the surface makes me think
  My origin more foul than rag or flesh.
The Queen. But you have passed through perils for my sake;
  Come a great distance. I permit the song.
The Swineherd. Kingdom and lady, if I sing the best?
  But who decides?
The Queen.   I and my heart decide.
  We say that song is best that moves us most.
  No song has moved us yet.
The Swineherd.   You must be won
  At a full moon in March, those beggars say.
  That moon has come, but I am here alone.
The Queen. No other man has come.
The Swineherd.   The moon is full.
The Queen. Remember through what perils you have come;
  That I am crueller than solitude,
  Forest or beast. Some I have killed or maimed
  Because their singing put me in a rage,
  And some because they came at all. Men hold
  That woman's beauty is a kindly thing,
  But they that call me cruel speak the truth,
  Cruel as the winter of virginity.
  But for a reason that I cannot guess
  I would not harm you. Go before I change.
  Why do you stand, your chin upon your breast?
The Swineherd. My mind is running on our marriage night,
  Imagining all from the first touch and kiss.

The Queen. What gives you that strange confidence? What makes
    You think that you can move my heart and me?
The Swineherd. Because I look upon you without fear.
The Queen. A lover in railing or in flattery said
    God only looks upon me without fear.
The Swineherd. Desiring cruelty, he made you cruel.
    I shall embrace body and cruelty,
    Desiring both as though I had made both.
The Queen. One question more. You bring like all the rest
    Some novel simile, some wild hyperbole
    Praising my beauty?
The Swineherd.   My memory has returned.
    I tended swine, when I first heard your name.
    I rolled among the dung of swine and laughed.
    What do I know of beauty?
The Queen.   Sing the best
    And you are not a swineherd, but a king.
The Swineherd. What do I know of kingdoms?
          [*Snapping his fingers*] That for kingdoms!
The Queen. If trembling of my limbs or sudden tears
    Proclaim your song beyond denial best,
    I leave these corridors, this ancient house,
    A famous throne, the reverence of servants—
    What do I gain?
The Swineherd.   A song—the night of love,
    An ignorant forest and the dung of swine.
         [*Queen leaves throne and comes down stage.*
The Queen. All here have heard the man and all have judged.
    I led him, that I might not seem unjust,
    From point to point, established in all eyes
    That he came hither not to sing but to heap
    Complexities of insult upon my head.
The Swineherd. She shall bring forth her farrow in the dung.
    But first my song—what nonsense shall I sing?
The Queen. Send for the headsman, Captain of the Guard.
Second Attendant [*speaking as Captain of the Guard*]. I have
    already sent. He stands without.

The Queen. I owe my thanks to God that this foul wretch,
  Foul in his rags, his origin, his speech,
  In spite of all his daring has not dared
  Ask me to drop my veil. Insulted ears
  Have heard and shuddered, but my face is pure.
  Had it but known the insult of his eyes
  I had torn it with these nails.
The Swineherd [*going up stage*]. Why should I ask?
  What do those features matter? When I set out
  I picked a number on the roulette wheel.
  I trust the wheel, as every lover must.
The Queen. Pray, if your savagery has learnt to pray,
  For in a moment they will lead you out
  Then bring your severed head.
The Swineherd.   My severed head.

                                              [*Laughs.*

  There is a story in my country of a woman
  That stood all bathed in blood—a drop of blood
  Entered her womb and there begat a child.
The Queen. A severed head! She took it in her hands;
  She stood all bathed in blood; the blood begat.
  O foul, foul, foul!
The Swineherd.   She sank in bridal sleep.
The Queen. Her body in that sleep conceived a child.
  Begone! I shall not see your face again.
  [*She turns towards him, her back to the audience, and
    slowly drops her veil.*
    The Attendants close the inner curtain.
Second Attendant. What do we sing?
First Attendant.   An ancient Irish Queen
  That stuck a head upon a stake.
Second Attendant.   Her lover's head;
  But that's a different queen, a different story.
First Attendant.
              He had famished in a wilderness,
              Braved lions for my sake,
              And all men lie that say that I
              Bade that swordsman take

His head from off his body
And set it on a stake.

He swore to sing my beauty
Though death itself forbade.
They lie that say, in mockery
Of all that lovers said,
Or in mere woman's cruelty
I bade them fetch his head.
                    [*They begin to part the inner curtain.*
O what innkeeper's daughter
Shared the Byzantine crown?
Girls that have governed cities,
Or burned great cities down,
Have bedded with their fancy-man
Whether a king or clown;

Gave their bodies, emptied purses
For praise of clown or king,
Gave all the love that women know!
O they had their fling,
But never stood before a stake
And heard the dead lips sing.
[*The Queen is discovered standing exactly as before, the
    dropped veil at her side, but she holds above her head
    the severed head of the Swineherd. Her hands are red.
    There are red blotches upon her dress, not realistically
    represented: red gloves, some pattern of red cloth.*
First Attendant. Her lips are moving.
Second Attendant.   She has begun to sing.
First Attendant. I cannot hear what she is singing.
    Ah, now I can hear.
                    [*singing as Queen*]
    Child and darling, hear my song,
    Never cry I did you wrong;
    Cry that wrong came not from me
    But my virgin cruelty.

Great my love before you came,
Greater when I loved in shame,
Greatest when there broke from me
Storm of virgin cruelty.

[*The Queen dances to drum-taps and in the dance lays
the head upon the throne.*

Second Attendant. She is waiting.
First Attendant.   She is waiting for his song.
The song he has come so many miles to sing.
She has forgotten that no dead man sings.
Second Attendant [*laughs softly as Head*]. He has begun to
laugh.
First Attendant.   No; he has begun to sing.
Second Attendant [*singing as Head*].

I sing a song of Jack and Jill.
Jill had murdered Jack;
The moon shone brightly;
Ran up the hill, and round the hill,
Round the hill and back.
A full moon in March.

Jack had a hollow heart, for Jill
Had hung his heart on high;
The moon shone brightly;
Had hung his heart beyond the hill,
A-twinkle in the sky.
A full moon in March.

[*The Queen in her dance moves away from the head,
alluring and refusing.*

First Attendant [*laughs as Queen*].
Second Attendant. She is laughing. How can she laugh,
Loving the dead?
First Attendant. She is crazy. That is why she is laughing.
                    [*Laughs again as Queen.*
[*Queen takes up the head and lays it upon the ground.
She dances before it—a dance of adoration. She takes
the head up and dances with it to drum-taps, which*

*grow quicker and quicker. As the drum-taps approach
their climax, she presses her lips to the lips of the head.
Her body shivers to very rapid drum-taps. The drum-
taps cease. She sinks slowly down, holding the head to
her breast. The Attendants close inner curtain, singing,
and then stand one on either side while the stage curtain descends.*

Second Attendant. Why must those holy, haughty feet de-
scend
From emblematic niches, and what hand
Ran that delicate raddle through their white?
My heart is broken, yet must understand.
What do they seek for? Why must they descend?

First Attendant. For desecration and the lover's night.

Second Attendant. I cannot face that emblem of the moon
Nor eyelids that the unmixed heavens dart,
Nor stand upon my feet, so great a fright
Descends upon my savage, sunlit heart.
What can she lack whose emblem is the moon?

First Attendant. But desecration and the lover's night.

Second Attendant. Delight my heart with sound; speak yet
again.
But look and look with understanding eyes
Upon the pitchers that they carry; tight
Therein all time's completed treasure is:
What do they lack? O cry it out again.

First Attendant. Their desecration and the lover's night.

THE END

THE HERNE'S EGG

The Herne's Egg

PERSONS IN THE PLAY

Congal, *King of Connacht*
Aedh, *King of Tara*
Corney, *Attracta's servant*
Mike, Pat, Malachi,
    Mathias, Peter, John,
    Connacht soldiers

Attracta, *A Priestess*
Kate, Agnes, Mary, *Friends of*
    Attracta
A Fool
Soldiers of Tara

Scene I

Mist and rocks; high up on backcloth a rock, its base hidden in mist; on this rock stands a great herne. All should be suggested, not painted realistically. Many men fighting with swords and shields, but sword and sword, shield and sword, never meet. The men move rhythmically as if in a dance; when swords approach one another cymbals clash; when swords and shields approach drums boom. The battle flows out at one side; two Kings are left fighting in the centre of the stage; the battle returns and flows out at the other side. The two Kings remain, but are now face to face and motionless. They are Congal, King of Connacht, and Aedh, King of Tara.

Congal. How many men have you lost?
Aedh. Some five-and-twenty men.
Congal. No need to ask my losses.
Aedh. Your losses equal mine.
Congal. They always have and must.
Aedh. Skill, strength, arms matched
Congal. Where is the wound this time?
Aedh. There, left shoulder-blade.
Congal. Here, right shoulder-blade.

171

Aedh. Yet we have fought all day.

Congal. This is our fiftieth battle.

Aedh. And all were perfect battles.

Congal. Come, sit upon this stone.
Come and take breath awhile.

Aedh. From daybreak until noon,
Hopping among these rocks.

Congal. Nothing to eat or drink.

Aedh. A story is running round
Concerning two rich fleas.

Congal. We hop like fleas, but war
Has taken all our riches.

Aedh. Rich, and rich, so rich that they
Retired and bought a dog.

Congal. Finish the tale and say
What kind of dog they bought.

Aedh. Heaven knows.

Congal.   You must have thought
What kind of dog they bought.

Aedh. Heaven knows.

Congal.   Unless you say,
I'll up and fight all day.

Aedh. A fat, square, lazy dog,
No sort of scratching dog.

SCENE II

*The same place as in previous scene. Corney enters, leading a
Donkey, a donkey on wheels like a child's toy, but life-size.*

Corney. A tough, rough mane, a tougher skin,
Strong legs though somewhat thin,
A strong body, a level line
Up to the neck along the spine.
All good points, and all are spoilt
By that rapscallion Clareman's eye!
What if before your present shape

You could slit purses and break hearts,
You are a donkey now, a chattel,
A taker of blows, not a giver of blows.
No tricks, you're not in County Clare,
No, not one kick upon the shin.
 [*Congal, Pat, Mike, James, Mathias, Peter, John, enter,
 in the dress and arms of the previous scene but without
 shields.*

Congal. I have learned of a great hernery
Among these rocks, and that a woman,
Prophetess or priestess, named Attracta,
Owns it—take this donkey and man,
Look for the creels, pack them with eggs.
Mike. Manners!
Congal.   This man is in the right.
I will ask Attracta for the eggs
If you will tell how to summon her.
Corney. A flute lies there upon the rock
Carved out of a herne's thigh.
Go pick it up and play the tune
My mother calls "The Great Herne's Feather."
If she has a mind to come, she will come.
Congal. That's a queer way of summoning.
Corney. This is a holy place and queer;
But if you do not know that tune,
Custom permits that I should play it,
But you must cross my hand with silver.
    [*Congal gives money, and Corney plays flute.*
Congal. Go pack the donkey creels with eggs.
   [*All go out except Congal and Mike. Attracta enters.*
Attracta. For a thousand or ten thousand years,
For who can count so many years,
Some woman has lived among these rocks,
The Great Herne's bride, or promised bride,
And when a visitor has played the flute
Has come or not. What would you ask?
Congal. Tara and I have made a peace;
Our fiftieth battle fought, there is need

Of preparation for the next;
He and all his principal men,
I and all my principal men,
Take supper at his principal house
This night, in his principal city, Tara,
And we have set our minds upon
A certain novelty or relish.

Mike. Herne's eggs.

Congal.   This man declares our need;
A donkey, both creels packed with eggs,
Somebody that knows the mind of a donkey
For donkey-boy.

Attracta.   Custom forbids:
Only the women of these rocks,
Betrothed or married to the Herne,
The god or ancestor of hernes,
Can eat, handle, or look upon those eggs.

Congal. Refused! Must old campaigners lack
The one sole dish that takes their fancy,
My cooks what might have proved their skill,
Because a woman thinks that she
Is promised or married to a bird?

Mike. Mad!

Congal.   Mad! This man is right,
But you are not to blame for that.
Women thrown into despair
By the winter of their virginity
Take its abominable snow,
As boys take common snow, and make
An image of god or bird or beast
To feed their sensuality:
Ovid had a literal mind,
And though he sang it neither knew
What lonely lust dragged down the gold
That crept on Danae's lap, nor knew
What rose against the moony feathers
When Leda lay upon the grass.

Attracta. There is no reality but the Great Herne.

Mike. The cure.

Congal.   Why, that is easy said;
  An old campaigner is the cure
  For everything that woman dreams—
  Even I myself, had I but time.

Mike. Seven men.

Congal.   This man of learning means
  That not a weather-stained, war-battered
  Old campaigner such as I,—
  But seven men packed into a day
  Or dawdled out through seven years—
  Are needed to melt down the snow
  That's fallen among these wintry rocks.

Attracta. There is no happiness but the Great Herne.

Congal. It may be that life is suffering,
  But youth that has not yet known pleasure
  Has not the right to say so; pick,
  Or be picked by seven men,
  And we shall talk it out again.

Attracta. Being betrothed to the Great Herne
  I know what may be known: I burn
  Not in the flesh but in the mind;
  Chosen out of all my kind
  That I may lie in a blazing bed
  And a bird take my maidenhead,
  To the unbegotten I return,
  All a womb and a funeral urn.

    [*Enter Corney, Pat, James, Mathias, etc., with Donkey.
    A creel packed with eggs is painted upon the side of
    the Donkey.*

Corney. Think of yourself; think of the songs:
  Bride of the Herne, and the Great Herne's bride,
  Grow terrible: go into a trance.

Attracta. Stop!

Corney.   Bring the god out of your gut;
  Stand there asleep until the rascals
  Wriggle upon his beak like eels.

Attracta. Stop!

Corney.   The country calls them rascals,
   I, sacrilegious rascals that have taken
   Every new-laid egg in the hernery.
Attracta. Stop! When have I permitted you
   To say what I may, or may not do?
   But you and your donkey must obey
   All big men who can say their say.
Congal. And bid him keep a civil tongue.
Attracta. Those eggs are stolen from the god.
   It is but right that you hear said
   A curse so ancient that no man
   Can say who made it, or any thing at all
   But that it was nailed upon a post
   Before a herne had stood on one leg.
Corney. Hernes must stand on one leg when they fish
   In honour of the bird who made it.

> "This they nailed upon a post,
> On the night my leg was lost,"
> *Said the old, old herne that had but one leg.*

> "He that a herne's egg dare steal
> Shall be changed into a fool,"
> *Said the old, old herne that had but one leg.*

> "And to end his fool breath
> At a fool's hand meet his death,"
> *Said the old, old herne that had but one leg.*

   I think it was the Great Herne made it,
   Pretending that he had but the one leg
   To fool us all; but Great Herne or another
   It has not failed these thousand years.
Congal. That I shall live and die a fool,
   And die upon some battlefield
   At some fool's hand, is but natural,
   And needs no curse to bring it.
Mike.   Pickled!

Congal. He says that I am an old campaigner,
   Robber of sheepfolds and cattle trucks,
   So cursed from morning until midnight
   There is not a quarter of an inch
   To plaster a new curse upon.
Corney.   Luck!
Congal. Adds that your luck begins when you
   Recall that though we took those eggs
   We paid with good advice; and then
   Take to your bosom seven men.
      [*Congal, Mike, Corney, Mathias, James, and Donkey go
         out. Enter timidly three girls, Kate, Agnes, Mary.*
Mary. Have all those fierce men gone?
Attracta. All those fierce men have gone.
Agnes. But they will come again?
Attracta. No, never again.
Kate. We bring three presents.
                    [*All except Attracta kneel.*
Mary. This is a jug of cream.
Agnes. This is a bowl of butter.
Kate. This is a basket of eggs.
         [*They lay jug, bowl, and basket on the ground.*
Attracta. I know what you would ask.
   Sit round upon these stones.
   Children, why do you fear
   A woman but little older,
   A child yesterday?
   All, when I am married,
   Shall have good husbands. Kate
   Shall marry a black-headed lad.
Agnes. She swore but yesterday
   That she would marry black.
Attracta. But Agnes there shall marry
   A honey-coloured lad.
Agnes. O!
Attracta.   Mary shall be married
   When I myself am married
   To the lad that is in her mind.

Mary. Are you not married yet?

Attracta. No. But it is almost come,
  May come this very night.

Mary. And must he be all feathers?

Agnes. Have a terrible beak?

Kate. Great terrible claws?

Attracta. Whatever shape he chose,
  Though that be terrible,
  Will best express his love.

Agnes. When he comes—will he?—

Attracta. Child, ask what you please.

Agnes. Do all that a man does?

Attracta. Strong sinew and soft flesh
  Are foliage round the shaft
  Before the arrowsmith
  Has stripped it, and I pray
  That I, all foliage gone,
  May shoot into my joy—

  [*Sound of a flute, playing "The Great Herne's Feather."*

Mary. Who plays upon that flute?

Agnes. Her god is calling her.

Kate. Look, look, she takes
  An egg out of the basket.
  My white hen laid it,
  My favourite white hen.

Mary. Her eyes grow glassy, she moves
  According to the notes of the flute.

Agnes. Her limbs grow rigid, she seems
  A doll upon a wire.

Mary. Her human life is gone
  And that is why she seems
  A doll upon a wire.

Agnes. You mean that when she looks so
  She is but a puppet?

Mary. How do I know? And yet
  Twice have I seen her so,
  She will move for certain minutes
  As though her god were there

Thinking how best to move
A doll upon a wire.
Then she will move away
In long leaps as though
He had remembered his skill.
She has still my little egg.

Agnes. Who knows but your little egg
  Comes into some mystery?

Kate. Some mystery to make
  Love-loneliness more sweet.

Agnes. She has moved. She has moved away.

Kate. Travelling fast asleep
  In long loops like a dancer.

Mary. Like a dancer, like a hare.

Agnes. The last time she went away
  The moon was full—she returned
  Before its side had flattened.

Kate. This time she will not return.

Agnes. Because she is called to her marriage?

Kate. Those leaps may carry her where
  No woman has gone, and he
  Extinguish sun, moon, star.
  No bridal torch can burn
  When his black midnight is there.

Agnes. I have heard her claim that they couple
  In the blazing heart of the sun.

Kate. But you have heard it wrong!
  In blue-black midnight they couple.

Agnes. No, in the sun.

Kate.   Blue-black!

Agnes. In the sun!

Kate.   Blue-black, blue-black!

Mary. All I know is that she
  Shall lie there in his bed.
  Nor shall it end until
  She lies there full of his might,
  His thunderbolts in her hand.

Scene III

Before the gates of Tara, Congal, Mike, Pat, Peter, James,
Mathias, etc., soldiers of Congal, Corney, and the Donkey.

Congal. This is Tara; in a moment
   Men must come out of the gate
   With a great basket between them
   And we give up our arms;
   No armed man can enter.
Corney. And here is that great bird
   Over our heads again.
Pat. The Great Herne himself
   And he in a red rage.
Mike. Stones.
Congal.   This man is right.
   Beat him to death with stones.

    [*All go through the motion of picking up and throwing*
       stones. There are no stones except in so far as their
       gestures can suggest them.

Pat. All those stones fell wide.
Corney. He has come down so low
   His legs are sweeping the grass.
Mike. Swords.
Congal.   This man is right.
   Cut him up with swords.
Pat. I have him within my reach.
Congal. No, no, he is here at my side.
Corney. His wing has touched my shoulder.
Congal. We missed him again and he
   Rises again and sinks
   Behind the wall of Tara.

    [*Two men come in carrying a large basket slung between*
       two poles. One is whistling. All except Corney, who is
       unarmed, drop their swords and helmets into the bas-
       ket. Each soldier when he takes off his helmet shows
       that he wears a skull-cap of soft cloth.

Congal. Where have I heard that tune?

Mike. This morning.

Congal.   I know it now,
  The tune of "The Great Herne's Feather."
  It puts my teeth on edge.

SCENE IV

*Banqueting hall. A throne painted on the backcloth. Enter
Congal, alone, drunk, and shouting.*

Congal. To arms, to arms! Connacht to arms!
  Insulted and betrayed, betrayed and insulted.
  Who has insulted me? Tara has insulted.
  To arms, to arms! Connacht to arms!
  To arms—but if you have not got any
  Take a table-leg or a candlestick,
  A boot or a stool or any odd thing.
  Who has betrayed me? Tara has betrayed!
  To arms, to arms! Connacht to arms!
    [*He goes out to one side. Music, perhaps drum and con-
      certina, to suggest breaking of wood. Enter, at the
      other side, the King of Tara, drunk.*

Aedh. Where is that beastly drunken liar
  That says I have insulted him?
              Congal enters with two table-legs

Congal. I say it!

Aedh.   What insult?

Congal.   How dare you ask?
  When I have had a common egg,
  A common hen's egg put before me,
  An egg dropped in the dirty straw
  And crowed for by a cross-bred gangling cock,
  And every other man at the table
  A herne's egg.   [*Throws a table-leg on the floor.*
            There is your weapon. Take it!
  Take it up, defend yourself.

An egg that some half-witted slattern
Spat upon and wiped on her apron!

Aedh. A servant put the wrong egg there.

Congal. But at whose orders?

Aedh.   At your own.
A murderous drunken plot, a plot
To put a weapon that I do not know
Into my hands.

Congal.   Take up that weapon.
If I am as drunken as you say,
And you as sober as you think,
A coward and a drunkard are well matched.

> [*Aedh takes up the table-leg. Connacht and Tara soldiers
> come in, they fight, and the fight sways to and fro.
> The weapons, table-legs, candlesticks, etc., do not
> touch. Drum-taps represent blows. All go out fighting.
> Enter Pat, drunk, with bottle.*

Pat. Herne's egg, hen's egg, great difference.
There's insult in that difference.
What do hens eat? Hens live upon mash,
Upon slop, upon kitchen odds and ends.
What do hernes eat? Hernes live on eels,
On things that must always run about.
Man's a high animal and runs about,
But mash is low, O, very low.
Or, to speak like a philosopher,
When a man expects the movable
But gets the immovable, he is insulted.

> *Enter Congal, Peter, Malachi, Mathias, etc.*

Congal. Tara knew that he was overmatched;
Knew from the start he had no chance;
Died of a broken head; died drunk;
Accused me with his dying breath
Of secretly practising with a table-leg,
Practising at midnight until I
Became a perfect master with the weapon.
But that is all lies.

Pat.   Let all men know
  He was a noble character
  And I must weep at his funeral.
Congal. He insulted me with a hen's egg,
  Said I had practised with a table-leg,
  But I have taken kingdom and throne
  And that has made all level again
  And I can weep at his funeral.
  I would not have had him die that way
  Or die at all, he should have been immortal.
  Our fifty battles had made us friends;
  And there are fifty more to come.
  New weapons, a new leader will be found
  And everything begin again.
Mike. Much bloodier.
Congal.   They had, we had
  Forgotten what we fought about,
  So fought like gentlemen, but now
  Knowing the truth must fight like the beasts.
  Maybe the Great Herne's curse has done it.
  Why not? Answer me that; why not?
Mike. Horror henceforth.
Congal.   This wise man means
  We fought so long like gentlemen
  That we grew blind.
     [*Attracta enters, walking in her sleep, a herne's egg in her
       hand. She stands near the throne and holds her egg
       towards it for a moment.*
Mathias.   Look! Look!
  She offers that egg. Who is to take it?
Congal. She walks with open eyes but in her sleep.
Mathias. I can see it all in a flash.
  She found that herne's egg on the table
  And left the hen's egg there instead.
James. She brought the hen's egg on purpose
  Walking in her wicked sleep.

Congal. And if I take that egg, she wakes,
Completes her task, her circle;
We all complete a task or circle,
Want a woman, then all goes—pff.

                [He goes to take the egg.

Mike. Not now.

Congal.   This wise man says "not now."
There must be something to consider first.

James. By changing one egg for another
She has brought bloodshed on us all.

Pat. He was a noble character,
And I must weep at his funeral.

James. I say that she must die, I say;
According to what my mother said,
All that have done what she did must die,
But, in a manner of speaking, pleasantly,
Because legally, certainly not
By beating with a table-leg
As though she were a mere Tara man,
Nor yet by beating with a stone
As though she were the Great Herne himself.

Mike. The Great Herne's bride.

Congal.   I had forgotten
That all she does he makes her do,
But he is god and out of reach;
Nor stone can bruise, nor a sword pierce him,
And yet through his betrothed, his bride,
I have the power to make him suffer;
His curse has given me the right,
I am to play the fool and die
At a fool's hands.

Mike.   Seven men.

    *[He begins to count, seeming to strike the table with the
table-leg, but table and table-leg must not meet, the
blow is represented by the sound of the drum.*

One, two, three, four,
Five, six, seven men.

Pat. Seven that are present in this room,
   Seven that must weep at his funeral.
Congal. This man who struck those seven blows
   Means that we seven in the name of the law
   Must handle, penetrate, and possess her,
   And do her a great good by that action,
   Melting out the virgin snow,
   And that snow image, the Great Herne;
   For nothing less than seven men
   Can melt that snow, but when it melts
   She may, being free from all obsession,
   Live as every woman should.
   I am the Court; judgment has been given.
   I name the seven: Congal of Tara,
   Patrick, Malachi, Mike, John, James,
   And that coarse hulk of clay, Mathias.
Mathias. I dare not lay a hand upon that woman.
   The people say that she is holy
   And carries a great devil in her gut.
Pat. What mischief can a Munster devil
   Do to a man that was born in Connacht?
Malachi. I made a promise to my mother
   When we set out on this campaign
   To keep from women.
John.   I have a wife that's jealous
   If I but look the moon in the face.
James. I am promised to an educated girl.
   Her family are most particular,
   What would they say—O my God!
Congal. Whoever disobeys the Court
   Is an unmannerly, disloyal lout,
   And no good citizen.
Pat.   Here is my bottle.
   Pass it along, a long, long pull;
   Although it's round like a woman carrying,
   No unmannerly, disloyal bottle,
   An affable, most loyal bottle.   [*All drink.*
Mathias. I first.

Congal.   That's for the Court to say.
    A Court of Law is a blessed thing,
    Logic, Mathematics, ground in one,
    And everything out of balance accursed.
    When the Court decides on a decree
    Men carry it out with dignity.
    Here where I put down my hand
    I will put a mark, then all must stand
    Over there in a level row.
    And all take off their caps and throw.
    The nearest cap shall take her first,
    The next shall take her next, so on
    Till all is in good order done.
    I need a mark and so must take
    The herne's egg, and let her wake.

    [*He takes egg and lays it upon the ground. Attracta
    stands motionless, looking straight in front of her. She
    sings. The seven standing in a row throw their caps
    one after another.*

Attracta.
        When I take a beast to my joyful breast,
        Though beak and claw I must endure,
        *Sang the bride of the Herne, and the Great
            Herne's bride,*
        No lesser life, man, bird or beast,
        Can make unblessed what a beast made blessed,
        Can make impure what a beast made pure.

        Where is he gone, where is that other,
        He that shall take my maidenhead?
        *Sang the bride of the Herne, and the Great
            Herne's bride,*
        Out of the moon came my pale brother,
        The blue-black midnight is my mother.
        Who will turn down the sheets of the bed?

        When beak and claw their work begin
        Shall horror stir in the roots of my hair?

Sang the bride of the Herne, and the Great
  Herne's bride,
And who lie there in the cold dawn
When all that terror has come and gone?
Shall I be the woman lying there?

SCENE V

Before the Gate of Tara. Corney enters with Donkey.
Corney. You thought to go on sleeping though dawn was up,
  Rapscallion of a beast, old highwayman.
  That light in the eastern sky is dawn,
  You cannot deny it; many a time
  You looked upon it following your trade.
  Cheer up, we shall be home before sunset.
                Attracta comes in
Attracta. I have packed all the uneaten or unbroken eggs
  Into the creels. Help carry them
  And hang them on the donkey's back.
Corney. We could boil them hard and keep them in the larder,
  But Congal has had them all boiled soft.
Attracta. Such eggs are holy. Many pure souls,
  Especially among the country-people,
  Would shudder if herne's eggs were left
  For foul-tongued, bloody-minded men.
              Congal, Malachi, Mike, etc., enter
Congal. A sensible woman; you gather up what's left,
  Your thoughts upon the cupboard and the larder.
  No more a herne's bride—a crazed loony
  Waiting to be trodden by a bird—
  But all woman, all sensible woman.
Mike. Manners.
Congal.   This man who is always right
  Desires that I should add these words,
  The seven that held you in their arms last night
  Wish you good luck.

Attracta.   What do you say?
   My husband came to me in the night.
Congal. Seven men lay with you in the night.
   Go home desiring and desirable,
   And look for a man.
Attracta.   The Herne is my husband.
   I lay beside him, his pure bride.
Congal. Pure in the embrace of seven men?
Mike. She slept.
Congal.   You say that though I thought,
   Because I took the egg out of her hand,
   That she awoke, she did not wake
   Until day broke upon her sleep—
   Her sleep and ours—did she wake pure?
   Seven men can answer that.
Corney. King though you are, I will not hear
   The bride of the Great Herne defamed—
   A king, a king but a Mayo man.
   A Mayo man's lying tongue can beat
   A Clare highwayman's rapscallion eye,
   Seven times a liar.
Mike.   Seven men.
Congal. I, Congal, lay with her last night.
Mathias. And I, Mathias.
Mike.   And I.
James.   And I.
Peter. And I.
John.   And I.
Pat.   And I; swear it;
   And not a drop of drink since dawn.
Corney. One plain liar, six men bribed to lie.
Attracta. Great Herne, Great Herne, Great Herne,
   Your darling is crying out,
   Great Herne, declare her pure,
   Pure as that beak and claw,
   Great Herne, Great Herne, Great Herne,
   Let the round heaven declare it.

[*Silence. Then low thunder growing louder. All except Attracta and Congal kneel.*

James. Great Herne, I swear that she is pure;
  I never laid a hand upon her.

Mathias. I was a fool to believe myself
  When everybody knows that I am a liar.

Pat. Even when it seemed that I covered her
  I swear that I knew it was the drink.

Attracta. I lay in the bride-bed,
  His thunderbolts in my hand,
  But gave them back, for he,
  My lover, the Great Herne,
  Knows everything that is said
  And every man's intent,
  And every man's deed; and he
  Shall give these seven that say
  That they upon me lay
  A most memorable punishment.

  [*It thunders. All prostrate themselves except Attracta and Congal. Congal had half knelt, but he has stood up again.*

Attracta. I share his knowledge, and I know
  Every punishment decreed.
  He will come when you are dead,
  Push you down a step or two
  Into cat or rat or bat,
  Into dog or wolf or goose.
  Everybody in his new shape I can see,
  But Congal there stands in a cloud
  Because his fate is not yet settled.
  Speak out, Great Herne, and make it known
  That everything I have said is true.

  [*Thunder. All now, except Attracta, have prostrated themselves.*

Attracta. What has made you kneel?

Congal.   This man
  That's prostrate at my side would say,

Could he say anything at all,
That I am terrified by thunder.
Attracta. Why did you stand up so long?
Congal. I held you in my arms last night,
We seven held you in our arms.
Attracta. You were under the curse, in all
You did, in all you seemed to do.
Congal. If I must die at a fool's hand,
When must I die?
Attracta.   When the moon is full.
Congal. And where?
Attracta.   Upon the holy mountain,
Upon Slieve Fuadh, there we meet again
Just as the moon comes round the hill.
There all the gods must visit me,
Acknowledging my marriage to a god;
One man will I have among the gods.
Congal. I know the place and I will come,
Although it be my death, I will come.
Because I am terrified, I will come.

Scene VI

A mountain-top, the moon has just risen; the moon of comic tradition, a round smiling face. A cauldron lid, a cooking-pot, and a spit lie together at one side of the stage. The Fool, a man in ragged clothes, enters carrying a large stone; he lays it down at one side and goes out. Congal enters carrying a wineskin, and stands at the other side of the stage. The Fool re-enters with a second large stone which he places beside the first.

Congal. What is your name, boy?
Fool.   Poor Tom Fool.
Everybody knows Tom Fool.
Congal. I saw something in the mist,
There lower down upon the slope,

I went up close to it and saw
A donkey, somebody's stray donkey.
A donkey and a Fool—I don't like it at all.
Fool. I won't be Tom the Fool after to-night.
  I have made a level patch out there,
  Clearing away the stones, and there
  I shall fight a man and kill a man
  And get great glory.
Congal.   Where did you get
  The cauldron lid, the pot and the spit?
Fool. I sat in Widow Rooney's kitchen,
  Somebody said, "King Congal's on the mountain
  Cursed to die at the hands of a fool."
  Somebody else said "Kill him, Tom."
  And everybody began to laugh
  And said I should kill him at the full moon,
  And that is to-night.
Congal.   I too have heard
  That Congal is to die to-night.
  Take a drink.
Fool.   I took this lid,
  And all the women screamed at me.
  I took the spit, and all screamed worse.
  A shoulder of lamb stood ready for the roasting—
  I put the pot upon my head.
  They did not scream but stood and gaped.
    [*Fool arms himself with spit, cauldron lid, and pot,
      whistling "The Great Herne's Feather."*
Congal. Hush, that is an unlucky tune!
  And why must you kill Congal, Fool?
  What harm has he done you?
Fool.   None at all.
  But there's a Fool called Johnny from Meath,
  We are great rivals and we hate each other,
  But I can get the pennies if I kill Congal,
  And Johnny nothing.
Congal.   I am King Congal,
  And is not that a thing to laugh at, Fool?

Fool. Very nice, O very nice indeed,
   For I can kill you now, and I
   Am tired of walking.
Congal.   Both need rest.
   Another drink apiece—that is done—
   Lead to the place you have cleared of stones.
Fool. But where is your sword? You have not got a sword.
Congal. I lost it, or I never had it,
   Or threw it at the strange donkey below,
   But that's no matter—I have hands.

    [*They go out at one side. Attracta, Corney, and Donkey
    come in. Attracta sings.*

Attracta.
       When beak and claw their work began
       What horror stirred in the roots of my hair?
       *Sang the bride of the Herne, and the Great
         Herne's bride.*
       But who lay there in the cold dawn,
       When all that terror had come and gone?
       Was I the woman lying there?

    [*They go out. Congal and Tom the Fool come. Congal
    is carrying the cauldron lid, pot, and spit. He lays them
    down.*

Congal. I was sent to die at the hands of a Fool.
   There must be another Fool on the mountain.
Fool. That must be Johnny from Meath.
   But that's a thing I could not endure,
   For Johnny would get all the pennies.
Congal. Here, take a drink and have no fear;
   All's plain at last; though I shall die
   I shall not die at a Fool's hand.
   I have thought out a better plan.
   I and the Herne have had three bouts,
   He won the first, I won the second,
   Six men and I possessed his wife.
Fool. I ran after a woman once.
   I had seen two donkeys in a field.
Congal. And did you get her, did you get her, Fool?

Fool. I almost had my hand upon her.
  She screamed, and somebody came and beat me.
  Were you beaten?
Congal.   No, no, Fool.
  But she said that nobody had touched her,
  And after that the thunder said the same,
  Yet I had won that bout, and now
  I know that I shall win the third.
Fool. If Johnny from Meath comes, kill him!
Congal. Maybe I will, maybe I will not.
Fool. You let me off, but don't let him off.
Congal. I could not do you any harm,
  For you and I are friends.
Fool.   Kill Johnny!
Congal. Because you have asked me to, I will do it,
  For you and I arc friends.
Fool.   Kill Johnny!
  Kill with the spear, but give it to me
  That I may see if it is sharp enough.

                                    [*Fool takes spit.*

Congal. And is it, Fool?
Fool.   I spent an hour
  Sharpening it upon a stone.
  Could I kill you now?
Congal.   Maybe you could.
Fool. I will get all the pennies for myself.
    [*He wounds Congal. The wounding is symbolised by a
        movement of the spit towards or over Congal's body.*
Congal. It passed out of your mind for a moment
  That we are friends, but that is natural.
Fool [*dropping spit*]. I must see it, I never saw a wound.
Congal. The Herne has got the first blow in;
  A scratch, a scratch, a mere nothing.
  But had it been a little deeper and higher
  It would have gone through the heart, and maybe
  That would have left me better off,
  For the Great Herne may beat me in the end.

Here I must sit through the full moon,
And he will send up Fools against me,
Meandering, roaring, yelling
Whispering Fools, then chattering Fools,
And after the morose, melancholy,
Sluggish, fat, silent Fools;
And I, moon-crazed, moon-blind,
Fighting and wounded, wounded and fighting.
I never thought of such an end.
Never be a soldier, Tom;
Though it begins well, is this a life?
If this is a man's life, is there any life
But a dog's life?
Fool.   That's it, that's it;
Many a time they have put a dog at me.
Congal. If I should give myself a wound,
Let life run away, I'd win the bout.
He said I must die at the hands of a Fool
And sent you hither. Give me that spit!
I put it in this crevice of the rock,
That I may fall upon the point.
These stones will keep it sticking upright.
                    [*They arrange stones, he puts the spit in.*
Congal [*almost screaming in his excitement*]. Fool! Am I
   myself a Fool?
For if I am a Fool, he wins the bout.
Fool. You are King of Connacht. If you were a Fool
   They would have chased you with their dogs.
Congal. I am King Congal of Connacht and of Tara,
   That wise, victorious, voluble, unlucky,
   Blasphemous, famous, infamous man.
   Fool, take this spit when red with blood,
   Show it to the people and get all the pennies;
   What does it matter what they think?
   The Great Herne knows that I have won.
      [*He falls symbolically upon the spit. It does not touch
      him. Fool takes the spit and wine-skin and goes out.*

It seems that I am hard to kill,
But the wound is deep. Are you up there?
Your chosen kitchen spit has killed me,
But killed me at my own will, not yours.

Attracta and Corney enter

Attracta. Will the knot hold?
Corney.   There was a look
About the old highwayman's eye of him
That warned me, so I made him fast
To that old stump among the rocks
With a great knot that he can neither
Break, nor pull apart with his teeth.
Congal. Attracta!
Attracta.   I called you to this place,
You came, and now the story is finished.
Congal. You have great powers, even the thunder
Does whatever you bid it do.
Protect me, I have won my bout,
But I am afraid of what the Herne
May do with me when I am dead.
I am afraid that he may put me
Into the shape of a brute beast.
Attracta. I will protect you if, as I think,
Your shape is not yet fixed upon.
Congal. I am slipping now, and you up there
With your long leg and your long beak.
But I have beaten you, Great Herne,
In spite of your kitchen spit—seven men—

[*He dies.*

Attracta. Come lie with me upon the ground,
Come quickly into my arms, come quickly, come
Before his body has had time to cool.
Corney. What? Lie with you?
Attracta.   Lie and beget.
If you are afraid of the Great Herne,
Put that away, for if I do his will,
You are his instrument or himself.

Corney. The thunder has me terrified.
Attracta. I lay with the Great Herne, and he,
    Being all a spirit, but begot
    His image in the mirror of my spirit,
    Being all sufficient to himself
    Begot himself; but there's a work
    That should be done, and that work needs
    No bird's beak nor claw, but a man,
    The imperfection of a man.

> [*The sound of a donkey braying.*

Corney. The donkey is braying.
    He has some wickedness in his mind.
Attracta. Too late, too late, he broke that knot,
    And there, down there among the rocks
    He couples with another donkey.
    That donkey has conceived. I thought that I
    Could give a human form to Congal,
    But now he must be born a donkey.
Corney. King Congal must be born a donkey!
Attracta. Because we were not quick enough.
Corney. I have heard that a donkey carries its young
    Longer than any other beast,
    Thirteen months it must carry it.

> [*He laughs.*

    All that trouble and nothing to show for it,
    Nothing but just another donkey.

THE END

PURGATORY

Purgatory

PERSONS IN THE PLAY

A Boy   An Old Man

A ruined house and a bare tree in the background.

Boy. Half-door, hall door,
   Hither and thither day and night,
   Hill or hollow, shouldering this pack,
   Hearing you talk.
Old Man.   Study that house.
   I think about its jokes and stories;
   I try to remember what the butler
   Said to a drunken gamekeeper
   In mid-October, but I cannot.
   If I cannot, none living can.
   Where are the jokes and stories of a house,
   Its threshold gone to patch a pig-sty?
Boy. So you have come this path before?
Old Man. The moonlight falls upon the path,
   The shadow of a cloud upon the house,
   And that's symbolical; study that tree,
   What is it like?
Boy.   A silly old man.
Old Man. It's like—no matter what it's like.
   I saw it a year ago stripped bare as now,
   So I chose a better trade.
   I saw it fifty years ago
   Before the thunderbolt had riven it,
   Green leaves, ripe leaves, leaves thick as butter,
   Fat, greasy life. Stand there and look,
   Because there is somebody in that house.
      [The Boy puts down pack and stands in the doorway.

Boy. There's nobody here.

Old Man.   There's somebody there.

Boy. The floor is gone, the windows gone,
 And where there should be roof there's sky,
 And here's a bit of an egg-shell thrown
 Out of a jackdaw's nest.

Old Man.   But there are some
 That do not care what's gone, what's left:
 The souls in Purgatory that come back
 To habitations and familiar spots.

Boy. Your wits are out again.

Old Man.   Re-live
 Their transgressions, and that not once
 But many times; they know at last
 The consequence of those transgressions
 Whether upon others or upon themselves;
 Upon others, others may bring help,
 For when the consequence is at an end
 The dream must end; if upon themselves,
 There is no help but in themselves
 And in the mercy of God.

Boy.   I have had enough!
 Talk to the jackdaws, if talk you must.

Old Man. Stop! Sit there upon that stone.
 That is the house where I was born.

Boy. The big old house that was burnt down?

Old Man. My mother that was your grand-dam owned it,
 This scenery and this countryside,
 Kennel and stable, horse and hound—
 She had a horse at the Curragh, and there met
 My father, a groom in a training stable,
 Looked at him and married him.
 Her mother never spoke to her again,
 And she did right.

Boy.   What's right and wrong?
 My grand-dad got the girl and the money.

Old Man. Looked at him and married him,
 And he squandered everything she had.

She never knew the worst, because
She died in giving birth to me,
But now she knows it all, being dead.
Great people lived and died in this house;
Magistrates, colonels, members of Parliament,
Captains and Governors, and long ago
Men that had fought at Aughrim and the Boyne.
Some that had gone on Government work
To London or to India came home to die,
Or came from London every spring
To look at the may-blossom in the park.
They had loved the trees that he cut down
To pay what he had lost at cards
Or spent on horses, drink, and women;
Had loved the house, had loved all
The intricate passages of the house,
But he killed the house; to kill a house
Where great men grew up, married, died,
I here declare a capital offence.

Boy. My God, but you had luck! Grand clothes,
And maybe a grand horse to ride.

Old Man. That he might keep me upon his level
He never sent me to school, but some
Half-loved me for my half of her:
A gamekeeper's wife taught me to read,
A Catholic curate taught me Latin.
There were old books and books made fine
By eighteenth-century French binding, books
Modern and ancient, books by the ton.

Boy. What education have you given me?

Old Man. I gave the education that befits
A bastard that a pedlar got
Upon a tinker's daughter in a ditch.
When I had come to sixteen years old
My father burned down the house when drunk.

Boy. But that is my age, sixteen years old,
At the Puck Fair.

Old Man.   And everything was burnt;
  Books, library, all were burnt.
Boy. Is what I have heard upon the road the truth,
  That you killed him in the burning house?
Old Man. There's nobody here but our two selves?
Boy. Nobody, Father.
Old Man.   I stuck him with a knife,
  That knife that cuts my dinner now,
  And after that I left him in the fire.
  They dragged him out, somebody saw
  The knife-wound but could not be certain
  Because the body was all black and charred.
  Then some that were his drunken friends
  Swore they would put me upon trial,
  Spoke of quarrels, a threat I had made.
  The gamekeeper gave me some old clothes,
  I ran away, worked here and there
  Till I became a pedlar on the roads,
  No good trade, but good enough
  Because I am my father's son,
  Because of what I did or may do.
  Listen to the hoof-beats! Listen, listen!
Boy. I cannot hear a sound.
Old Man.   Beat! Beat!
  This night is the anniversary
  Of my mother's wedding night,
  Or of the night wherein I was begotten.
  My father is riding from the public-house,
  A whiskey-bottle under his arm.
              [A *window is lit showing a young girl.*
  Look at the window; she stands there
  Listening, the servants are all in bed,
  She is alone, he has stayed late
  Bragging and drinking in the public-house.
Boy. There's nothing but an empty gap in the wall.
  You have made it up. No, you are mad!
  You are getting madder every day.

Old Man. It's louder now because he rides
  Upon a gravelled avenue
  All grass to-day. The hoof-beat stops,
  He has gone to the other side of the house,
  Gone to the stable, put the horse up.
  She has gone down to open the door.
  This night she is no better than her man
  And does not mind that he is half drunk,
  She is mad about him. They mount the stairs.
  She brings him into her own chamber.
  And that is the marriage-chamber now.
  The window is dimly lit again.

  Do not let him touch you! It is not true
  That drunken men cannot beget,
  And if he touch he must beget
  And you must bear his murderer.
  Deaf! Both deaf! If I should throw
  A stick or a stone they would not hear;
  And that's a proof my wits are out.
  But there's a problem: she must live
  Through everything in exact detail,
  Driven to it by remorse, and yet
  Can she renew the sexual act
  And find no pleasure in it, and if not,
  If pleasure and remorse must both be there,
  Which is the greater?
                      I lack schooling.
  Go fetch Tertullian; he and I
  Will ravel all that problem out
  Whilst those two lie upon the mattress
  Begetting me.
                  Come back! Come back!
  And so you thought to slip away,
  My bag of money between your fingers,
  And that I could not talk and see!
  You have been rummaging in the pack.
                  [*The light in the window has faded out.*

Boy. You never gave me my right share.
Old Man. And had I given it, young as you are,
   You would have spent it upon drink.
Boy. What if I did? I had a right
   To get it and spend it as I chose.
Old Man. Give me that bag and no more words.
Boy. I will not.
Old Man   I will break your fingers.
      [*They struggle for the bag. In the struggle it drops, scat-
         tering the money. The Old Man staggers but does not
         fall. They stand looking at each other. The window is
         lit up. A man is seen pouring whiskey into a glass.*
Boy. What if I killed you? You killed my grand-dad,
   Because you were young and he was old.
   Now I am young and you are old.
Old Man [*staring at window*]. Better-looking, those sixteen
      years—
Boy. What are you muttering?
Old Man.   Younger—and yet
   She should have known he was not her kind.
Boy. What are you saying? Out with it!
                        [*Old Man points to window.*
   My God! The window is lit up
   And somebody stands there, although
   The floorboards are all burnt away.
Old Man. The window is lit up because my father
   Has come to find a glass for his whiskey.
   He leans there like some tired beast.
Boy. A dead, living, murdered man!
Old Man. "Then the bride-sleep fell upon Adam":
   Where did I read those words?
                        And yet
   There's nothing leaning in the window
   But the impression upon my mother's mind;
   Being dead she is alone in her remorse.
Boy. A body that was a bundle of old bones
   Before I was born. Horrible! Horrible!
                        [*He covers his eyes.*

Old Man. That beast there would know nothing, being
    nothing,
  If I should kill a man under the window
  He would not even turn his head.   [*He stabs the Boy.*
  My father and my son on the same jack-knife!
  That finishes—there—there—there—
            [*He stabs again and again. The window grows dark.*
  "Hush-a-bye baby, thy father's a knight,
  Thy mother a lady, lovely and bright."
  No, that is something that I read in a book,
  And if I sing it must be to my mother,
  And I lack rhyme.
      [*The stage has grown dark except where the tree stands
        in white light.*
                          Study that tree.
  It stands there like a purified soul,
  All cold, sweet, glistening light.
  Dear mother, the window is dark again,
  But you are in the light because
  I finished all that consequence.
  I killed that lad because had he grown up
  He would have struck a woman's fancy,
  Begot, and passed pollution on.
  I am a wretched foul old man
  And therefore harmless. When I have stuck
  This old jack-knife into a sod
  And pulled it out all bright again,
  And picked up all the money that he dropped,
  I'll to a distant place, and there
  Tell my old jokes among new men.
          [*He cleans the knife and begins to pick up money.*
  Hoof-beats! Dear God,
  How quickly it returns—beat—beat—!

  Her mind cannot hold up that dream.
  Twice a murderer and all for nothing,
  And she must animate that dead night
  Not once but many times!

O God,
Release my mother's soul from its dream!
Mankind can do no more. Appease
The misery of the living and the remorse of the dead.

THE END

THE DEATH OF CUCHULAIN

and for law

The Death of Cuchulain

PERSONS IN THE PLAY

Cuchulain	An Old Man
Eithne Inguba	A Blind Man
Aoife	A Servant
Emer	A Singer, a Piper, and
The Morrigu, *Goddess*	a Drummer
of *War*	

A bare stage of any period. A very old man looking like something out of mythology.

Old Man. I have been asked to produce a play called *The Death of Cuchulain*. It is the last of a series of plays which has for theme his life and death. I have been selected because I am out of fashion and out of date like the antiquated romantic stuff the thing is made of. I am so old that I have forgotten the name of my father and mother, unless indeed I am, as I affirm, the son of Talma, and he was so old that his friends and acquaintances still read Virgil and Homer. When they told me that I could have my own way, I wrote certain guiding principles on a bit of newspaper. I wanted an audience of fifty or a hundred, and if there are more, I beg them not to shuffle their feet or talk when the actors are speaking. I am sure that as I am producing a play for people I like, it is not probable, in this vile age, that they will be more in number than those who listened to the first performance of Milton's *Comus*. On the present occasion they must know the old epics and Mr. Yeats' plays about them; such people, however poor, have libraries of their own. If there are more than a hundred I won't be able to escape people who are educating themselves out of the Book Societies and the like, sciolists all, pickpockets and opinionated bitches. Why pickpockets? I will explain that, I will make it all quite clear.

[*Drum and pipe behind the scene, then silence.*
That's from the musicians; I asked them to do that if I was getting excited. If you were as old you would find it easy to get excited. Before the night ends you will meet the music. There is a singer, a piper, and a drummer. I have picked them up here and there about the streets, and I will teach them, if I live, the music of the beggar-man, Homer's music. I promise a dance. I wanted a dance because where there are no words there is less to spoil. Emer must dance, there must be severed heads—I am old, I belong to mythology—severed heads for her to dance before. I had thought to have had those heads carved, but no, if the dancer can dance properly no wood-carving can look as well as a parallelogram of painted wood. But I was at my wit's end to find a good dancer; I could have got such a dancer once, but she has gone; the tragi-comedian dancer, the tragic dancer, upon the same neck love and loathing, life and death. I spit three times. I spit upon the dancers painted by Degas. I spit upon their short bodices, their stiff stays, their toes whereon they spin like peg-tops, above all upon that chambermaid face. They might have looked timeless, Rameses the Great, but not the chambermaid, that old maid history. I spit! I spit! I spit!

[*The stage is darkened, the curtain falls. Pipe and drum begin and continue until the curtain rises on a bare stage. Half a minute later Eithne Inguba enters.*

Eithne. Cuchulain! Cuchulain!

Cuchulain enters from back
                    I am Emer's messenger,
I am your wife's messenger, she has bid me say
You must not linger here in sloth, for Maeve
With all those Connacht ruffians at her back
Burns barns and houses up at Emain Macha:
Your house at Muirthemne already burns.
No matter what's the odds, no matter though

Your death may come of it, ride out and fight.
The scene is set and you must out and fight.
Cuchulain. You have told me nothing. I am already armed,
  I have sent a messenger to gather men,
  And wait for his return. What have you there?
Eithne. I have nothing.
Cuchulain.   There is something in your hand.
Eithne. No.
Cuchulain. Have you a letter in your hand?
Eithne. I do not know how it got into my hand.
  I am straight from Emer. We were in some place.
  She spoke. She saw.
Cuchulain.   This letter is from Emer,
  It tells a different story. I am not to move
  Until to-morrow morning, for, if now,
  I must face odds no man can face and live.
  To-morrow morning Conall Caernach comes
  With a great host.
Eithne.   I do not understand.
  Who can have put that letter in my hand?
Cuchulain. And there is something more to make it certain
  I shall not stir till morning; you are sent
  To be my bedfellow, but have no fear,
  All that is written, but I much prefer
  Your own unwritten words. I am for the fight,
  I and my handful are set upon the fight;
  We have faced great odds before, a straw decided.
     The Morrigu enters and stands between them
Eithne. I know that somebody or something is there,
  Yet nobody that I can see.
Cuchulain.   There is nobody.
Eithne. Who among the gods of the air and upper air
  Has a bird's head?
Cuchulain.   Morrigu is headed like a crow.
Eithne [*dazed*]. Morrigu, war goddess, stands between.
  Her black wing touched me upon the shoulder, and
  All is intelligible.   [*The Morrigu goes out.*
        Maeve put me in a trance.

Though when Cuchulain slept with her as a boy
She seemed as pretty as a bird, she has changed,
She has an eye in the middle of her forehead.

Cuchulain. A woman that has an eye in the middle of her
forehead!
A woman that is headed like a crow!
But she that put those words into your mouth
Had nothing monstrous; you put them there yourself;
You need a younger man, a friendlier man,
But, fearing what my violence might do,
Thought out these words to send me to my death,
And were in such excitement you forgot
The letter in your hand.

Eithne. Now that I wake
I say that Maeve did nothing out of reason;
What mouth could you believe if not my mouth?

Cuchulain. When I went mad at my son's death and drew
My sword against the sea, it was my wife
That brought me back.

Eithne. Better women than I
Have served you well, but 'twas to me you turned.

Cuchulain. You thought that if you changed I'd kill you for it,
When everything sublunary must change,
And if I have not changed that goes to prove
That I am monstrous.

Eithne. You're not the man I loved,
That violent man forgave no treachery.
If, thinking what you think, you can forgive,
It is because you are about to die.

Cuchulain. Spoken too loudly and too near the door;
Speak low if you would speak about my death,
Or not in that strange voice exulting in it.
Who knows what ears listen behind the door?

Eithne. Some that would not forgive a traitor, some
That have the passion necessary to life,
Some not about to die. When you are gone
I shall denounce myself to all your cooks,
Scullions, armourers, bed-makers, and messengers,

Until they hammer me with a ladle, cut me with a knife,
Impale me upon a spit, put me to death
By what foul way best please their fancy,
So that my shade can stand among the shades
And greet your shade and prove it is no traitor.
Cuchulain. Women have spoken so, plotting a man's death.
                    Enter a Servant
Servant. Your great horse is bitted. All wait the word.
Cuchulain. I come to give it, but must ask a question.
   This woman, wild with grief, declares that she
   Out of pure treachery has told me lies
   That should have brought my death. What can I do?
   How can I save her from her own wild words?
Servant. Is her confession true?
Cuchulain.   I make the truth!
   I say she brings a message from my wife.
Servant. What if I make her swallow poppy-juice?
Cuchulain. What herbs seem suitable, but protect her life
   As if it were your own, and should I not return
   Give her to Conall Caernach because the women
   Have called him a good lover.
Eithne.   I might have peace that know
   The Morrigu, the woman like a crow,
   Stands to my defence and cannot lie,
   But that Cuchulain is about to die.

   [*Pipe and drum. The stage grows dark for a moment.
   When it lights up again, it is empty. Cuchulain enters
   wounded. He tries to fasten himself to a pillar-stone
   with his belt. Aoife, an erect white-haired woman,
   enters.*

Aoife. Am I recognised, Cuchulain?
Cuchulain.   You fought with a sword,
   It seemed that we should kill each other, then
   Your body wearied and I took your sword.
Aoife. But look again, Cuchulain! Look again!
Cuchulain. Your hair is white.
Aoife.   That time was long ago,
   And now it is my time. I have come to kill you.

Cuchulain. Where am I? Why am I here?

Aoife.   You asked their leave,
When certain that you had six mortal wounds,
To drink out of the pool.

Cuchulain.   I have put my belt
About this stone and want to fasten it
And die upon my feet, but am too weak.
Fasten this belt.   [*She helps him to do so.*
                         And now I know your name,
Aoife, the mother of my son. We met
At the Hawk's Well under the withered trees.
I killed him upon Baile's Strand, that is why
Maeve parted ranks that she might let you through.
You have a right to kill me.

Aoife.   Though I have,
Her army did not part to let me through.
The grey of Macha, that great horse of yours
Killed in the battle, came out of the pool
As though it were alive, and went three times
In a great circle round you and that stone,
Then leaped into the pool; and not a man
Of all that terrified army dare approach,
But I approach.

Cuchulain.   Because you have the right.

Aoife. But I am an old woman now, and that
Your strength may not start up when the time comes
I wind my veil about this ancient stone
And fasten you to it.

Cuchulain.   But do not spoil your veil.
Your veils are beautiful, some with threads of gold.

Aoife. I am too old to care for such things now.
                    [*She has wound the veil about him.*

Cuchulain. There was no reason so to spoil your veil:
I am weak from loss of blood.

Aoife.   I was afraid,
But now that I have wound you in the veil
I am not afraid. But—how did my son fight?

Cuchulain. Age makes more skilful but not better men.

Aoife. I have been told you did not know his name
   And wanted, because he had a look of me,
   To be his friend, but Conchubar forbade it.
Cuchulain. Forbade it and commanded me to fight;
   That very day I had sworn to do his will,
   Yet refused him, and spoke about a look;
   But somebody spoke of witchcraft and I said
   Witchcraft had made the look, and fought and killed him.
   Then I went mad, I fought against the sea.
Aoife. I seemed invulnerable; you took my sword,
   You threw me on the ground and left me there.
   I searched the mountain for your sleeping-place
   And laid my virgin body at your side,
   And yet, because you had left me, hated you,
   And thought that I would kill you in your sleep,
   And yet begot a son that night between
   Two black thorn-trees.
Cuchulain.   I cannot understand.
Aoife. Because about to die!
                  Somebody comes,
   Some countryman, and when he finds you here,
   And none to protect him, will be terrified.
   I will keep out of his sight, for I have things
   That I must ask questions on before I kill you.
     [*She goes. The Blind Man of "On Baile's Strand"
       comes in.*
     *He moves his stick about until he finds the standing
       stone; he lays his stick down, stoops and touches
       Cuchulain's feet. He feels the legs.*
Blind Man. Ah! Ah!
Cuchulain.   I think you are a blind old man.
Blind Man. A blind old beggar-man. What is your name?
Cuchulain. Cuchulain.
Blind Man.   They say that you are weak with
   wounds.
   I stood between a Fool and the sea at Baile's Strand
   When you went mad. What's bound about your hands
   So that they cannot move? Some womanish stuff.

I have been fumbling with my stick since dawn
And then heard many voices. I began to beg.
Somebody said that I was in Maeve's tent,
And somebody else, a big man by his voice,
That if I brought Cuchulain's head in a bag
I would be given twelve pennies; I had the bag
To carry what I get at kitchen doors,
Somebody told me how to find the place;
I thought it would have taken till the night,
But this has been my lucky day.

Cuchulain.   Twelve pennies!

Blind Man. I would not promise anything until the woman,
The great Queen Maeve herself, repeated the words.

Cuchulain. Twelve pennies! What better reason for killing a
    man?
You have a knife, but have you sharpened it?

Blind Man. I keep it sharp because it cuts my food.

    [*He lays bag on ground and begins feeling Cuchulain's
    body, his hands mounting upward.*

Cuchulain. I think that you know everything, Blind Man.
My mother or my nurse said that the blind
Know everything.

Blind Man.   No, but they have good sense.
How could I have got twelve pennies for your head
If I had not good sense?

Cuchulain.   There floats out there
The shape that I shall take when I am dead,
My soul's first shape, a soft feathery shape,
And is not that a strange shape for the soul
Of a great fighting-man?

Blind Man.   Your shoulder is there,
This is your neck. Ah! Ah! Are you ready, Cuchulain!

Cuchulain. I say it is about to sing.

                                    [*The stage darkens.*

Blind Man.   Ah! Ah!

    [*Music of pipe and drum, the curtain falls. The music
    ceases as the curtain rises upon a bare stage. There is
    nobody upon the stage except a woman with a crow's*

head. She is the Morrigu. She stands towards the back.
She holds a black parallelogram, the size of a man's
head. There are six other parallelograms near the
backcloth.

The Morrigu. The dead can hear me, and to the dead I speak.
This head is great Cuchulain's, those other six
Gave him six mortal wounds. This man came first;
Youth lingered though the years ran on, that season
A woman loves the best. Maeve's latest lover,
This man, had given him the second wound,
He had possessed her once; these were her sons,
Two valiant men that gave the third and fourth:
These other men were men of no account,
They saw that he was weakening and crept in;
One gave him the sixth wound and one the fifth;
Conall avenged him. I arranged the dance.

    [*Emer enters. The Morrigu places the head of Cuchulain*
    upon the ground and goes out. Emer runs in and begins
    to dance. She so moves that she seems to rage against
    the heads of those that had wounded Cuchulain, per-
    haps makes movements as though to strike them, going
    three times round the circle of the heads. She then
    moves towards the head of Cuchulain; it may, if need
    be, be raised above the others on a pedestal. She moves
    as if in adoration or triumph. She is about to prostrate
    herself before it, perhaps does so, then rises, looking
    up as if listening; she seems to hesitate between the
    head and what she hears. Then she stands motionless.
    There is silence, and in the silence a few faint bird
    notes.

    The stage darkens slowly. Then comes loud music, but
    now it is quite different. It is the music of some Irish
    Fair of our day. The stage brightens. Emer and the
    head are gone. . . . There is no one there but the three
    musicians. They are in ragged street-singers' clothes;
    two of them begin to pipe and drum. They cease. The
    Street-Singer begins to sing.

Singer.

> The harlot sang to the beggar-man.
> I meet them face to face,
> Conall, Cuchulain, Usna's boys,
> All that most ancient race;
> Maeve had three in an hour, they say.
> I adore those clever eyes,
> Those muscular bodies, but can get
> No grip upon their thighs.
> I meet those long pale faces,
> Hear their great horses, then
> Recall what centuries have passed
> Since they were living men.
> That there are still some living
> That do my limbs unclothe,
> But that the flesh my flesh has gripped
> I both adore and loathe.

[Pipe and drum music.

> Are those things that men adore and loathe
> Their sole reality?
> What stood in the Post Office
> With Pearse and Connolly?
> What comes out of the mountain
> Where men first shed their blood?
> Who thought Cuchulain till it seemed
> He stood where they had stood?
> No body like his body
> Has modern woman borne,
> But an old man looking back on life
> Imagines it in scorn.
> A statue's there to mark the place,
> By Oliver Sheppard done.
> So ends the tale that the harlot
> Sang to the beggar-man.

[Music from pipe and drum.

THE END

CATHLEEN NI HOOLIHAN

Cathleen Ni Hoolihan

PERSONS IN THE PLAY

Peter Gillane
Michael Gillane, *His son, going to be married*
Patrick Gillane, *A lad of twelve, Michael's brother*
Bridget Gillane, *Peter's wife*
Delia Cahel, *Engaged to Michael*
The Poor Old Woman
Neighbours

Interior of a cottage close to Killala, in 1798. Bridget is standing at a table undoing a parcel. Peter is sitting at one side of the fire, Patrick at the other.

Peter. What is that sound I hear?

Patrick. I don't hear anything. [*He listens.*] I hear it now. It's like cheering. [*He goes to the window and looks out.*] I wonder what they are cheering about. I don't see anybody.

Peter. It might be a hurling match.

Patrick. There's no hurling to-day. It must be down in the town the cheering is.

Bridget. I suppose the boys must be having some sport of their own.

Patrick. There is an old woman coming down the road. I don't know is it here she's coming.

Bridget. It will be a neighbour coming to hear about Michael's wedding. Can you see who it is?

Patrick. I think it is a stranger, and she's not coming to the house. She has not turned up the path. She's turned into the gap that goes down where Maurteen and his sons are shearing sheep [*He turns towards them*]. Do you remember what Winnie of the Cross Roads was saying the other night

about the strange woman that goes through the country the
time there's war or trouble coming?

Bridget. Don't be bothering us about Winnie's talk, but go
and open the door for your brother. I hear him coming up
the path.

Bridget. Come over here, Peter, and look at Michael's wedding clothes. [*Peter shifts his chair to table.*] Those are
grand clothes, indeed.

Bridget. You hadn't clothes like that when you married me,
and no coat to put on of a Sunday more than any other
day.

Peter. That is true, indeed. We never thought a son of our
own would be wearing a suit of that sort at his wedding, or
have so good a place to bring a wife to.

Patrick [*who is still at the window*]. Here is Michael coming
back, father.

Peter. I hope he has brought Delia's fortune with him safe,
for fear her people might go back of the bargain, and I
after making it. Trouble enough I had making it.

[*Patrick opens the door, and Michael comes in.*

Bridget. What kept you, Michael? We were looking out for
you this long time.

Michael. I went round by the priest's house to bid him be
ready to marry us to-morrow.

Bridget. Did he say anything?

Michael. He said it was a very nice match, and that he was
never better pleased to marry two in his parish than myself
and Delia Cahel.

Peter. Have you got the fortune, Michael?

Michael. Here it is.

[*He puts bag on the table and goes over and leans against
chimney jamb. Bridget who has been all this time ex-
amining the clothes, pulling the seams and trying the
lining of the pockets, etc., puts the clothes on the
dresser.*

Peter [*getting up and taking the bag in his hand and turning
out the money*]. Yes, I made the bargain well for you,
Michael. Old John Cahel would sooner have kept a share

of this a while longer. "Let me keep the half of it till the first boy is born," says he. "You will not," says I. "Whether there is or is not a boy, the whole hundred pounds must be in Michael's hands before he brings your daughter to the house." The wife spoke to him then, and he gave in at the end.

Bridget. You seem well pleased to be handling the money, Peter.

Peter. Indeed, I wish I'd had the luck to get a hundred pounds, or twenty pounds itself, with the wife I married.

Bridget. Well, if I didn't bring much I didn't get much. What had you the day I married you but a flock of hens and you feeding them, and a few lambs and you driving them to the market at Ballina. [*She is vexed, and bangs a jug on the dresser.*] If I brought no fortune I worked it out in my bones, laying down the baby—Michael, that is standing there now, on a stook of straw, while I dug the potatoes, and never asking big dresses or anything, but to be working.

Peter. That is true, indeed.   [*He pats her arm.*

Bridget. Leave me alone now till I ready the house for the woman that is to come into it.

Peter. You are the best woman in Ireland, but money is good, too. [*He begins handling the money again and sits down.*] I never thought to see so much money within my four walls. We can do great things now we have it. We can take the ten acres of land we have a chance of since Jamsie Dempsey died, and stock it. We will go the fair of Ballina to buy the stock. Did Delia ask any of the money for her own use, Michael?

Michael. She did not, indeed. She did not seem to take much notice of it, or to look at it at all.

Bridget. That's no wonder. Why would she look at it when she had yourself to look at—a fine strong young man; it is proud she must be to get you; a good, steady boy, that will make use of the money, and will not be running through it, or spending it on drink, like another.

Peter. It's likely Michael himself was not thinking much of the fortune either, but of what sort the girl was to look at.

Michael [*coming over towards the table*]. Well, you would like a nice comely girl to be beside you, and to go walking with you. The fortune only lasts for a while, but the woman will be there always.

Patrick [*turning round from the window*]. They are cheering again down in the town. Maybe they are landing horses from Enniscrone. They do be cheering when the horses take the water well.

Michael. There are no horses in it. Where would they be going and no fair at hand! Go down to the town, Patrick, and see what is going on.

Patrick [*opens the door to go out, but stops for a moment on the threshold*]. Will Delia remember, do you think, to bring the greyhound pup she promised me when she would be coming to the house?

Michael. She will surely. [*Patrick goes out, leaving the door open.*

Peter. It will be Patrick's turn next to be looking for a fortune, but he won't find it so easy to get it, and he with no place of his own.

Bridget. I do be thinking sometimes, now things are going so well with us, and the Cahels such a good back to us in the district, and Delia's own uncle a priest, we might be put in the way of making Patrick himself a priest some day, and he so good at his books.

Peter. Time enough, time enough; you have always your head full of plans.

Bridget. We will be well able to give him learning, and not to send him tramping the country like a poor scholar that lives on charity.

Michael. They're not done cheering yet.

[*He goes over to the door and stands there for a moment, putting up his hand to shade his eyes.*

Bridget. Do you see anything?

Michael. I see an old woman coming up the path.

Bridget. Who is it, I wonder?

Michael. I don't think it's one of the neighbours, but she has her cloak over her face.

Bridget. Maybe it's the same woman Patrick saw a while ago. It might be some poor woman heard we were making ready for the wedding, and came to look for her share.

Peter. I may as well put the money out of sight. There's no use leaving it out for every stranger to look at.

[*He goes over to a large box by the wall, opens it and puts the bag in, and fumbles with the lock.*

Michael. There she is, father! [*An old woman passes the window slowly. She looks at Michael as she passes.*] I'd sooner a stranger not to come to the house the night before the wedding.

Bridget. Open the door, Michael, don't keep the poor woman waiting.

[*The old woman comes in, Michael stands aside to make way for her.*

Old Woman. God save all here!

Peter. God save you kindly.

Old Woman. You have good shelter here.

Peter. You are welcome to whatever shelter we have.

Bridget. Sit down there by the fire and welcome.

Old Woman [*warming her hands*]. There's a hard wind outside.

[*Michael watches her curiously from the door. Peter comes over to the table.*

Peter. Have you travelled far to-day?

Old Woman. I have travelled far, very far; there are few have travelled so far as myself.

Peter. It is a pity, indeed, for any person to have no place of their own.

Old Woman. That is true for you, indeed, and it is long I am on the road since I first went wandering. It is seldom I have any rest.

Bridget. It is a wonder you are not worn out with so much wandering.

Old Woman. Sometimes my feet are tired and my hands are quiet, but there is no quiet in my heart. When the people see me quiet they think old age has come on me, and that all the stir has gone out of me.

Bridget. What was it put you astray?

Old Woman. Too many strangers in the house.

Bridget. Indeed you look as if you had had your share of trouble.

Old Woman. I have had trouble indeed.

Bridget. What was it put the trouble on you?

Old Woman. My land that was taken from me.

Peter. Was it much land they took from you?

Old Woman. My four beautiful green fields.

Peter [*aside to Bridget*]. Do you think could she be the Widow Casey that was put out of her holding at Kilglas a while ago?

Bridget. She is not. I saw the Widow Casey one time at the market in Ballina, a stout, fresh woman.

Peter [*to old woman*]. Did you hear a noise of cheering, and you coming up the hill?

Old Woman. I thought I heard the noise I used to hear when my friends came to visit me.

[*She begins singing half to herself.*

     I will go cry with the woman,
     For yellow-haired Donough is dead;
     With a hempen rope for a neckcloth
     And a white cloth on his head.

Michael [*coming from the door*]. What is that you are singing, ma'am? [*She goes on singing, much louder.*

Old Woman. Singing I am about a man I knew one time, yellow-haired Donough, that was hanged in Galway.

     I am come to cry with you, woman,
     My hair is unwound and unbound;
     I remember him ploughing his field,
     Turning up the red side of the ground.

     And building his barn on the hill
     With the good mortared stone;
     O! we'd have pulled down the gallows
     Had it happened in Enniscrone!

Michael. What was it brought him to his death?

Old Woman. He died for love of me; many a man has died for love of me.

Peter [*aside to Bridget*]. Her trouble has put her wits astray.

Michael. Is it long since that song was made? Is it long since he got his death?

Old Woman. Not long, not long. But there were others that died for love of me a long time ago.

Michael. Were they neighbours of your own, ma'am?

Old Woman. Come here beside me and I'll tell you about them. [*Michael sits down beside her at the hearth.*] There was a red man of the O'Donells from the North, and a man of the O'Sullivans from the South, and there was one Brian that lost his life at Clontarf, by the sea, and there were a great many in the West, some that died hundreds of years ago, and there are some that will die to-morrow.

Michael. Is it in the West that men will die to-morrow?

Old Woman. Come nearer, nearer to me.

Bridget. Is she right, do you think? or is she a woman from the North?

Peter. She doesn't know well what she's talking about, with the want and the trouble she has gone through.

Bridget. The poor thing, we should treat her well.

Peter. Give her a drink of milk, and a bit of the oaten cake.

Bridget. Maybe we should give her something along with that to bring her on her way; a few pence, or a shilling itself, and we with so much money in the house.

Peter. Indeed, I'd not begrudge it to her if we had it to spare, but if we go running through what we have, we'll soon have to break the hundred pounds, and that would be a pity.

Bridget. Shame on you, Peter. Give her the shilling and your blessing with it, or our own luck will go from us.

[*Peter goes to the box and takes out a shilling.*

Bridget [*to the old woman*]. Will you have a drink of milk?

Old Woman. It is not food or drink that I want.

Peter [*offering the shilling*]. Here is something for you.

Old Woman. That is not what I want. It is not silver I want.

Peter. What is it you would be asking for?

Old Woman. If anyone would give me help he must give me himself, he must give me all.

    [*Peter goes over to the table staring at the shilling in his hand in a bewildered way and stands whispering to Bridget.*

Michael. Have you no man of your own, ma'am?

Old Woman. I have not. With all the lovers that brought me their love, I never set out the bed for any.

Michael. Are you lonely going the roads, ma'am?

Old Woman. I have my thoughts and I have my hopes.

Michael. What hopes have you to hold to?

Old Woman. The hope of getting my beautiful fields back again; the hope of putting the strangers out of my house.

Michael. What way will you do that, ma'am?

Old Woman. I have good friends that will help me. They are gathering to help me now. I am not afraid. If they are put down to-day, they will get the upper hand to-morrow. [*She gets up.*] I must be going to meet my friends. They are coming to help me, and I must be there to welcome them. I must call the neighbours together to welcome them.

Michael. I will go with you.

Bridget. It is not her friends you have to go and welcome, Michael; it is the girl coming into the house you have to welcome. You have plenty to do; it is food and drink you have to bring to the house. The woman that is coming is not coming with empty hands; you would not have an empty house before her. [*To the old woman.*] Maybe you don't know, ma'am, that my son is going to be married to-morrow.

Old Woman. It is not a man going to his marriage that I look to for help.

Peter [*to Bridget*]. Who is she, do you think, at all?

Bridget. You did not tell us your name yet, ma'am.

Old Woman. Some call me the Poor Old Woman, and there are some that call me Cathleen ni Hoolihan.

Peter. I think I knew some one of that name once. Who was it, I wonder? It must have been someone I knew when I was a boy. No, no, I remember I heard it in a song.

Old Woman [*who is standing in the doorway*]. They are wondering that there were songs made for me; there have been many songs made for me. I heard one on the wind this morning. [*She sings.*

> Do not make a great keening
> When the graves have been dug to-morrow,
> Do not call the white-scarfed riders
> To the burying that shall be to-morrow.
>
> Do not spread food to call strangers
> To the wakes that shall be to-morrow;
> Do not give money for prayers
> For the dead that shall die to-morrow. . . .

They will have no need of prayers, they will have no need of prayers.

Michael. I do not know what that song means; but tell me something I can do for you.

Peter. Come over to me, Michael.

Michael. Hush, father; listen to her.

Old Woman. It is a hard service they take that help me. Many that are red-cheeked now will be pale-cheeked; many that have been free to walk the hills and the bogs and the rushes will be sent to walk hard streets in far countries; many a good plan will be broken; many that have gathered money will not stay to spend it; many a child will be born and there will be no father at its christening to give it a name. They that had red cheeks will have pale cheeks for my sake; and for all that they will think they are well paid.

[*She goes out. Her voice is heard outside singing.*

> They shall be remembered for ever;
> They shall be alive for ever;
> They shall be speaking for ever;
> The people shall hear them for ever.

Bridget [*to Peter*]. Look at him, Peter; he has the look of a man that has got the touch. [*Raising her voice.*] Look here, Michael, at the wedding clothes. [*Taking clothes from dresser.*] You have a right to fit them on now; it would be a pity to-morrow if they did not fit; the boys would be laughing at you. Take them, Michael, and go into the room and fit them on.   [*She puts them on his arm.*

Michael. What wedding are you talking of? What clothes will I be wearing to-morrow?

Bridget. These are the clothes you are going to wear when you marry Delia Cahel to-morrow.

Michael. I had forgotten that.

[*He looks at the clothes and turns towards the inner room, but stops at the sound of cheering outside.*

Peter. There is the shouting come to our own door. What is it has happened?

[*Neighbours come crowding in, Patrick and Delia with them.*

Patrick. There are ships in the bay; the French are landing at Killala.

[*Peter takes his pipe from his mouth and his hat off and stands up. The clothes slip from Michael's arm.*

Delia. Michael! [*He takes no notice.*] Michael! [*He turns towards her.*] Why do you look at me like a stranger?

[*She drops his arm. Bridget goes over towards her.*

Patrick. The boys are all hurrying down the hillsides to meet the French.

Delia. Michael won't be going to join the French.

Bridget [*to Peter*].Tell him not to go, Peter.

Peter. It's no use. He doesn't hear a word we're saying.

Bridget. Try, Delia, and coax him over to the fire.

Delia. Michael, Michael, you won't leave me! You won't join the French and we going to be married to-morrow!

[*She puts her arms about him. He turns to her as if about to yield.*

Old woman's voice outside:
They shall be remembered for ever;
The people shall hear them for ever.

[*Michael breaks away from Delia and goes towards neigh-
    bours at the door.*

Michael. Come, we have no time to lose; we must follow her.
                    [*Michael and the neighbours go out.*

Peter [*laying his hand on Patrick's arm*]. Did you see an old
    woman going down the path?

Patrick. I did not; but I saw a young girl, and she had the
    walk of a queen.

THE END

NOTES

On Baile's Strand

Yeats began to write this play in 1901, having thought it out while walking in the Seven Woods of Coole Park, Lady Gregory's seat in Galway. It is based on her translation of "The Only Son of Aoife" in *Cuchulain of Muirthemne* (1902). The original version was first published in 1903; its main revision occurs in the version published in 1906. It was first performed at the opening of the Abbey Theatre, Dublin, on 27 December 1904. It is dedicated to William Fay, an Irish working man who with his brother Frank, an accountant's clerk, had formed a company of actors. They were distinctive actors and were members of the Abbey company until 1907, when they resigned in protest against Miss Horniman's reorganization of the company. See W. G. Fay and Catherine Carswell, *The Fays and the Abbey Theatre* (1935).

p. 18   *William Fay:* (1872–1947), Irish actor.

p. 19   *Cuchulain, King of Muirthemne:* the warrior hero of the *Táin Bó Cuálnge*, or "The Cattle Raid of Cooley," a Gaelic epic, contained in the Red Branch or Ulster cycle of tales. These were probably transmitted orally in the early Christian period, then written down by monks, and incorporated in late MSS. in the eleventh and fifteenth centuries.

      Muirthemme: area ruled by Cuchulain in modern Co. Louth. Early versions of the play show that Conchubar and other kings had come to consult Cuchulain about the rebuilding of Emain, burned down after the deaths of Deirdre and Naoise, told in tale of "The Fate of the Sons of Usna," one of the remscéla of the *Táin Bó Cuálnge*.

      Conchubar: King of Uladh, or Ulster.

      Dundealgan: modern Dundalk, Co. Louth.

p. 20   *Boann* (or *Boand*): Irish goddess, wife of Naada of the Silver Hand, who gave her name to the River Boyne which rose out of a secret well into which Boann looked, though this was not allowed. The water rose and drowned her. Cf. Eleanor Hull, *A Text-book of Irish Literature*

(Dublin, 1906), I, pp. 8–9. For derivation of the name, perhaps "Cow-white goddess," see T. F. O'Rahilly, *Early Irish History and Mythology* (Dublin, 1946), p. 3. See also Kuno Meyer, *The Voyage of Bran* (1895), p. 214.

Fand (or *Fann*): wife of Manannán Mac Lir, god of the sea. She fell in love with Cuchulain, when her husband forsook her; but he claimed her again and brought her back to his realm. Her name may mean a tear, or the moisture of the eye. Cf. Eleanor Hull, *ibid.*, p. 22.

p. 21   *a young man*: Conlaech, Cuchulain's son by Aoife.

p. 22   *Aoife's country*: Aoife was a warrior queen in Scotland, who was an enemy of Scathach (see note, p. 234). Cuchulain conquered her, and forced her to grant him three wishes. She was to become Scathach's vassal, to sleep one night with him, and to bear him a son.

Banachas and Bonachas: demons of the air, that screamed around warriors in combat.

Fomor: head of the Fomorians, gods of darkness, finally overthrown by the Tuatha de Danaan, gods of life and light.

p. 25   *Maeve of Cruachan*: Queen of Connacht, married to Ailill; she was an amorous and warlike woman. Cruachan (modern Rathcrogan, Co. Roscommon) was the capital of Connacht.

the northern pirates: Norse invaders, whose power was finally crushed by Brian Boru in the Battle of Clontarf, 1014.

Sorcha: part of the Gaelic Otherworld.

p. 26   *your father*: one tradition held that Cuchulain was the son of Lugh, the god of light. In *At the Hawk's Well* his father is Sualtam.

p. 27   *Country-under-Wave*: Tir-fa-tonn, Otherworld in Gaelic mythology.

p. 36   *Laegaire*: or Laeghaire Buadach, Leary the Triumphant, a hero of the Red Branch.

p. 41   *Scathach*: warrior woman of the Island of Skye who taught Cuchulain the art of war.

Uathach: daughter of Scathach, who was attracted by Cuchulain's beauty and made him welcome when he visited Scathach; he rewarded her by attacking her and killing the champion who came to her aid.

Alba: Scotland.

p. 42   *Dubthach the Chafer*: character in *Táin Bó Cuálnge*. He was sent by Conchubar as an emissary with Fergus (see

Deirdre, pp. 47–49 to bring Deirdre, Naoise and his brothers back from Scotland. After the murder of Naoise and death of Deirdre he joined Queen Maeve.

DEIRDRE

Yeats probably began to write this play in prose; he was working on it in 1905 and 1906, largely at Coole Park. He was aware of the story of "The Tragical Fate of the Sons of Usna" in many forms (there were prose translations, by O'Flanagan in the *Transactions of the Iberno-Celtic Society* and by O'Curry in *Atlantis*; Sir Samuel Ferguson wrote his version in verse) but based his play on Lady Gregory's *Cuchulain of Muirthemne* (1902). It was first published in 1907 and first performed at the Abbey Theatre, Dublin, on 26 November 1906. The dedication is to Mrs. Patrick Campbell who took the part of Deirdre in 1906, 1907, and 1908.

p. 46   *Mrs. Patrick Campbell:* (1867–1940), famous actress.

   Robert Gregory: (1881–1918), son of Lady Gregory, painter and designer, shot down over Italy in 1918; for praise of his versatility see Yeats's poem "In Memory of Major Robert Gregory."

p. 47   *Fergus:* MacRoy or Son of Rogh, former king of Ulster who was tricked out of his crown by Ness, the mother of Conchubar. He was the poet of the Red Branch cycle of tales.

   Naoise: son of Usna; one of Conchubar's warriors.

   Deirdre: formerly Conchubar's ward whom he kept in the hills in the care of an old nurse Lavarcham, intending to marry her. Naoise, one of his warriors, saw her, fell in love with her, and ran away with her to Scotland, accompanied by his brothers Ainle and Ardan. Deirdre prophesied she would bring suffering on Ulster.

p. 51   *Lugaidh Redstripe:* a hero of the Red Branch.

   Queen Edain: or Etáin, a beautiful woman, wooed, won, and taken to the Otherworld by King Midir. Here, she is changed into a fly by Fuamorach, Midir's wife, who blows her into this world, where she is reborn three times before Midir, in a game of chess, finally wins her back to the Otherworld. The account of this forms one of the major tales in the mythological cycle, *The Wooing of Etáin.*

p. 53   *a king of Surracha:* possibly Sorcha, Gaelic Otherworld. O'Rahilly explains the name as originally *Syriaca*, Syria, influenced by the native word *Sorcha*, bright. In later romantic literature it denotes an exotic country with no precise geographical position.

p. 56   *The hot Istain stone, And the cold stone of Fanes*: Professor David Greene suggests that these may come from some medieval lapidary and have nothing to do with Irish tradition.

p. 58   *a golden tongue*: Fergus was occasionally called "Honey-mouth."

p. 68   *The daughter of the King of Leodas*: G. B. Saul, *Prolegomena to the Study of Yeats's Plays* (1958), p. 46, suggests Leodas may be "an imaginary Pictish king?—the 'Lord of Duntreon'?" Dún Treóin is in Argyll. Leodas is from Leòdhas, Gaelic name of the Isle of Lewis. Since rhyme in modern Irish is that of vowels only Treóin and Leòdhais (gen. of Leòdhas) would be interchangeable in the verse quoted, if it translated an original. In versions of the Deirdre story the woman who causes jealousy is the daughter of the Earl of Dún Treóin. I am indebted to Professor David Greene for this information.

THE PLAYER QUEEN

Yeats began to write this play in 1907 (cf. *Plays in Prose and Verse*, 1922, p. 429) with the intention of making a verse tragedy of it. He finished a prose draft in 1908, and was working on a further prose scenario in 1909. He continued to work on the play in 1914 and 1916. The first performance was at the King's Hall, Covent Garden, London, on 25 May 1919; the first published version is that of 1922.

p. 79   *Kubla Khan, or Kublai Khan*: founder of Mongol dynasty in the thirteenth century.

p. 82   *the Bible says: Exodus* 22, 18.
        Candlemas: celebrated on 2 February.

p. 86   *the donkey*: see *Matthew* 21, 2–10.

p. 88   *"The Tragical History of Noah's Deluge"*: probably *Noah and the Flood*, a Chester miracle play.

p. 90   *Saint Octema*: an invented character.

p. 91   *Sleep of Adam: Genesis* 2, 21.

p. 98   *Pasiphae*: in mythology the daughter of Helios, married to Minos of Crete who, in order to secure the throne, prayed to Poseidon to send him a bull from the sea to sacrifice. The bull was so beautiful that Minos would not kill it, whereupon Pasiphae fell in love with it, disguised herself as a cow, and bore the Minotaur, half-man, half-bull, which lived in the labyrinth at Crete.

Leda: in mythology the mother of the Dioscuri and Helen. Zeus approached her in the shape of a swan and begat Helen. Leda was also the mother of Clytemnestra.

p. 99   *Cato*: Marcius Porcius Cato Uticensis (95–46 B.C.) was a Roman stoic who supported Pompey and, after his defeat, joined the Pompeians in Africa. After Caesar's victory at Thapsus, he committed suicide at Pharsalus.

Cicero: Marcius Tullius Cicero (106–43 B.C.), Roman orator, author, politician, led the opposition to Antony and faced death bravely after Octavian took Rome.

Demosthenes: (384–322 B.C.), Athenian orator who, while in exile, tried to organise combined action against Macedon after the death of Alexander. He returned to Athens, which was subsequently occupied by a Macedonian garrison, and a decree for his execution was passed. He took refuge in a temple; being pursued there, sucked poison concealed in his pen and died.

Petronius Arbiter: Roman, author of *Cena Trimalchicius*, a former proconsul and Nero's *arbiter elegantiae*, who, when Nero was turned against him by Tigellinus, committed suicide, writing a document denouncing Nero and his accomplices.

p. 100 *Xanadu*: where Kubla Khan decreed a lordly pleasure house, in Coleridge's "Kubla Khan"; the source is *Purchas his Pilgrimes* (1625).

Agamemnon: husband of Clytemnestra, brother of Menelaus, and leader of Greek armies against Troy. He sacrificed his daughter Iphigenia at Aulis, was murdered on his return to Argos by Clytemnestra and Aegisthus, her paramour.

Helen: wife of Menelaus, who went to Troy with Paris, son of Priam, and was thus the cause of the Trojan war.

p. 102 *Ionian music . . . Dorian scale*: Yeats is making the normal distinction here between these modes of Greek music: the Ionic soft and effeminate, the Dorian simple and solemn.

Delphi: situated on slopes of Mount Parnassus, was the seat of a temple of Apollo and of a famous oracle, very influential between eighth and fifth centuries B.C.

p. 103 *The Christian era . . . an end*: an idea expressed by Yeats in

A *Vision* and in many poems, that history consists of
opposing gyres, one age being the reversal of another.

THE ONLY JEALOUSY OF EMER

Yeats began this play in 1916 and finished it in January 1918. The
story probably derives from the legendary tale *The Sickbed* [or
Wasting-away] *of Cuchulain* which is the basis for Lady Gregory's
"The Only Jealousy of Emer" in *Cuchulain of Muirthemne* (1902).
The play was first published in *Poetry* (Chicago), January 1919,
then in *Two Plays for Dancers* (1919). There were several revisions,
the major ones contained in the version included in *Collected Plays*
(1934). The play was first publicly performed in Holland with
masks by Hildo van Krop. Cf. W. B. Yeats, *Wheels and Butterflies*
(1934), p. 69. A prose version, *Fighting the Waves*, written in 1928,
was performed at the Abbey Theatre, Dublin on 13 August 1929.

p. 113 *Cuchulain*: see note, p. 233.

       Emer: Cuchulain's wife whom he won after a series of trials.

       Eithne Inguba: Cuchulain's young mistress.

       Sidhe: the gods of ancient Ireland.

       Archimedes: (287–212 B.C.), of Syracuse, a mathematician
       and inventor.

p. 115 *Baile's tree*: a reference to the story of Baile and Aillinn,
       lovers, to each of whom Aengus, the god of love, gave
       false news of the other's death. They died of broken
       hearts and were changed into white swans linked by a
       golden chain. A yew tree grew where Baile's body lay,
       a wild apple where Aillinn's.

p. 116 *Manannan, son of the sea*: Manannán Mac Lir, the god of
       the sea.

p. 118 *Bricriu*: the figure is here distinguishing itself from Concho-
       bar's poet Bricriu, known for his bitterness.

p. 122 *a hawk flew*: this refers to Yeats's play *At the Hawk's Well*,
       where Cuchulain is deceived by the guardian of the well,
       half-hawk, half-woman.

p. 123 *Fand*: wife of Manannán Mac Lir, see note p. 234.

THE RESURRECTION

Yeats drafted this play in 1925. It was first published in June 1927
in the *Adelphi*, then in *Stories of Michael Robartes and His Friends*
(1921), and later in *Wheels and Butterflies* (1934). The first performance was at the Abbey Theatre, Dublin, on 30 July 1934.

p. 128 *Junzo Sato*: a Japanese who met Yeats after a lecture in

Portland, Oregon, and gave him a sword which is mentioned in "Meditations in Time of Civil War, III," and in "A Dialogue of Self and Soul."

p. 129 *the Peacock Theatre:* a small theatre (sometimes used for rehearsals) attached to the Abbey Theatre, Dublin.

Dionysus: Greek god of an emotional religion which particularly affected women, who seized an animal or a child at the height of their ecstasy and, tearing it apart, ate the pieces, believing they were incorporating the god and his power within themselves in so doing. These lines draw a parallel between the myth of Dionysus and the death and resurrection of Christ. Ellmann (*Identity of Yeats,* 1954, p. 260) draws on Sir James Frazer's *The Golden Bough* (which Yeats read) for this explanation: Dionysus, child of a mortal, Persephone, and an immortal, Zeus, was torn to pieces by the Titans. Athene (the "staring virgin" of the poems: "staring" indicating that she acts as if in a trance because the events are preordained) snatched the heart from his body, brought it on her hand to Zeus, who killed the Titans, swallowed the heart, and begat Dionysus again, upon another mortal, Semele.

that beating heart: in his introduction to this play Yeats gives Sir William Crookes's *Studies in Psychical Research* as a source for this image.

p. 130 *Magnus Annus:* this passage is explained by a passage in *A Vision* (1926), page 149, where Yeats quotes Virgil's Fourth Eclogue: "the cycles in their vast array begin anew; virgin Astrea comes, the reign of Saturn comes, and from the heights of Heaven a new generation of mankind descends . . . Apollo now is king, and in your consulship, in yours, Pollio, the age of glory shall commence." The verses state Yeats's idea that Christianity brought a radical violence into the world and ushered in a new historical period. See also *A Vision* (1937), pages 243–54, where he discusses the idea of a Great Year. The Muses sing of Magnus Annus as a play because they regard the ritual death and rebirth of the god as a recurring event, part of the cycles of history. Ellmann points out that "both Gods had died and been reborn in March when the sun was between the Ram and the Fish, and when the moon was beside the constellation Virgo, who carries the star Spica in her hand." In these stanzas Yeats is thinking of Virgil, *Eclogue*, IV, 6 "Iam redit et Virgo . . ." where Virgo, daughter of Jupiter and Themis, is the last to leave Earth at the end of the golden age; but will return, bringing back the golden age. This Virgilian prophecy was later read as fortelling the coming of Mary (as Virgo) and Christ, the star of Bethlehem (as Spica).

Argo's: Argo was the ship in which Jason sailed to fetch the Golden Fleece. The idea of a second Argo is in Virgil's Fourth Eclogue and also in Shelley's *Hellas*.

The Roman Empire stood appalled: because though there were but six million Christians in the Roman Empire's sixty million, the world was to become Christian, and the Empire to be destroyed by Christianity (a view Yeats shared with Gibbon).

that fierce virgin: Mary. Here R. Ellmann, *ibid*., p. 261, remarks that these lines daringly assert a parallelism and even identity between the three pairs, Astraea and Spica, Athene and Dionysus, and Mary and Christ. Cf. Lady Gregory, *Journal*, 263, for an early version reading "Virgo [the constellation] and the mystic star."

the fabulous darkness: probably derived from a description of Christianity by Proclus, a fourth-century neo-Platonic philosopher (whom Yeats read in Thomas Taylor's translation of 1816, cf. F. A. C. Wilson, *Yeats and Tradition*, p. 59). Cf. *A Vision* (1937), pp. 277, 278, and *A Vision* (1926), pp. 185 *seq*.:

". . . The irrational force that would create confusion and uproar as with the cry 'The Babe, the Babe, is born'—the women speaking unknown tongues, the barbers and weavers expounding Divine revelation with all the vulgarity of their servitude, the tables that move or resound with raps—but creates a negligible sect. All about it is an *antithetical* aristocratic civilisation in its completed form, every detail of life hierarchical, every great man's door crowded at dawn by petitioners, great wealth everywhere in few men's hands, all dependent upon a few, up to the Emperor himself who is a God dependent upon a greater God, and, everywhere in court, in the family, an inequality made law, and floating over all the Romanised Gods of Greece in their physical superiority. . . . The world became Christian, 'that fabulous formless darkness' as it seemed to a philosopher of the fourth century, blotted out 'every beautiful thing,' not through the conversion of crowds or general change of opinion, or through any pressure from below, for civilisation was *antithetical* still, but by an act of power."

the Eleven: the disciples, minus Judas.

p. 131 *thirteen:* Christ and the twelve disciples.

Jesus divided bread and wine: see *Matthew* 26, 26–27.

Peter: see *Matthew* 26, 37–75.

p. 133 *born of a woman:* see *Isaiah* 7, 14.

p. 135 *Astrea's:* Astrea, a daughter of Zeus, was said to have lived on earth and been a source of blessing to men during the Golden Age. She is mentioned in the passage from Virgil quoted above. G. B. Saul, *op. cit.*, p. 85, remarks, "Astræa: goddess of justice, sometimes regarded as the daughter of the Titan Astraeus by Eos; in her heavenly transformation, Virgo."

the goddess: Athene. Cf. W. B. Yeats "The Phases of the Moon," *Collected Poems,* p. 185.

Achilles: son of Peleus and Thetis, bravest of the Greeks in the Trojan war, was wounded in his heel (the only vulnerable part of his body, by which Thetis had held him when plunging him in the Styx) by Paris and died.

Lucretius: Titus Lucretius Carus (*c.* 99–55 B.C.), Roman poet and author of *De Rerum Naturae*, a philosophical poem in which he tries to show that the course of the world can be explained without divine intervention.

p. 139 *the heart of a phantom,* see note p. 239.

p. 140 *Heracleitus:* of Ephesus, wrote a work "Concerning Nature" in which he asserted all things were in a state of flux.

Galilean turbulence: foretold by astronomers in Babylon who reduce man's status by their science; Man is being taught that he is nothing in comparison to the universe; He is becoming featureless: cf. *A Vision* (1937), pp. 273 *seq.*:

"The mind that brought the change, if considered as man only, is a climax of whatever Greek and Roman thought was most a contradiction to its age; but considered as more than man He controlled what Neo-Pythagorean and Stoic could not—irrational force. He could announce the new age, all that had not been

thought of, or touched, or seen, because He could sub-
stitute for reason, miracle."

Everything that man esteems: a praise of man, who goes on
creating heroically despite the fact that all things pass
away. Cf. W. B. Yeats, *Autobiographies*, p. 315.

THE WORDS UPON THE WINDOW-PANE

The starting-point for this play, according to Allan Wade, *The
Letters of W. B. Yeats* (1954), p. 891 *n.*, was Yeats's finding in
1910 an inscription cut on a window in Oliver St. John Gogarty's
Dublin house "Fairfield." He wrote the play when he was reading
deeply in Swift during 1930; it was finished in October and performed at the Abbey Theatre, Dublin, on 17 November 1930. It
was first published in 1934.

p. 142 *Lady Gregory*: Lady Augusta Gregory (1852–1932), Irish
playwright, widow of Sir William Gregory; she co-
operated with Yeats in establishing the Abbey Theatre.

p. 143 *the Corbets of Ballymoney*: Yeats had Corbet relatives, but
this name and that of Ballymoney (there are many vil-
lages or towns with this name in Ireland, for instance,
in Co. Antrim, Co. Cork, Co. Wexford) are probably
taken to indicate a young man of some social and intellectual standing.

p. 144 *Myers' "Human Personality"*: written by F. W. H. Myers
(1843–1901) and published in 1903 in two volumes.

a wild book: either *A New Revelation* (1918) or a *History
of Spiritualism* (2 vols., 1926) by Sir Arthur Conan
Doyle, perhaps more widely known for his Sherlock
Holmes detective stories.

Lord Dunraven, then Lord Adare: introduced to "place"
Dr. Trench. The full title of this Irish peerage created
for the Quin family was Earl of Dunraven and Viscount
Adare. This reference is probably to the third Earl,
Edward Wyndham-Quin, a scholar of literature and
archaeology.

David Home: presumably Daniel D. Home (1833–86),
Scottish medium and spiritualist.

Emanuel Swedenborg: (1688–1772), Swedish scientist and
mystic philosopher, devoted his life after 1745 to inter-
preting the scriptures, his being a theosophical system.

p. 145 *Harold's Cross*: Dublin suburb and situation of dog-racing
track.

Grattan: Henry Grattan (1746–1820), Irish barrister and M.P.; carried an address demanding legislative independence in 1782. The Irish parliament which lasted until 1800 was known as Grattan's parliament.

Curran: John Philpot Curran (1750–1817), Irish barrister and M.P., who defended the prisoners in the 1798 trials and opposed the Union.

Jonathan Swift: (1667–1745), Dean of St. Patrick's Cathedral, Dublin, wrote *Journal to Stella,* a series of letters from 1710 to 1713 to Esther Johnson and Rebecca Dingley, her companion.

Stella: Swift's name for Esther Johnson (1681–1728), whom he met in Sir William Temple's household when he was secretary there; they remained close friends till her death. He was buried by her side in St. Patrick's Cathedral.

Vanessa: Swift's name for Esther Vanhomrigh (1690–1723), whom he met in London in 1708; she fell in love with him, and Swift's poem "Cadenus and Vanessa" is an account of their unhappy relationship.

p. 146 *Bolingbroke:* Henry St. John Bolingbroke, first Viscount (1678–1751), friend of Swift, author, orator, politician, in charge of the negotiations leading to the Peace of Utrecht in 1710. Dismissed on the accession of George I, he fled to France, but returned in 1723.

Robert Harley: first Earl of Oxford (1661–1724), friend of Swift, a moderate Tory who persuaded his party to pass the Act of Settlement. He remained in a Whig ministry until 1708. In 1710 he and St. John led the Tory Ministry which brought about the Treaty of Utrecht (1713). He was dismissed in 1714 through the Jacobite intrigues of his colleague.

Ormonde: James Butler, Duke of Ormonde (1610–88), born of an ancient Anglo-Irish family, distinguished himself in the Strafford administration and in the rebellions of 1640 was appointed chief commander of the army. James Butler, second Duke of Ormonde (1665–1746), served in the army against Monmouth, at the Battle of the Boyne; Lord Lieutenant of Ireland three times 1703–13; impeached for high treason 1705, retired to Avignon. The Duke was greatly admired by Swift. Benjamin Yeats married into the Butler family in 1773, and the Yeats family always valued this connection, using "Butler" frequently as a Christian name.

Brutus: Marcius Junius Brutus (85–42 B.C.) joined Pompey, but was pardoned by Caesar after the battle of Pharsalia. Joined the conspiracy against Caesar; after the latter's murder Brutus and Cassius were defeated at Philippi and Brutus committed suicide.

Jean Jacques Rousseau: (1712–78), born at Geneva, author and philosopher. His *Du Contrat Social* (1762) prepared the way for the French Revolution.

p. 147 *Saeva indignatio:* a reference to Swift's epitaph in St. Patrick's Cathedral, Dublin, which runs

Hic depositum est Corpus
IONATHAN SWIFT S.T.D.
Hujus Ecclesiae Cathedralis
Decani,
Ubi saeva Indignatio
Ulterius
Cor lacerare nequit.
Abi Viator
Et imitare, si poteris,
Strenuum pro virili
Libertatis Vindicatorem.

Yeats translated it in "Swift's Epitaph," *Collected Poems*, p. 277.

Cato: see note, p. 237.

p. 149 *the quotation: Job 4, 13–15:* In thoughts from the visions of the night, when deep sleep falleth on men, Fear came upon me, and trembling which made all my bones to shake. Then a spirit passed before my face; the hair of my flesh stood up.

p. 151 *the Lord Treasurer:* Robert Harley, first Earl of Oxford (1661–1724). See note on p. 243.

Plutarch: (c. A.D. 46–120), Greek biographer, wrote parallel lives of twenty-three Greeks and twenty-three Romans.

p. 152 *Dr. Arbuthnot:* Dr. John Arbuthnot (1667–1735) was Queen Anne's doctor, an author, and a friend of Swift and Pope.

a line of Dryden's: "great wits are sure to madness / Near allied," from Dryden's *Absalom and Achitophel*, I. 163.

p. 155 *Chrysostom:* St. John (c. A.D. 345–407), eloquent (Chrysostom = golden-mouthed) Greek Father of the Church, wrote commentaries on the Gospel of St. Matthew and the Epistles to the Romans and Corinthians.

p. 157 *His brain had gone:* probably not correct, but for an expert view of Swift's health see T. G. Wilson, "Swift's Personality and Death Masks," *A Review of English Literature,* July 1962.

p. 158 *perish the day:* from *Job* 3, 3: Let the day perish wherein I was born.

A FULL MOON IN MARCH

Yeats developed this play, first published in 1935, from *The King of the Great Clock Tower* (1934), which was first written in prose, and on which he was working in 1933. He may have begun to work on the idea about 1929.

p. 162 *Pythagoras:* a Greek philosopher of the sixth century B.C. who thought the universe had a mathematical basis. He believed in the Orphic doctrine of metempsychosis, the purificatory or punishing process in which souls transmigrated from man to man, or man to animal or animal to man.

p. 165 *An ancient Irish Queen:* Queen Maeve of Connacht.

an innkeeper's daughter: the Empress Theophano, married by Romanus II, c. A.D. 956.

THE HERNE'S EGG

Yeats began to write this play in 1935. It was first published in 1938 and first performed by Lord Longford's company in 1939; it was later performed at the Abbey Theatre on 29 October and 5 November 1950. Mr. Austin Clarke has suggested that the play is founded on a passage in Sir Samuel Ferguson's *Congal* (1872).

p. 171 *a great herne:* a heron.

Congal: an Ulster king who rebelled against the High King Domnal in an attempt to reassert paganism; he was defeated at the Battle of Moyra.

Connacht: one of the five ancient kingdoms of Ireland, its capital being Cruachan.

Aedh: Irish for Hugh.

Tara: a hill in Co. Meath, seat of government of the High Kings of Ireland.

p. 174 *Danae's lap:* Danae was the daughter of Acrisius, king of Argos, who shut her in a brazen tower as an oracle foretold he would be killed by his daughter's son. Zeus fell in love with her and visited her in a shower of gold; their son was Perseus, who eventually did kill his grandfather by accident.

p. 185 *Munster:* southern province of Ireland.

p. 190 *Slieve Fuadh:* (modern Sliabh Fuaid) the highest mountain in the Fews range in Armagh. Cuchulain when setting off from Dundalk to Emain Macha as a boy was told by his mother that he would have a hard journey as Slieve Fuadh lay in between.

PURGATORY

Yeats wrote this play between March and May 1938. It was first published in *Last Poems and Two Plays* (1939) and first performed at the Abbey Theatre, Dublin on 10 August 1938.

p. 200 *the Curragh:* district in Co. Kildare, famous for its race-course and as a breeding and training ground for race-horses.

p. 201 *Aughrim and the Boyne:* two battles crucial in Irish and European history. At the Boyne on 1 July 1690, William defeated James and thus brought about the triumph of Louis' European opponents. At Aughrim, twelve days later, Ginkle, William's Dutch commander, broke the Irish army, 11,000 men of which left for France after the Siege of Limerick ended in October 1690.

p. 201 *the Puck Fair:* an annual festival lasting three days and nights (Gathering Day, Market or Fair Day and Scatter-ing Day), held at Kilorglin, Co. Kerry. A goat is still crowned king as part of the ceremonies, which are attended by many of the tinkers of Ireland.

p. 203 *Tertullian:* Quintus Septimus Florens Tertullianus (*c.* A.D. 160–225), lawyer and author, native of the Roman prov-ince of Africa, was converted to Christianity; his *Apology* rebuts charges against Christianity.

THE DEATH OF CUCHULAIN

Yeats began this play in the autumn of 1938, ending it before Christ-mas of that year. It was first published in *Last Poems and Two Plays* (1939) and first performed at the Abbey Theatre, Dublin, in 1949.

p. 209 *Cuchulain:* see note, p. 233.

Eithne Inguba: see note, p. 238.

Aoife: see note, p. 234.

Emer: see note, p. 238.

Talma: François Joseph Talma (1763–1826), French tragedian.

p. 210 *Hilaire Germaine Edgar Degas:* (1834–1917), French painter.

Rameses the Great: (1311–1245 B.C.), Pharaoh of Egypt.

Maeve: see note, p. 234.

Emain Macha: capital of Ulster sited near modern Armagh, said to have been burnt in A.D. 332.

p. 211 *Conall Caernach:* an Ulster hero, greatest in prowess after Cuchulain.

p. 213 *The Morrigu:* a crow-headed war goddess.

p. 214 *At the Hawk's Well:* Yeats began *At the Hawk's Well* in 1915; it was first performed in Lady Cunard's drawing-room in London in March 1916, first published in 1917. This play tells how Cuchulain is lured away by the woman of the well and begets a son on her.

On Baile's Strand: Yeats's play (see pp. 19–43) tells the story of how Cuchulain kills this son.

p. 214 *The grey of Macha:* one of Cuchulain's two chariot horses, a kelpie or lake-horse.

p. 217 *Maeve's latest lover:* the Queen was notoriously amorous.

her sons . . . these other men: It is likely that Yeats is using poetic licence here. In the oldest version of the legend the hero is killed by Lugaid mac Con Roí and Erc mac Coirbri, by three magic spears prepared by the three sons of Calatín. Later versions add MacNiad mac Finn maic Rosa, to make one man for each spear. The fathers of all six had been killed by Cuchulain; this is the reason given for their combining to kill him.

p. 218 *Usna's boys:* Naoise and his brothers, Ardan and Ainle, who had accompanied him into Scotland when he ran away with Deirdre, King Conchubar's ward.

the Post Office: The General Post Office, Dublin, was held by the insurgents in the Easter Rising 1916, and was the scene of their surrender.

Pearse: Patrick Henry Pearse (1879–1916), Irish poet and leader, shot for taking part in the 1916 Rising, when he was president of the provisional government.

Connolly: James Connolly (1870–1916), Irish trade-union

leader and organiser of the Irish Citizen Army, shot for his part in the 1916 Rising.

Oliver Sheppard: (d. 1941), Irish sculptor.

CATHLEEN NI HOOLIHAN

Yeats, in a note dated 1903 and addressed to Lady Gregory, gives the source of this play (the title is later spelt as Cathleen ni Houlihan) as a dream he had "almost distinct as a vision, of a cottage where there was well-being and firelight and talk of a marriage and into the midst of that cottage there came an old woman in a long cloak. She was Ireland herself, that Cathleen ni Hoolihan for whom so many songs have been sung and about whom so many stories have been told and for whose sake so many have gone to their death." The play was first published in *Samhain*, October 1902, and first performed at St. Teresa's Total Abstinence Association Hall, Dublin, on 2 April 1902, with Maud Gonne in the title-rôle.

p. 221 *Kathleen (or Cathleen) ni Houlihan*: a symbol of Ireland.

Killala: in Co. Mayo, where a French force under General Humbert landed on 22 August 1798.

p. 223 *Ballina*: town in Co. Mayo.

p. 224 *Enniscrone*: G. B. Saul, *op. cit.*, p. 35, suggests Inchicronan, Co. Clare, but Enniscrone, now a small seaside resort, is in the extreme west of Co. Sligo not far from Ballina.

p. 226 *too many strangers*: the English in Ireland.

four beautiful green fields: the four provinces of Ireland.

Kilglas: village near Killala, spelt Kilglass in later versions.

p. 227 *a red man*: probably "Red" Hugh Roe O'Donnell (*c.* 1571–1602), escaped from prison in Dublin, overran Connacht, shared in victory of Yellow Ford, failed to reduce Kinsale, went to Spain for aid, and was poisoned there.

a man of the O'Sullivans: probably Donal O'Sullivan Beare (1560–1618), received Spanish garrison in his castle of Dunboy, 1601; Carew demolished it. O'Sullivan fought his way to Ulster, then went to London, but failing to obtain restitution from James, went to Spain, where he was killed by a refugee.

Brian Boru: (926–1014), High King of Ireland, killed in victorious battle with the Danes at Clontarf, Dublin, 1014.

p. 229 *keening*: Irish form of mourning over the dead.

white-scarfed riders: white-robed priests at funerals.

SELECT BIBLIOGRAPHY

EDITIONS OF YEATS'S PLAYS

The Collected Works in Verse and Prose of William Butler Yeats (8 vols., 1908)
Volumes II, III, and IV contain the texts of plays and notes.

Plays in Prose and Verse for an Irish Theatre (1922)
Contains brief notes on the plays.

Plays and Controversies (1923)
Contains essays on "The Irish Dramatic Movement" and "A People's Theatre."

Wheels and Butterflies (1934)
Contains very useful introduction.

Collected Plays (1934)

Last Poems and Plays (1940)

Collected Plays (1952)
A good edition, though the dates supplied are misleading. Peter Ure, *Yeats the Playwright* (1963) gives useful information on the dates of composition, publication and performance; see also Allan Wade, *A Bibliography of the Writings of W. B. Yeats* (1951; rev. ed., 1958).

Russell K. Alspach (ed.), *The Variorum Edition of the Plays of W. B. Yeats* (1966).

CRITICISM AND BIOGRAPHY

W. B. Yeats, *Essays and Introductions* (1961); *Explorations* (1962)
These two volumes contain essays by Yeats on the theatre and on particular plays and dramatists. Selections are contained in Pocket Papermacs, *Selected Criticism* (1964) and *Selected Prose* (1964).

Joseph Hone, *W. B. Yeats 1865–1939* (1943; rev. ed., 1963).

A. Norman Jeffares, *Yeats: Man and Poet* (1949; rev. ed., 1962).

Birgit Bjersby, *The Interpretation of the Cuchulain Legend in the Works of W. B. Yeats* (1950).

T. R. Henn, *The Lonely Tower* (1950; rev. ed., 1965).

G. B. Saul, *Prolegomena to the Plays of W. B. Yeats* (1958).

F. A. C. Wilson, *W. B. Yeats and Tradition* (1958).

F. A. C. Wilson, *Yeats's Iconography* (1960).

A. G. Stock, *W. B. Yeats. His Poetry and Thought* (1961; rev. ed., 1964).

A. Norman Jeffares (ed.), *A Review of English Literature* [Yeats number] (July 1963).

Peter Ure, *Yeats* [in *Writers and Critics* series] (1963).

Peter Ure, *Yeats the Playwright* (1963).

Helen Vendler, *Yeats's Vision and the Later Plays* (1963).

Denis Donoghue (ed.), *The Integrity of Yeats* (1964).

Edward Engelberg, *The Vast Design* (1964).

M. C. Bradbrook, *English Dramatic Form: A History of its Development* (1965).

Curtis Bradford, *Yeats at Work* (1965).

S. B. Bushrui, *Yeats's Verse Plays: The Revisions 1900–1910* (1965).

Denis Donoghue and J. R. Mulryne (eds.), *An Honoured Guest: New Essays on W. B. Yeats* (1965).

A. Norman Jeffares and K. G. W. Cross (eds.), *In Excited Reverie* (1965).

D. E. S. Maxwell and S. B. Bushrui (eds.), *W. B. Yeats 1865–1965: Centenary Essays* (1965).

Shotaro Oshima, *W. B. Yeats and Japan* (1965).

B. Rajan, *W. B. Yeats: A Critical Introduction* (1965).

Corinna Salvadori, *Yeats and Castiglione: Poet and Courtier* (1965).

Robin Skelton and Ann Saddlemyer (eds.), *The World of W. B. Yeats* (1965).